YEW TREE GARDENS

Sisters Mattie, Nell and Renie have escaped from their bullying father. Building new lives for themselves, the youngest sister, Renie, lives with the newly married Nell. Working as a waitress at the King's Head Hotel, she becomes increasingly harassed by the new assistant manager, Mr Judson. So, also eager to escape from Nell's unpleasant husband, Renie is delighted to be offered a new job in London. Making new friends she soon settles, yet worries about how Nell is treated by her husband. When tragedy strikes Nell and her family, Renie feels horrified and helpless; finding her only comfort in her growing friendship with the injured Gil. But can their relationship progress from just friendship? And how will the return of the threatening Judson affect their future?

ANNA JACOBS

YEW TREE GARDENS

Complete and Unabridged

CHARNWOOD
Leicester

First published in Great Britain in 2012 by
Allison & Busby Limited
London

First Charnwood Edition
published 2013
by arrangement with
Allison & Busby Limited
London

A catalogue record for this book is available
from the British Library.

ISBN 978–1–4448–1516–0

Published by
F. A. Thorpe (Publishing)
Anstey, Leicestershire

Set by Words & Graphics Ltd.
Anstey, Leicestershire
Printed and bound in Great Britain by
T. J. International Ltd., Padstow, Cornwall
This book is printed on acid-free paper

In loving memory of Leonie Knight, a very dear friend and fellow novelist, taken from us far too soon.

With gratitude and thanks to Chris Barker, Archivist of the Model T Ford Register of Great Britain, for his wonderful help with the details of Model T Fords.

1910

Prologue

Swindon, Wiltshire; March

Renie woke with a start as her sisters shook her. She stared at them for a few moments, then realised it was morning and the adventure had begun. They were all running away from home today to escape their bully of a father.

Then she remembered that her eldest sister Mattie was going somewhere on her own, while Renie had to go with Nell. As she got dressed, she tried one last time to persuade them otherwise. 'I really ought to go with Mattie. If I don't, she'll be on her own.'

'Shh! You'll wake Dad.'

Renie lowered her voice but didn't give up. 'Yes, but you've got Cliff, and you know he doesn't really want me living with you two after you're married. Please. It's not too late for us to change our plans.'

Mattie put one arm round her shoulders and whispered hoarsely, 'We went through all this last night. I don't know where I'll be going or what I'll be doing. You'll be much safer with Nell and Cliff. He has a good trade and will always be able to get a job.' She broke off to cough.

When Renie opened her mouth to argue, worried about how ill Mattie still looked, Nell came to her other side. 'Shh, love. Do you want to wake Dad? If he finds out what we're doing . . .'

Nell didn't have to finish the sentence. Renie shivered at the mere thought of that. If Dad found out they were running away, he'd beat them senseless. He'd done that to Mattie once, when she started courting and insisted she was going to get married. She still bore the marks of his belt buckle on her back. Dad had lamed her fellow, who had left Swindon for good — without Mattie.

Dad didn't want any of them to marry, just earn him money and then look after him as he grew older. That wouldn't be much of a life, would it?

But though Renie was eager to get away, she wasn't looking forward to living with Cliff, either. There was something mean about him. She didn't think he'd thump her or anything — he'd better not even try — but she didn't think he'd be kind, either.

She couldn't say that to Nell, of course, because her sister loved him and thought he was wonderful. Anyway, Nell had no choice about marrying him now, because she was expecting his child. But he didn't seem even a tiny bit pleased about that.

Renie wasn't going to let any man have his way with her. She wasn't sure exactly what that meant, but it sounded awful. She'd heard some of the married women at work talking about their husbands and how they had to put up with them in bed, always 'at it'.

She had decided not even to walk out with a fellow. She was only sixteen, after all, and there was time to enjoy life before she settled down

4

— if she ever did settle down. Oh, she wanted so much more from life than marriage and children and housework; she wanted adventure, travel, excitement.

She read about it in books, the sort of life people from her part of town rarely managed. And whatever anyone said, she was going to —

'Renie!'

Mattie shook her again, smiling. 'Stop daydreaming and finish getting ready.'

1

Lancashire, April 1910

It was hard settling down in Lancashire and Renie missed Swindon and her eldest sister greatly. She missed Wiltshire, too. It was much softer countryside than here, prettier.

Cliff's relatives in Rochdale were not helpful, and looked down on Renie's sister Nell for being in the family way. As if she'd done that on her own!

But help had come from the congregation of a small Methodist church, and Cliff had found a job with one of its members.

Renie helped her sister scrub out their new house, but she hated it and knew Nell wasn't happy with it, either. Cliff had chosen to live in Milnrow, near Rochdale, because he'd found a place that was cheap and close to where he worked.

The five small houses in Willow Court opened on to a yard and shared one old-fashioned lavatory, situated right next to the only entrance to the yard. They were back-to-back houses, which meant they had no rear doors, just a front one, with one big room and a scullery downstairs, and two bedrooms upstairs.

'You'd think Cliff could find us somewhere better than this to live,' she grumbled. 'It's horrible, as well as filthy.'

'He wants to be near his new job.' Nell sighed

7

as she looked round. 'It's only for a few months. I'll look for somewhere better later, once he's settled in his job. He'll be happier then.'

Later, as they finished scrubbing the floors, Nell said, 'As soon as this is dry, I want to whitewash all the walls.'

'Wallpaper would look nicer.'

'Bugs can live in wallpaper. Whitewash is cleanest in a place like this.'

A *slum*, Renie thought. That was what it was, a slum.

★   ★   ★

A few days later, Nell married Cliff and they all moved into Willow Court. Renie hated living there from the start: the smell, the slovenly neighbours, the way Cliff acted like lord of the world, tossing out orders, telling her off for nothing. He wasn't *her* husband!

It was a relief when the minister's wife helped her find a job working in the canteen of a local mill. At least it got her out of the house all day and stopped Cliff complaining of how much she was costing him for food. The job was more pleasant than her old one in the laundry, but the wages were the same.

Cliff wanted to take all her money to pay for her keep, just like her father had. He and Nell had a big row about that, but for once Nell won. If she hadn't, Renie would have moved into lodgings rather than hand over all her money.

At the canteen, she had to peel mountains of potatoes and wash the same dishes and pans day after day. Her hands were just as red and raw as they had been in the laundry. But at least she made friends with the other girls and they had a bit of fun together.

After they'd served the meals to the millhands, two of them had to clean the tables and mop the floor in the canteen, while the rest cleared up the kitchen and got it ready for the night shift. Daytime workers could either bring their own dinners or buy food cheaply. The night shift had to bring their own food, but one of the lads made them tea and coffee.

In the morning Renie had to start all over again, cleaning up after the men who worked at night and who always tramped dirt in and left the tables in a mess. They should at least have thrown their rubbish in the bin, not left it lying around. That encouraged mice.

One of the best things about this job was that she didn't have to provide her own midday meals, because the canteen staff could eat the leftovers free. By the time her birthday came in August, she had grown a full inch and some of her clothes were too tight.

She and Nell celebrated her birthday together. Cliff didn't care whether it was her birthday or not, just whether his food was ready on time and his clothes washed and ironed, so they left him out.

She continued to eat well at work and Cook even let them take leftovers home now and then, so Nell benefited too. Renie noticed Cook always had food to take home, but knew better than to comment on that.

She felt as if she had grown up very quickly and learnt a lot since they left Swindon. She missed it, wished they were still living there. Lancashire just didn't feel like home.

★ ★ ★

After a few weeks, one of the women at the canteen took Renie aside. 'I've been watching you. You're a real hard worker.'

'Thanks, Mary.'

'I wondered if you'd like an extra job on Saturday nights. It'd earn you three shillings.'

'Doing what?'

'Working in the kitchen at the King's Head Hotel in Rochdale. It's mostly washing up, but if they think you're worth it, they'll teach you to do other things, like they did me. I've been learning waitressing. They're always on the lookout for good workers, you see, because the owners have other hotels. They're called Mr and Mrs Carling and the King's Head was the first hotel they ever owned. They've got a hotel in London and three others, I think, only they call them the Rathleighs. I got confused at first about that.' She laughed. 'I'm going to give notice at the canteen tomorrow and work in this hotel full-time as a waitress.'

'You lucky thing!'

'It's not just luck. I've earned my new job by hard work and you can too. Waitresses get tips as well as wages, and they don't ruin their hands. One day I want to work as a housekeeper in a big hotel. I'm never getting married. I don't want to spend my life running round after a fellow and going without to feed the kids, like my sister does.'

Renie was happy to hear another woman say she wasn't getting married. Whenever she said that, people laughed at her and told her she'd change when she met the right man. But she wouldn't. Watching how unhappy Cliff made her sister proved how chancy marriage could be. Her father had made her mother unhappy too.

'It's really kind of you to think of me, Mary, and I'd love to try for it.'

'Like I said, you're a good worker.'

'How do we get back after work?'

'The last train and then we have to walk home from the station. They make sure I can leave on time for that and they give me my fare. They're good employers. Have you ever been inside the hotel?'

'No. I walked past the door one day and it looked very posh.'

'It is. People of our sort don't go there, just rich folk. You should hear how they talk.' She stuck her nose in the air and said, 'How do you do?' in a plummy voice, making Renie laugh.

'The hotel guests eat meals in the restaurant, three courses at least, the lucky things, and they stay the night in fancy bedrooms. The house-keeper let me have a peep at them. They're lovely.' Mary's eyes grew dreamy for a moment. 'One day I'm going to sleep in a bedroom like that.'

She shook her head and smiled. 'Listen to me going on. I can take you to meet the housekeeper after work, if you like, to see if she'll take you on. I've already told her about you.'

Renie nearly said yes, then looked down at herself. 'Not today. I'll look a mess by then and this is my oldest skirt. How about tomorrow? I can bring some clean clothes to change into after work.'

She didn't tell Nell about this chance of an extra job, because Cliff might find out and stop her even trying. He didn't want anyone to be happy, that one didn't.

* * *

The next day after work, Mary took her into Rochdale and they went into the King's Head by a rear entrance. She explained to a man in a black suit that she was taking Renie for an interview with Mrs Berton.

The further into the hotel they went, the more nervous Renie became. What was a girl like her doing in a place like this?

The housekeeper's room was so grand she wanted to clutch Mary's arm. But then she realised she was being a coward, so took a deep breath and stood up straight. Her sister Mattie said you had to face things you were afraid of. Her heart clenched, as it always did, at the thought of Mattie and she wondered where her eldest sister was.

'This is Renie, Mrs Berton.'

After a series of questions, the housekeeper said, 'I'll give you a trial, Renie, because Mary speaks well of you and you look like a strong, healthy sort of girl.' She frowned. 'Is Renie short for Irene?'

'Yes, Mrs Berton.'

'Then I think we'll use your full name here. Renie sounds rather common.'

When they got out of the hotel, Renie said indignantly, 'Fancy changing my name!'

'They do things like that in posh hotels. Everything has to sound right, as well as look right. What does it matter? You'll be earning three shillings every Saturday.'

Three whole shillings for herself. She'd not give a farthing of it to Cliff.

Nell was delighted for her, but *he* threw a fit about her being out late. After Renie told him she'd be coming home with Mary, he said the three shillings would be very welcome.

'I'm not giving you any more money. It doesn't cost you anything for me to work in Rochdale.'

'I'm the head of this household and you'll do as you're told, young woman.'

'I won't go to work there at all if you take my money.'

'Don't be cheeky. You live under my roof and you'll do as I say.'

'I'm not being cheeky, but it's my money. And if you don't like me living here, I can always go into lodgings.'

'Cliff, let her do it. She'll be saving me the meal on Saturday night, because they give her something to eat, so we do benefit.'

The dirty look he gave Renie said he'd not forget this, but she'd had enough of him and his grasping ways and she didn't care. Nell might have to put up with him, but she didn't.

13

It was hard on the hands washing up all evening, but Renie did the best she could, grating the soap carefully and shaking it up in a bottle of hot water to dissolve it. She made sure she rinsed the dishes and got them sparkling clean, because she was desperate to be kept on.

To her surprise, the cook was a man and insisted on being called 'Sheff' (she found out later it was spelt 'chef'). He came to inspect her work every hour or so the first night.

After his third visit to the scullery he said, 'You're very thorough. Keep that up and you'll get the job permanently, young Irene.'

'Thank you, Chef.'

He went back to his cooking. She saw the meals sometimes when she went to collect the dirty dishes from the side bench just inside the kitchen door. She'd never seen food like he and his assistants made.

When he offered her something to eat in the middle of the evening, she accepted gratefully. Another girl, who was also eating, explained what the food was and taught her some French words.

Renie felt very grown up, catching the train home. She walked to Willow Court from the station with Mary, who lived nearby, feeling tired but exhilarated. Best of all were the florin and shilling wrapped in her handkerchief and bumping against her leg.

She found the house in darkness, so lit a candle and made her way up to her bedroom. She wasn't going to let the money out of her sight until she could open a savings bank account of her own. Maybe Cook at the canteen would let her nip along the street to do that in her lunch break.

★ ★ ★

Nell's daughter was born in late September and was a little darling. Renie loved cuddling her, but Cliff never even picked her up, complaining that he'd wanted a son.

The following week the manager at the King's Head summoned Renie to his office before she started work. Another man was sitting next to the desk.

'This is Mr Judson, who's going to be working here for a while as my assistant.'

She nodded to the stranger and clasped her hands in front of her, hoping they didn't look too reddened.

'We're very pleased with your work, Irene. When you stepped in for Janet you did well on the waitressing too, which is why we let you try that out a few times.'

Renie had guessed they were testing her out.

'We've decided to offer you a job here full-time as a waitress. We'll train you in our ways.'

She couldn't hide her delight. 'Oh, I'd love to do that! Thank you very much. I'll work really hard.'

He smiled and turned to the man next to him. 'We have some good workers here in Lancashire.'

The man nodded, but the way his eyes ran over Renie's body made her feel uncomfortable.

Even when she found she'd be earning less

15

money at first, till she was trained, she didn't care. She'd get out of the canteen and not have such rough hands, and if she did her work well, there would be tips and maybe one day she could go to work in London, or in one of the other Rathleigh hotels.

She twirled round as she walked back to the kitchen and one of the waiters laughed at her. She didn't care.

She might even go back to Wiltshire one day, but not near her father. She didn't think Mattie would have gone too far away from home.

Renie rushed home that night and burst into the house, delighted to see her sister still up, just finishing feeding the baby. 'Guess what! They're going to keep me on at the hotel as a waitress, because I've given satisfaction. Isn't that marvellous?'

'That's what you wanted, isn't it?'

'Yes.' She cuddled up against Nell and the baby for a moment or two. 'And one day I'll go and work in London. I really will.'

'I'm glad for you, but I don't want you to go to London. I'll miss you in the evenings as it is.'

'Will you be all right on your own?'

'Of course I will. I have my library books, don't I? It'll make me very happy to see you getting such a good chance. And I'll have Sarah to keep me company. I won't be on my own any more.'

They didn't tell Cliff till the next evening.

'You'll not last long,' he said at once. 'You're too clumsy to be a waitress.'

She raised her chin and stared at him the way

16

Chef stared at someone when they'd made a mistake. She'd been practising that in front of the broken piece of mirror in her bedroom. She'd been practising speaking better too. 'The manager doesn't think so.'

Nell moved closer to her as if to protect her, only Renie was taller than her now, nearly as tall as Cliff. She'd grown in the past few months, thanks to the excellent food she'd been eating. She was no longer afraid of him physically, either. If he hit her, she'd thump him right back.

'How much are they paying you?' he asked.

'None of your business.'

'It is while you're under my roof.'

'Enough to pay my keep, don't worry. And I'll get food to eat, all except my breakfast, so I'll cost you less.'

'We should take less money from you, then,' Nell said at once.

He rounded on her. 'You'll do no such thing! You still do her washing, don't you? And clean up after her?'

Renie tried to turn his anger away from his wife. 'They let some of the girls live in, only I told them I wanted to stay here to help my sister. But they said there would always be a bed for me there.'

He went red and his hands clenched into fists. All hung in the balance for a moment or two. 'Well, don't try to pay any less for your keep.'

'I won't. I know you keep Nell short and she needs every penny I can give her to make ends meet.'

He did walk across to her then, but she stood her ground. 'Don't you dare lay a finger on me

17

or I'll definitely leave!'

'I wouldn't waste my energy on you. You're useless. No wonder you're not walking out with anyone like the other girls.'

'It's not for lack of chances. I don't want to get married.'

'You will. That's what all women want, a man to work his fingers to the bone providing for them and their children.' After glaring at her and then at Nell, he went out to the pub, slamming the door behind him.

'I wish you'd be more careful how you talk to him,' her sister said once his footsteps had faded into the distance. 'What if he'd hit you?'

'I'd have hit him back. Where it hurts. And then I'd have moved out. Never mind him, look what I've brought you as a present for giving me such a lovely little niece.' She brandished a Fry's Chocolate Cream bar. 'What's more, we're not saving him any.'

Nell's eyes filled with tears and the two sisters hugged.

★　★　★

The first time Mr Judson pressed himself against her, Renie shoved him away hard. She'd met men like him before and you had to make it plain from the start that you'd not put up with it. 'Stop that!'

He stood still for a moment, smiled, then walked away whistling.

When he touched her body again, she kicked him hard in the shin. If he'd been anyone else except the assistant manager, she'd have kicked him where it hurt a lot more.

He looked furious, but she was angry too.

They stood glaring at one another for a few moments, then he straightened up and said, 'You'll be sorry for that.'

'And you'll be sorry if you touch me like that again!'

The housekeeper was passing just then and stopped to stare at them.

'And don't you be cheeky to me again, young woman,' he said and walked away.

Renie looked at the housekeeper. 'I wasn't being cheeky to him.'

'I didn't think you had been. You're not the cheeky sort. Is he giving you any trouble?'

She shrugged. 'He tries to touch some of us. I don't like it and I won't let him do it, not even if I lose my job for it.'

'You won't. I'll make sure of that.' The housekeeper patted her shoulder. 'You carry on sticking up for yourself, young Irene.' She hesitated, looking over her shoulder before asking, 'Has he given anyone else any trouble?'

'He grabbed Nellie's breast the other day and hurt her. She cried about that in the back pantry.'

The housekeeper breathed deeply. 'I'll have a word with the manager. We employ decent girls here and I'm not having them treated like . . . like the other sort.'

Things got better then and Mr Judson stopped touching the women staff, but the looks he gave Renie said he blamed her and he'd not forget what she'd done. Luckily, he wasn't in charge of the dining room staff, but worked in the office — she didn't know what he did there. Some of the time, he stood in Reception and fussed over customers when they arrived.

Smarmy devil, he was to them.

There was always a worm in the apple, wasn't there? Nothing ever went smoothly. Renie was learning that. She was learning a lot about life since they'd fled from Swindon.

⋆　⋆　⋆

Renie loved being a waitress, helping people, seeing the pleasure on their faces as they ate the delicious food Chef produced. She'd never had a job as interesting as this before, hadn't realised food could be so wonderful.

Six weeks after she'd started, the manager summoned her with a flick of the finger. 'A word, Irene.'

She cast a quick glance over the restaurant, but it was quiet now after the lunchtime rush and she'd cleared up all her tables. She followed Mr Sewell into his office to one side of the foyer, frowning as she tried to work out what she'd done wrong. Nothing that she could think of.

He sat down behind his desk and stared at her over his steepled fingers. 'We've been very pleased with how you've settled in, Irene, and how quickly you've learnt the job. I've not seen anyone pick it up as quickly as you. And the customers like you, too. That's important.'

'Oh. Well, thank you. I do enjoy my work.' She could feel herself flushing with pleasure at the compliment. Mr Sewell wasn't noted for handing them out too often, so it really meant something.

'I overheard you the other day talking about how you'd like to see more of the world.'

She looked at him warily. What had that to do with working here?

'The company has an opening in London for a waitress, and since they're very particular about who they employ, they've asked the managers of our regional hotels if we have any staff with potential. I don't want to lose you so quickly, but I can find someone else for our level of waitressing. The London Rathleigh is a very fine hotel and the restaurant there maintains a much higher standard than this one can — though we do quite well for a small provincial hotel.'

She was surprised at that. To her, the King's Head seemed the last word in luxury — and large, not small.

'You'd learn things from continuing your training in London which you could never learn here. However, it is my hope that one day you may come back here as head waitress. Your family lives in the area, after all.'

The offer took her breath away and for a moment she couldn't put two words together. Then they tumbled out in a rush. 'Oh, I'd love to go to London! Thank you so much for thinking of me, Mr Sewell.'

'There's just one thing: are you courting? It'd be a waste us putting all this effort into you if you're going to get married in a year or two.'

'I don't have a young man because I don't want to get married.' Though she'd been asked to walk out with fellows three times now. 'I've seen how unhappy my sister is with her husband.'

He looked surprised at her frankness. When would she learn to keep quiet about her personal life? Mary had told her the other day that managers and head waiters didn't want to know that sort of thing.

He didn't comment, apart from, 'That's all right, then. Now, to practicalities. We need you to start next week, Irene, so that you're trained in London ways by the Christmas rush. It takes a very special girl to do that so quickly, but I know you won't let me down.'

'I can do it, sir, I know I can. But where will I live in London? Will they help me find lodgings?'

He smiled. 'You'll live in at the Rathleigh, of course. They employ so many young women, they have dormitories for them. They'll deduct the cost of living in from your wages, but I think you'll find it much cheaper than London lodgings.'

She beamed at him. 'That's all right, then. I'll do my very best to give satisfaction, sir.'

'We'd like you to leave on Monday. You'll be provided with a train ticket and your taxi fare from the station to the London hotel.'

That took her breath away. Her, riding in a taxi.

She floated out of his room, and when Mary asked her what was making her smile, she told her. Then she realised that Mary had been there longer and was struggling not to appear jealous. 'I'm sorry. I owe this to you. I wish you were coming too.'

'So do I. Perhaps another time.'

She gave Mary a hug. 'Thank you so much. If I can ever put in a good word for you, I will.'

It was only when she was walking home that Renie had time to think how this would affect her sister. Poor Nell would be very lonely then. The thought of that made her feel guilty, but she couldn't bear to turn down this golden opportunity and she knew dear Nell wouldn't want her to.

Renie sighed happily. She'd dreamt of escaping from Milnrow and her brother-in-law, and now she was going to do it, she really was.

⋆ ⋆ ⋆

Cliff threw a fit when Renie said she'd be leaving and instantly forbade her to go. He and Nell had a row about it later and of course, in such a small house, Renie heard every word.

'I forbid her to go!' he yelled.

'Why?'

'Because I bloody well say so, that's why.'

The baby began to cry, frightened by the loud voices. Renie heard Cliff yell, 'Stop that brat squalling!' and then the bed frame creaked as he turned over. Poor Nell had to get up to comfort little Sarah. She took the baby downstairs, as she often did.

Renie wondered whether to go down and join her, but was tired and couldn't resist closing her eyes.

⋆ ⋆ ⋆

23

Once Cliff had gone to work the next day, Nell said, 'Just pack up and go on Monday. You've only a few days to wait. He needn't know anything till after you've left.'

'He'll get mad at you then.'

Nell shrugged. 'He's always getting mad. I can't do anything right these days, especially when Sarah wakes him up at night.'

'Oh, Nell.' Renie hesitated, wondering whether to say something about this sham of a marriage, but her sister turned round and started clattering pots and pans, so she held her peace.

Cliff seemed to take for granted that she'd do as he told her and stay in Milnrow. Luckily, he never poked his head into her bedroom, so he didn't see the trunk she'd bought with money from her savings. Not that the trunk was full, but it was on the list of items she had to provide. She wasn't going to buy any new clothes till she got to London, where she'd keep her eyes open for good quality, second-hand ones. If she'd dressed well here, Cliff would have demanded more money from her.

On the Monday Cliff went off to work as usual, but somehow, while she finished her packing and got her trunk taken to the station, Renie kept thinking he'd find out and try to stop her.

It wasn't till the second train pulled out of Manchester that she began to feel safe. Her spirits lifted and she began to take an interest in the places they were passing through. Nell had packed her some sandwiches, an apple and a bottle of cold tea for the journey, so she wouldn't need to spend any of her money on food.

She felt as if she'd grown suddenly older, thrown on her own resources like this. She only had her savings to fall back on if anything went wrong, so she was determined to be very careful.

She still winced when she remembered how careless she'd been with the few pennies that came her way when she was younger. Such a waste! Now, thanks to her tips, every penny of which she'd saved, she had nearly ten pounds tucked away for a rainy day because she would never ask Cliff for help, no matter how desperate she was.

She could live on that money for weeks, if the worst came to the worst. But if she worked hard, she should be all right. The hotel owners treated their staff well.

But oh, she was going to miss Nell so much. She missed her eldest sister too. Surely a woman as clever as Mattie would be managing all right?

And one day the three of them would be reunited, Renie had to believe that. When they ran away, they'd agreed to try to make contact after two years through Cliff's family. But Cliff was refusing to contact his family. In March next year the two years would have passed and maybe somehow, whatever Cliff said, they could find a way to get in touch with Mattie.

2

In November, Gilbert Rycroft flung himself out of the house after yet another row with his father. Marriage! Was that all his parents could think of? He was twenty-five and enjoying life. Why should he marry when he had two older brothers quite willing to provide heirs for the family estate in Hampshire?

He had no desire whatsoever to settle down. He loved visiting friends, hunting, shooting, whatever each season brought.

'You shouldn't be riding when you're in such a temper, Master Gil,' the head groom said.

'I'll be calmer when I get back, Walter.'

'You'll have to give in to them one day, Master Gil.'

'I'm *not* marrying Amelia Frensham and that's flat. It'd be like marrying my sister.' He looked at the ageing man, who'd been more like a father to him than his own father had, and said quietly, 'I just can't do it with her, Walter.'

'They shouldn't have brought you up together.'

'I don't know that it'd have made any difference. There are some women you want in bed and others you don't want, however nice they are.'

'Then go and ride it off, but treat that horse gently. It's muddy underfoot after all the rain we've had lately.'

Impatient to get out into the fresh air, Gil

26

mounted and rode off across the nearby meadow, sailing over the fence at the other side of it.

Walter watched him go, shaking his head. 'They're pressing him too hard,' he muttered. 'No good will come of it.'

That lad didn't have enough to keep him busy and use up his energy. They should have found him a job instead of encouraging him to live in idleness. Money didn't always bring true happiness, as Walter had seen in this household.

★　★　★

Two hours later the son of a local farmer came galloping into the stable yard, yelling loudly. 'Come quick! Master Gil's hurt bad.'

Walter sent one groom up to the house, the other to fetch the doctor, then set off to find out what had happened to his lad, not forgetting to take his rifle. If the accident had been a bad one, there might be a horse to put out of its misery.

The sound of a horse groaning, a hoarse anguished sound, reached them before they got to the scene of the accident. A rifle shot cracked out and the sound cut off abruptly.

Walter shook his head, tears rising in his eyes. He'd bred that mare himself and she was one of his favourites. 'Damn fool! I'll give him what for.'

But there was no scolding Gil, who was lying on the damp ground, white and only half-conscious, his left arm and leg twisted at unnatural angles.

★　★　★

27

London terrified Renie. The buildings were so tall, and even Euston Station was like a palace, with a high ceiling full of glass panels like a giant's greenhouse. She was jostled by crowds of rushing people, who all seemed to know where they were going, which was more than she did.

She was relieved when a kindly older porter took pity on her and carried her luggage, showing her where to get a cab.

She knew she was supposed to tip him because she'd seen guests at the hotel tipping people, but wasn't sure how much.

When she offered him sixpence, he smiled and closed her hand round the coin. 'Keep it, lass. You're the same age as my granddaughter, I should think, and about as short of money.'

'Thank you.'

As he helped load her luggage into the cab, he added, 'Good luck in London. I hope you're going to a good place. In service, are you?'

'No. I'm going to work in a hotel, the Rathleigh.'

'The one round the corner from Yew Tree Gardens? Nice hotel, that. You'll be all right there if you work hard. I've heard they treat their staff decently.'

She looked back at the station as they pulled away. The porter had told her to look at the famous arch in front of it. Big columns of stone were topped by a roof like a flattened triangle. She'd never seen anything like it before.

It felt very grand to be riding in a cab.

The horse slowed down and the cab driver called out, 'These are the gardens. The hotel is just round the corner. You'll be able to walk round them when you're free. They were left for the use of everyone.'

She was a bit disappointed but didn't say so. Yew Tree Gardens were in the centre of a square, and weren't very big, only a scrubby oblong of grass about two hundred yards long and a hundred wide, with a few trees and flower beds round the edges, all enclosed by iron railings. The yew trees formed dark clumps here and there. Not her favourite sort of tree.

The horse speeded up again and turned a corner which led to a terrace of buildings. These weren't small houses like those in the terraces she knew, but very large ones, built for rich people, she was sure. They were all five storeys high and exactly the same in style, looking quietly elegant, as if they knew and were proud of their place in the world.

'They bought the end four houses,' the cab driver called, 'and made them into a hotel. It goes round the corner, too.'

She'd have liked to go up the wide steps to the big front entrance of the hotel, but of course she knew better than to do that. So did the driver, who turned into a narrow street between the side part of the hotel and the next row of large houses.

A bored-looking pageboy came out of the hotel as she was paying the driver and called, 'Can I help you?'

'I'm starting work here.'

'Right-o.' He vanished and reappeared with a trolley, on to which he and the driver unloaded her trunk and bag. Then the lad wheeled them inside without even looking at her.

Before she followed him, she looked up at the building in awe. It was surprisingly big with the wing down the side.

'Hurry up, you!' the lad yelled.

She rushed inside and followed him to the housekeeper's room, feeling nervous. This woman could make her life pleasant or miserable.

He knocked on the door and when a voice called, 'Come!' he led the way inside.

'The new girl's here, Mrs Tolson. Shall I take her things up?' This time his voice was quiet and respectful.

'Yes please, Billy. She's in Dormitory Two, the bed next to the door on the right.' She turned to study the newcomer.

Mrs Tolson was so elegant she took Renie's breath away. She looked more like a lady than a housekeeper.

'Welcome to the London Rathleigh, Irene. You come highly recommended by Mr Sewell.'

'Thank you, Mrs Tolson.'

'He says you're a hard worker, but you still have a lot to learn, so I'll put you under Maud's wing. She's our senior waitress and a very good teacher, so be sure to listen to her carefully and do what she tells you.'

'I'll do my very best, I promise.'

'Tell me about your family.'

This question surprised Renie, but she explained the situation quickly.

'And what do you like to do in your spare time?'

'Read. Is there a library near here that I can join?'

Mrs Tolson nodded approvingly. 'A very good pastime and one we encourage. We have two bookcases full of books in the women's sitting room for the use of our female staff. When you've finished reading those that interest you, you might need to go to the local library, which isn't far away. Not many of our women staff bother much with reading, I'm afraid.'

She rang a small silver bell and another woman arrived, about forty and very thin. 'This is Irene Fuller, who is starting as a waitress. Irene, this is Miss Pilkins, who is the assistant housekeeper in charge of the hotel rooms, and also the women staff and their accommodation. Take Irene upstairs, please, Miss Pilkins, and check that she has the correct clothes. If not, fit her out from the spares, then take her down to meet Maud. By the time you've done that, it'll be nearly mealtime and you can show her where to go.'

Miss Pilkins led the way at a brisk pace. 'This is the staff lift and those are the staff stairs. We never use the customers' lifts or stairs.'

Renie had never ridden in a lift before and she felt a little nervous because the iron grill, which was pulled across to form a door, allowed her to see all the workings as well as each floor they passed through. She had an urge to clutch Miss Pilkins, but didn't give in to it.

'This is the fifth floor, the top one. The women staff's accommodation is to the right. You are never, ever to go to the left, which is the men's area.'

'Yes, Miss Pilkins.'

Just before they turned into Dormitory Two, which was apparently for the younger women, Miss Pilkins indicated a door. 'That's my room. If you need help in the night, you're to knock me up. You're not to bring anyone else up here, even if they're related to you.'

'I don't know anyone in London.'

'Very well. If you'll open your trunk, I'll check your working clothes.'

Feeling a bit ashamed of how little she had, Renie took the key off the chain round her neck and unlocked her trunk.

'You'll need more than that.' Miss Pilkins pulled a little notebook out of her pocket and made a quick list. 'Let's go and sort out what you need. Mrs Tolson keeps some spares. They're second hand but of good quality. You'll be charged for them at a shilling a week out of your wages.'

An hour later, Renie owned more clothes than ever in her life before. They were made of good, hard-wearing fabrics and Miss Pilkins took care to find ones that fitted her properly, too. She wished she had something half as good for her off-duty clothes.

So many new things to learn, she thought as Miss Pilkins showed her how to tie the apron. 'Aprons belong to the hotel and are laundered by them. You will be given a clean one every day. If there's an accident and you need another clean one, ask Maud. Now, take the uniform off and change into your normal clothes.'

She led the way briskly down to the foyer and introduced Renie to Maud, who was supervising the clearing up of the tea shop.

'I'm just finishing,' Maud said. 'If you wait over there, you can watch what we do, then we'll go for our meal.'

In the staff dining room, which was at the rear of the building in the rear wing, Maud handed her over to Daphne, who was a year or two older than Renie, rather plump, with a cheerful expression and brown hair with a frizzy fringe.

'Call me Daff, everyone does when I'm not on duty,' she said as soon as Maud had gone off to the senior staff dining room for her own meal.

Renie sat quietly at the table, enjoying the food, of which you could eat as much as you wanted. She noticed how daintily the girls used their cutlery, and kept an eye on them to make sure she was doing things the right way. But her time waitressing in the King's Head had taught her to use her knives and forks properly, thank goodness.

After they'd cleared the table, Daff explained about the roster for clearing up the staff dining rooms, then took Renie to the attic sitting room, where both the housekeeping and waitressing female staff sat in the evenings.

'Girls, this is Irene. She's from Lancashire.' Daff frowned at her. 'You don't sound like a northerner.'

'I'm from Wiltshire really. I've only been living in Lancashire because my sister and her husband moved there.'

'Parents dead?'

'Well, my mother is. I don't get on with my father.'

They spent a few minutes asking Renie questions about herself, then left her in peace. At nine o'clock, two girls went out to fetch jugs of cocoa and supper, which was whatever cakes and biscuits had been left in the tea shop. Soon afterwards the women started going to bed, so Renie followed Daff.

She felt shy about undressing in front of strangers, but she quickly realised that they didn't stare at one another and most used a nightdress to cover themselves as they finished undressing.

She was so tired she didn't even remember pulling the covers up, and could only stare round, bewildered by her surroundings, when Daff woke her at seven o'clock in the morning.

★ ★ ★

Walter fell to his knees beside Gil and tried to comfort his lad while they waited for help after the accident. He felt more a father to Gil than Mr Rycroft had ever been. If Walter had ever been blessed with children, he'd have treated them more lovingly. All show and no go, that was the master. Appearances and 'doing the right thing' counted more than people's feelings, especially with an unimportant third son.

Dr Lawrence arrived a few minutes later and, to Walter's annoyance, he'd been drinking. At this hour of the morning, too! If there had been anyone else to send for, Walter would have done it.

A short examination and the doctor shook his

head. 'It's a bad one, this. Send for a cart with plenty of straw. It's going to hurt to move him.'

'I sent for one already.'

'His left arm's out of its socket and it's broken as well. Let's get that shoulder back in place first, then we'll find something to splint the arm.'

He did this so quickly that Walter didn't have time to protest. But surely more care should have been taken? It was the second time Gil's shoulder had popped out in the past year and his scream of pain was so loud and agonised, Walter felt sick to think how rough the doctor had been.

To his relief the cart arrived then.

Back at the house, Walter had a quiet word with the master, begging him to send for a London specialist doctor to set the arm and leg properly, not Dr Lawrence.

'Why do you say that?'

'He's been drinking, sir.'

Mr Rycroft went across to the local doctor, recoiling at the smell of alcohol. 'You've been drinking.'

'Just a quick nip to keep out the cold.' But the doctor was swaying slightly and his eyes weren't in proper focus.

'More than a nip. You're not fit to care for anyone. Leave my house this minute!' Mr Rycroft himself escorted the doctor to the door.

As he watched his master use the telephone to call for a London doctor, Walter decided there was some use to the newfangled apparatus after all.

He was concerned about the mistress, who was sitting by Gil's side, looking as if she might faint at any moment.

But there was nothing any of them could do except wait. And pray for their poor lad.

★　★　★

By the time a specialist arrived from London three hours later, accompanied by his assistant, Gil was tossing and moaning. Walter stood by the bed, occasionally trying to comfort him, but Mr Rycroft remained by the window, looking round in disapproval as his son groaned in pain.

It was left to Walter to explain exactly what had happened.

The specialist stared down at his patient. 'I'll have to examine the arm and leg, and I'm afraid I'm going to hurt you, Mr Rycroft.'

He was gentle and careful, very different from the local doctor, but though Gil tried hard to bear the pain in silence, he couldn't help crying out and Walter had to help the doctor's assistant hold him still as the arm and leg were checked.

When he'd finished, the specialist turned to the master. 'Only time will tell for sure, Mr Rycroft, but some fool's handled your son's arm roughly. The leg's a nasty break, but it would be much worse if someone hadn't straightened it carefully.'

'I did that. I've dealt with animals with broken limbs,' Walter said.

'You did well. Now, I'll need to use chloroform on your son to deal with the broken limbs.' The specialist looked towards Mr Rycroft, who had come as far as the foot of the bed now, but still wasn't looking at his son. 'Is there a nurse for afterwards?'

'We can send for one.'

'There's me,' Walter said quietly. 'I've had a lot to do with sick and injured animals.'

'This is not a job for a groom,' the master said at once.

Walter was already disgusted by the way he was treating his son and had difficulty speaking politely. 'With respect, sir, I've known Master Gil since he was a babe in arms. He'll do as I tell him where he won't listen to others.'

'You're not — '

The specialist interrupted, speaking with a lowered voice, but Walter could hear what he said and was sure Gil could too.

'It's not likely your son will recover full use of that arm and shoulder, Mr Rycroft. I suspect there could be some nerve damage. We'll have to wait and see. If your man here feels he can best deal with your son, I'm happy to have him help us and then leave him in charge. You can tell he's a man of sense by the way he dealt with the situation today. I'm sure you can get him a nurse to assist him.'

'That means I'll lose my head groom.'

The specialist couldn't hide his surprise at this.

Walter managed to speak quietly and politely, because it'd do no good to speak sharply to the master, who had sacked men for less. 'Mark can take charge, sir. I have absolute confidence in him.'

'Oh, very well!'

'Perhaps you'd like to leave us to it, then, sir?' the specialist suggested. 'If you could put a maid at our disposal to fetch hot water or anything else we need?'

'Very well. I'll be down in the library when you've finished.'

Walter could see Gil relax slightly after his father had left.

Once the room had been organised, the assistant brought out the necessary equipment. He put a mask over the patient's nose and mouth, then dropped liquid on to it. Walter had to help hold Gil at first, because he clearly didn't enjoy the sensation.

'They feel as if they're smothering,' the assistant said quietly, 'but they're not. There. He's unconscious now.'

The specialist worked quickly to set the leg, working by feel, then dealt with the arm, frowning and shaking his head. 'I fear he'll never have full use of this.'

Walter watched with interest as the assistant helped encase the limbs in bandages impregnated with plaster of Paris.

'I've never seen those before,' he said. 'How clever.'

The specialist nodded acknowledgement of the compliment. 'They were introduced during the Crimean War, but of course I make my own and we manage rather better nowadays. There. That should do it.'

Gradually Gil regained consciousness, moaning and trying to move.

The specialist seemed to have lost interest and

was now taking off the smock he'd worn to keep his clothes clean, so Walter went to the head of the bed. 'Hold still, lad. It's over now.'

'Over ... thank heaven. Don't let my father — '

'I'll keep him away from you as much as I can.'

The specialist listened to this with raised eyebrows. 'Should you speak like that about your master?'

'Mr Rycroft is no good with sick people, sir, because he's never had a day's illness in his life. I'm the one who's looked after Master Gil since he was ten.'

'I see. Well, I'll leave you two to clear up, and go and report. Is there another doctor in the neighbourhood apart from the one who first attended Mr Rycroft?'

'Yes, sir. Dr Laver was away in London when it happened but he should be back tomorrow.'

'I'll write him a note and he can telephone me if he needs more information or is worried about anything.' He looked at his assistant. 'Usual painkillers.'

The doctor went to take his leave of Mr Rycroft senior, who had joined his wife in her sitting room.

The assistant finished putting away the equipment, then took a box containing folded pieces of paper out of one of the leather bags. 'These powders are to be taken in half a glass of water, one only, morning and evening, to help with the pain. If you need more, you can get them from the local doctor. It's written on the

39

box what's in them.'

Once he'd gone, Gil opened his eyes and looked at Walter. 'I heard what he said.'

'I thought you did.'

'I'm going to be a cripple, aren't I?'

'You'll have one bad arm, lad. That's not exactly a cripple.'

'I won't be able to ride, though, will I?' Gil turned his head away. 'And it's all my own fault for losing my temper.'

There was nothing you could say to that.

★ ★ ★

The day following Renie's arrival in London, she went to work under Maud. The morning light wasn't flattering to the head waitress, who was extremely thin, with a rather pointed nose and lightly greying hair.

She studied the newcomer for a moment or two then nodded. 'You've tied your apron properly, but let me just show you how to fix the cap on so that it doesn't slip.' She took Renie to a mirror and smiled at her in it. 'Bewildering, isn't it?'

'Yes, very. But I'll do my best to learn quickly.'

'I'm sure you will. Mr Sewell hasn't sent us a bad 'un yet. Now, let's get to work.'

The waitresses staffed the tea shop during the day, leaving the male waiters to see to customers who took luncheon and dinner in the elegant restaurant.

Renie found her first full day at the Rathleigh bewildering. They did things so differently here and were fussy about every tiny detail. She tried her best to remember what she was shown and was relieved when Maud said in her quiet way as they finished clearing up, 'You did well for a first day, Irene.'

'Thank you. I won't forget about the plates next time.'

'I'm sure you won't.'

Renie joined the other girls in the staff sitting room after her meal, listening more than talking, which was unusual for her. They seemed mostly quiet people, with Daff the liveliest and loudest. Renie guessed that she was the youngest, but Daff could only be a couple of years older. Even she quietened down when one of the older women stared across at her, said her name and shook her head slightly.

After a while, Renie went over to the bookcase to find something to read.

'Not another bookworm,' Daff teased. She was embroidering a blouse, sighing every now and then as her thread got knotted, or she had to pull out a stitch.

'I like reading.' Renie studied the titles of the books.

A woman nearby pointed to one book with a brightly coloured cover. 'I really enjoyed this one.'

Renie picked it up. *Helen With The High Hand*. 'What a strange title. I haven't read any books by Arnold Bennett before.' She studied the first page, then nodded. 'Looks as if it'll be good.'

'You have to put your name on the borrowers' list when you borrow a book and cross it out

41

when you bring it back.'

Renie did as she was shown then put the book down by her chair. 'I need to write a letter to my sister first. I'll go and get my writing things.'

'No need to do that if it's to your family,' the same woman said. 'They encourage us to write home. They not only provide paper and envelopes, but pay postage too. Though don't try to slip in a letter to a friend. They know all our families' addresses.'

'How kind of them!'

'They're not all of them kind,' Daff muttered.

Renie ignored that remark. People she'd met had been very kind indeed. She wrote a quick letter to Nell. The same woman took her out to show her where to leave the letter for collection in the morning.

'Don't take too much notice of Daff. She always finds something to complain about. They're very fair employers here, even though they work you hard. Mr Greaves might be old, but he's a good manager and keeps everyone on their toes.'

As the days passed, Renie was surprised not to receive a reply by return of post, but perhaps it would arrive tomorrow. She planned to write to Nell every week without fail, knowing how her letters would cheer her sister up.

When no reply had arrived after three days, Renie wrote again, and this time she did hear from her sister, explaining what had happened and how Cliff had destroyed the letter and address. She was furious to think her brother-in-law had thrown her letter in the fire and not for the first time wished poor Nell hadn't had to marry Cliff.

Nell hadn't said whether Cliff was angry about Renie leaving, but he must have been, and he'd have taken it out on his wife.

But there was nothing she could do about her sister's situation except make sure she was never a burden to Nell, let alone in Cliff's power. And she'd never, ever let either of her sisters down by misbehaving. Mattie had taught them both the right way to behave and why Nell had given herself to Cliff out of wedlock still puzzled Renie. But that wasn't something you could ask about, certainly not in a letter that he might get his hands on.

She was missing little Sarah as well as her sister. That child was such a little love.

Renie had never even been inside a big hotel like this one. The King's Head in Rochdale, bought when the Carlings were just starting up, apparently, was nothing to this place. She felt very ignorant during her first few weeks there, but with temporary staff around, hired just for the festive season, she wasn't the only one needing to ask her way, so at least she didn't stick out like a sore thumb.

★　★　★

Gil refused to join his family in London for Christmas and Walter couldn't change his mind, whatever he said or did. Gil didn't share his family's love of the social whirl. He preferred a quieter life in the country.

Mrs Rycroft came down to see her youngest son one day, staying overnight, but she had to rush back to London for a ball the following evening.

She made time to speak to Walter. 'He's very depressed, isn't he?'

'Yes, ma'am. I do my best, but he's had to face some big changes, and he was never an indoor lad.'

'No. If you need anything, think of anything we can send, just let me know.'

'I will, ma'am.'

He watched her go, wishing they'd insisted on Gil joining them in London.

It was going to be a very quiet Christmas.

*   *   *

The Rathleigh was almost completely booked out for Christmas, and there were parties held in several of the big private dining rooms every evening.

The female waitresses, normally kept away from serving dinner, had to work in the evenings as well, but they were paid extra for it, so Renie didn't mind. Of course, she was too junior to actually wait on the posh customers who dined there, but she fetched and carried for the waiters, watching wide-eyed as beautiful women in clothes such as she'd never seen before were shown to their seats.

'Look at that one,' Daff hissed as she passed, carrying a steaming tureen of vegetables.

Renie tried not to stare. She wasn't sure what

44

she thought about peg-top skirts, whose material was bulky and pleated round the hips, then narrowed as it crossed at the front in two panels. It left a 'V' bare near the feet, fully revealing not only the ankles but the lower legs in their silk stockings. Some people thought that was shocking, but at least this lady had neat ankles.

'Look how low that neckline over there is,' she whispered to Daff when their paths next crossed. 'It's not respectable. My sister would have a fit if I wore something like that.'

'I've seen lower necklines. She looks pretty, though. I wish I had a tiny waist like hers.'

The evening gowns were made in beautiful fabrics like velvet and silk, which Renie had never seen close up before. They seemed to come in more colours than the rainbow and she wished she could buy something more colourful to wear. Not silk or anything impractical, but still, a pretty, bright material would cheer you up.

She tried to describe the clothes in her next letter to Nell, but knew she couldn't do them justice.

★   ★   ★

After Christmas, the big pot of tips from happy customers was divided between those who'd worked so hard to serve them.

Mrs Tolson herself came into the women's sitting room to speak to the women staff. 'I'm very pleased with you all. You've worked hard. Mr Greaves and I have counted the tips and

45

divided it up between you. Also, Mr Carling wishes all employees to have a small bonus, as usual, in appreciation of your hard work over the year.'

She called out the names and women came forward one by one to receive small envelopes and to take a chocolate from a big box.

Renie was called out last.

'Irene Fuller.'

Daff had to nudge her to remind her that this was her. She still sometimes forgot to answer to her full name.

She peeped into the envelope, which clinked nicely, expecting shillings, and finding three guineas and some change. In addition, she had a bonus on top of her wages paid by the owners, the smallest of any member of the permanent staff, which was only fair because she was a newcomer. But still, it was an extra three shillings, because they got a two shillings bonus for each month of service.

And the chocolate was wonderful. Even better than a Fry's Chocolate Cream bar. She sucked it slowly to make it last.

When Mrs Tolson had left, one of the older women said, 'Mean devils!'

Renie looked at her in surprise.

'I mean the Carlings, young Irene. They've earned hundreds of pounds from our hard work and we have to be grateful for a few shillings extra. It's the customers' tips that have given us our real bonus.'

'If you met my brother-in-law, you'd think the Carlings very generous.' Renie spoke without thinking, but to her surprise this led to one or two other women talking about relatives who were also treated badly by their stingy husbands.

'Don't ever marry, young Irene!' said Miss Plympton, who was in charge of the cakes in the tea shop. 'The only way you'll keep the money you earn is to stay single.'

Another woman tossed her head. 'Well, I don't agree. My Jimmy isn't like that and I can't wait to get married, but we've agreed to wait two years so that we can save up for our furniture.'

When the women got talking in the evenings, Renie learnt quite a lot about life.

She didn't join in the complaints about the Rathleigh. She'd never stopped being thankful for this job. Whatever anyone else thought of their employers, the Carlings had taken her away from the grinding poverty and constant nastiness of her life with her brother-in-law.

She wished she could take Nell away, too. And little Sarah.

There were so many things she hoped for, now she was in London. Who knew what would happen to her in such an exciting place? She'd taken the first step out of poverty, and would work hard to go further yet.

1911

3

After Christmas, Renie still occasionally got lost in the areas of the hotel where guests were not to be found, and got teased a lot about that. But she couldn't help it. It was easy enough to find your way round the main part of the hotel where the guests stayed, but there were two levels of cellars below that, where employees did dirty or menial jobs, mending, cleaning, fetching and carrying coal and oil. Only they were called 'basements' because 'cellar' was considered a rather common word.

Worst of all was going down to the lower basement, which was mainly storerooms, because there were very few people around and it gave her the shivers as her footsteps echoed on the stone paving. Once she let a door slam behind her and couldn't open it again because the wood was damp and it had stuck fast.

She thought she'd be trapped there for hours till someone noticed she was missing and her lamp wouldn't last that long and she'd be alone in the dark. She nearly panicked, but fortunately she heard footsteps in the corridor and called for help. And even more fortunately, it wasn't one of the pageboys.

After that, she made sure to prop the doors open carefully before she went into a storeroom. It was her job and she had to do it, so she gritted her teeth and tried not to jump at strange noises, because if the pageboys found out she was afraid, they'd make her life hell, she knew. When she had been new to the hotel, they'd played a few nasty tricks on her until Maud had had a word with them. No one would dare play tricks on Maud.

The front cellars connected at several points with the side basement beneath the hotel's rear wing. There was one wide passage and several narrow sets of stairs. The wing had been built later to extend the hotel and the guest rooms here were not as spacious — or as expensive — and were used mostly for guests' servants, who had their own dining room and sitting room.

Three worlds under one roof, she thought: guests, staff and visiting servants. And in each world there were several different groups as well, such as upper and lower servants, who didn't sit down to eat together. It could be very confusing to a girl from the country.

★ ★ ★

As he started to recover, Gil, who had almost lived out of doors and been very active, fretted at sitting around inside the house and wasn't the easiest of patients.

His mother came to see him morning and evening when she was at home, and for her he held back his frustration, but she could tell how he was feeling.

She stopped Walter in the corridor one day to say, 'I don't know what we'd do without you. My

52

husband means well and I love my son dearly, but neither of us is any use in the sickroom.'

No wonder. The master had never bothered to get to know his children, just barked orders at them, Walter thought. Mr Rycroft might lavish money on his children, but that wasn't the same as loving someone.

The mistress cared for her children in the way most upper-class ladies did, from a distance. After all, Mrs Rycroft had a busy social life with her husband and they spent most of the year in London.

A nanny had brought up their three sons, young nursemaids had played with them or taken them for walks. As he grew older Gil became mad about horses and spent a lot of time in the stables with Walter. It was a pity old Nurse had died a few years ago. She'd have been a great help just now.

Walter left his deputy in charge of the stables, and tried to keep his lad from plunging into deepest despair.

When Gil was allowed to get up, he had to be lifted into a wheeled chair by Walter and the nurse, because the broken arm and leg were still in plaster. Dr Laver would remove that after a month or so.

Mr Rycroft, a stout gentleman who puffed going up stairs, had wanted to install a newfangled invention in his country house, as he had in his town house: a lift. But with no electricity in the country, this wasn't possible.

Gil refused point-blank to be moved to the London house, so they brought in men to carry him up and down the stairs morning and evening.

When the plaster was cut away, Dr Laver said the bones had healed well. 'Try walking a few steps.'

Gil found to his horror that he couldn't walk evenly. 'What's wrong?'

'It was a bad break. You'll have to consult the specialist as to whether anything else can be done.'

Walter had seen it before. A break that healed to leave one leg shorter than the other. He didn't say that to Gil, but he doubted a specialist could perform a miracle.

They'd have to wait and see. At least going to London would get the lad out of the house.

★ ★ ★

They went up to London by train a few days later, but Gil was still limping badly and needed to use a stick. They had a compartment to themselves, and when they got out of the train, Gil avoided looking round or making eye contact with anyone.

At the last minute Mr Rycroft was called away to an important meeting, so it was Walter who went with Gil to the specialist.

'The leg's healed well, Mr Rycroft.'

'But I'm still limping,' Gil protested.

'It sometimes happens that a leg is shortened by such an accident. I'm afraid you'll always limp, Mr Rycroft. There's nothing that can be done unless you want to undergo a series of operations — and even then, nothing can be guaranteed. I'd not advise it in your case. The bones were badly damaged.'

Silence, then, 'And my arm?' Gil scowled down at it. 'It twitches. I can't control that.'

'I'm afraid the rough treatment you received after the accident has injured nerves in that arm. It may improve a little, but I doubt it'll ever be fully right again.'

There was a long silence, but Walter could see how his lad's shoulders slumped. He knew how embarrassed Gil was by the way the arm jerked involuntarily.

Other people weren't always tactful about how they reacted to it, either. His mother hated to see it and couldn't hide how she felt. His father had once or twice said sharply, 'Can't you control that damned arm?'

After that interview with the specialist, there were no more tears, but there were no smiles, either. Gil limped round the country house like a white-faced ghost, spending hours staring out of the window or sitting in the summer house. He still tired quickly and retreated to his bedroom on the slightest excuse.

The family continued to lead their normal life, spending most of their time in London and coming less and less frequently to Hampshire. The two older brothers were married and no longer living at home. It seemed clear to Walter that the Rycrofts were avoiding their previously handsome, athletic son.

Well, the lad was still handsome. The accident hadn't harmed his face.

One day Walter took the bull by the horns. 'How about going to London for a few days? There's more to do there.'

'There's nothing *I* want to do. Do you think I want to be seen by the fashionable world like this?' He tried to gesture to himself, and as the damaged arm jerked sideways, he let out a bitter laugh. 'I'm like a badly strung puppet.'

'Your father's talking about consulting other specialists to see if they can help.'

'I doubt anyone can. We've already seen the supposedly best man.'

'Well, a dicky arm isn't the end of the world.'

'No. And what can't be cured must be endured. Only . . . it's the end of my world. I don't know how to bear this, Walter. I just . . . don't know how.' His voice broke.

★ ★ ★

As the months passed, Renie settled into her new life. The work was hard and not very interesting, but there were more people to talk to and a lot to do in London on her day off. Even if she had only an hour off, she often nipped out to walk round Yew Tree Gardens, glad to be among greenery and to see a few flowers. She enjoyed watching children play there.

In June, the city was filled with spectators for the coronation of King George V. Fortunately the summer had been fine and the coronation could take place in style.

Renie was surprised at the fuss that the staff of the Rathleigh made about it, hardly talking about anything else for weeks. They couldn't go to watch the procession, of course, but most of them managed to see the preparations, the stands for spectators and the decorations along the route to be taken to Westminster Abbey on the 22nd.

The day after the coronation, she overheard one of the guests talking about it, and it didn't sound at all like what she'd seen when she sneaked a look at one of the guests' newspapers.

'Just a procession of men in fancy uniforms riding expensive horses,' the old lady said scornfully. 'And the route was soon covered in dung. Those animals have no respect for the Queen and King, or for anyone else except Mother Nature.' She laughed heartily at her own joke, but her companions seemed embarrassed.

The staff of the hotel knew better, of course, than to criticise the royal family in any way, but the younger ones had been surprised when the poor queen had to give up her own name Victoria and become Queen Mary. The older staff said there would never be another like dear Queen Victoria and forbade them to speak of either queen disrespectfully.

It wasn't disrespectful to wonder why things were done, Renie thought mutinously, but she'd changed since she was a girl and didn't burst out with her thoughts. Living with Cliff and being afraid of being thrown out of his house had taught her to hold her tongue and made her grow up quickly.

Far more important to Renie was that little Sarah was very ill with diarrhoea that same month, and Nell could only send her sister a couple of brief notes to assure her that Sarah hadn't succumbed. So many children died of stomach upsets that Renie had tears of sheer relief in her eyes when she heard that Sarah was well and truly better.

It was living in that nasty little house that had done it. How could Cliff make his family live in a slum? It wouldn't cost him much more to rent a decent house.

*   *   *

In September Renie took her annual week's holiday, going to spend it with her sister in Lancashire. It was wonderful to be with Nell, to be able to talk about anything and everything, and she loved playing with little Sarah, who was just starting to walk, clinging to the furniture, not moving on her own yet.

Cliff was as nasty as ever, demanding Renie pay him for the food she ate and the washing she would cause. 'I'll buy my own food,' she told him. 'I'm not giving you any money. Anyway, you don't do the shopping.'

For a minute he glared at her so fiercely she wondered if she'd said too much and was afraid he might throw her out. Instead, he looked at his wife. 'You'd better not keep me short to feed her.'

'Of course not, Cliff.'

Nell's voice was toneless and she kept her eyes down. That upset Renie.

Once he'd gone out to the pub, she asked,

'Why do you let him treat you like that?'

'Because it's easier. He's out all day and at the pub several evenings, so I don't have to put up with him for long.'

Renie didn't comment but that phrase upset her. *Put up with him!* She remembered when Nell had thought herself in love and loved by Cliff. What an unhappy life she led now.

All Renie could do was buy her sister and niece treats. One afternoon she took them to see a moving picture show.

But the week passed so quickly, and Nell looked so unhappy as she said goodbye, that Renie knew she'd go home and cry.

There was nothing she could do to help Nell, except stay independent. She knew her sister was very pleased about that and wanted nothing but the best for her.

But was being a waitress the best life had to offer?

Renie still wanted so much more.

* * *

She bought Christmas presents to send to her sister and niece from a nearby market Daff showed her, where there was a second-hand stall selling clothes that were better than average, though of course more expensive.

Daff always studied the clothes carefully, fingering them and sighing in envy. 'One day I'm going to have lots of clothes like these. Till then, I keep my eyes open for bargains.'

'Is this where you bought the blue skirt and

jacket you wear on Sundays for church?'

'Yes. Oh, look at this. That's good value. Wool as fine as that usually costs a fortune. It'd really suit you.'

Renie was nearly tempted into buying the dark-red skirt and jacket, then thought of Nell, how hard she worked, how work-worn her poor hands were. 'It's lovely but I can't afford it, and when would I wear it anyway?'

'To church.'

'Who for?'

'You might meet someone you like.'

'I don't want a fellow.'

The owner of the stall sidled up to her. 'This would suit you even better, love.' He held out a blouse and skirt and Renie sighed. He was right.

'It would, but I can't afford it, thanks.'

He looked at her shrewdly. 'New to London, are you? Come out dancing with me one night and I'll sell this to you for half a crown.'

She knew what he really meant by that invitation and drew herself up. 'No, thank you. I don't accept favours from strangers.' She walked off before he could say anything else, muttering, 'The cheek of him!'

She had seen girls get tempted into trouble by easy ways like that to get things they wanted, but nothing would persuade Renie to give her body to a fellow till she was married — if she ever did marry. She didn't intend to wind up like Nell, tied for life to a mean-spirited man who didn't care for her or his own child.

At the moment Renie was enjoying life hugely, in spite of her worries about her sister, even though she'd never worked as hard in her life before. It was enough. She was only eighteen, after all, though sometimes she felt older.

★   ★   ★

In November 1911, a year after Gil's accident, Mr Rycroft came down to visit his son and told him over dinner, 'I've made an appointment in London with a specialist in the rehabilitation of injuries like yours. He's been studying in France and has recently returned. Daniel Seaborne is very well thought of. Maybe he can do something for you.'

Gil stared at him across the end of the large, shiny mahogany table that could seat ten people even without extra leaves. 'Do you think this one will be able to perform miracles, then? The others couldn't.'

'We have to keep trying.'

'I don't agree. I'm fed up of being mauled around. If this chappie doesn't help, I'll not go to any others, whatever you threaten.'

'You'll do what I say. You're still dependent on me and don't you forget it.'

Gil raised the glass of wine to his lips in a mocking gesture and drained it.

His father took the bottle away from him before he could refill his glass. 'You're drinking too much. You can have water with your meals from now on. And make sure you're on time for breakfast tomorrow. We don't want to miss our train.'

Gil didn't say how easy it would be, once his

father had returned to London, to nip down to the wine cellar and take a bottle or two from where they'd not be noticed. Even a lame man could move quietly enough to manage that. And Walter didn't often spend the evenings in the house because his quarters were still over the stables, so he didn't know everything.

The physical pain had gone now, but Gil was desperately unhappy. He couldn't even go for a brisk walk. He wasn't used to sitting around the house and had never been interested in books.

The drink blurred the edges of his misery as nothing else seemed to do. He had nothing else to turn to.

No, that wasn't true. He had Walter, didn't know what he'd have done without the kindly old man.

But what worried him most was what he was going to do with the rest of his life. He wasn't trained for any profession. He was useless.

★ ★ ★

At breakfast, Gil's father took charge of the post and studied one letter with a frown, before passing it to his son. 'Who'd be writing to you from Swindon? It's good-quality notepaper. Who do you know there?'

'I don't know anyone.'

'Shall I open it for you? I've got my letter opener here. It must be awkward for you.'

'No, thanks. I'll read it later.' Gil reached for the letter, saw his father hesitate, and kept his hand outstretched.

'Oh, very well.' His father slapped the envelope on to his hand.

Gil stuffed it into his pocket.

'Aren't you going to read it?' his father pressed.

He tried to hold back his anger. 'I'll read it later. I'm not expecting anything important.'

'I'd appreciate you letting me know what it's about. I like to keep an eye on what comes to my house.'

Gil stood up so hastily he knocked his chair over. He bent to pick it up before his father could do that for him and by that time he'd bitten back a sarcastic comment that he was twenty-six years old, not six. As Walter kept telling him, it did no good to upset the master. 'I'd better get ready for this useless trip to London you're insisting on.'

'What's the matter?' Walter asked as soon as he went into the bedroom.

'My father. As usual. Wants to know what my mail is about now.' He tossed the unopened letter on to the bed. 'I'll see what that is later. I'd better get ready now or I'll be late. Has he decided whether you're coming up to London with us?'

'Yes. He wants me to help you with your luggage and keep an eye on you. Look . . . your father does care about you, you know.'

Gil sighed. 'I know. In his own way, always in his own way, as if a son is a possession. It's just . . . I'd do better if he left me alone. He treats me like a child, and I'm not.'

'Then don't act like one.'

Walter was right, really, but Gil didn't tell him that. He did sometimes behave childishly, couldn't seem to help himself when everything got him down.

★ ★ ★

Their appointment was the first one the following day. The specialist had fitted him in at the early hour of eight o'clock to please Mr Rycroft senior.

At least Gil's father didn't come into the examination room with him.

Seaborne poked Gil around, hummed and hawed, then sat down with him in his office. 'Do you want to call your father in now?'

'Not yet, if you don't mind. I'd like to talk to you on my own. I want . . . need to know the truth.'

'I'm not going to offer you false hope. You'll never regain full use of that arm, Mr Rycroft. There is no way known of reversing nerve damage like yours. The doctor who caused it was a fool.'

There was silence as Seaborne looked at him sympathetically. 'As for the leg, you'll always have a limp, though you can probably reduce it by gently building up the strength of the limb with exercises, and reinforcing that by walking regularly. I'll give you the name of a man who specialises in this sort of exercise. And if you get your right shoe built up by a shoemaker I know, that'll also help minimise the limp. I don't know why someone hasn't suggested it before. The exercising will be painful to start off with, though.'

Gil felt as if he'd been given good news, for the first time in ages. Perhaps now his father would listen to the specialist and allow the built-up shoe. It didn't matter what it looked like as long as it helped minimise the limp. And he didn't care whether the exercising hurt or not. 'I'll definitely do that, then. Thank you.'

Seaborne's voice softened. 'It takes time to get used to changes like this, but at least you're a young man and healthy in every other way. Hard as it is to face a different future from what you'd planned, you've the time and money to find some other path in life. Be thankful for what you've got. Others are not as fortunate.'

Gil knew that, of course he did, but it didn't make him *feel* any better, so he just nodded. 'I wonder if you'd do me a favour, Mr Seaborne? Could you please make my father understand that it's no use consulting other specialists?'

'I'll try, simply because you're right: it isn't any use. He must care a lot about you.'

'Not really. He cares more about how having a son like me reflects on the family. When someone else suggested building up my shoe, he took offence, said it'd look bad.'

The specialist looked at Gil in surprise, then pity. 'Well, I'll do my best to change his mind about that. It happens sometimes that relatives have trouble adjusting, as well as those directly affected. You can't . . . get away from him, make a life of your own?'

'Unfortunately, I'm totally dependent on him financially.'

After his father had come in to listen to the

65

specialist, Gil walked out with him.

'I suppose we'd better get your shoes built up, then. It'll look bad, but there you are. Go and see this chappie. You won't need me for that.'

'Thank you.'

'Fancy lunch at my club?'

Gil shook his head, seeing the quick flash of relief on his father's face. 'No, thanks. I'm a bit tired now.'

'Well, you go home and have a nice long rest.'

A nice long rest was the last thing Gil wanted. What was 'nice' about lounging around doing nothing?

When he got back to the London house, it was only half past nine and he wondered what to do with himself for the rest of the day. Most of his old friends lived in the country and he wasn't one for museums and art galleries. Anyway, he'd lost touch with people, now that they no longer shared interests.

He went up to his room to find Walter waiting for him.

'What did this fellow say, lad?'

'Same as the other specialists, except he managed to persuade my father to stop dragging me round to anyone else. Oh, and he also obtained permission for me to get my shoe built up to help minimise the limp.'

'About time too. I don't know why your father was so against that.'

'Appearances.' Gil went to stand at the window and stare out at the grey day. 'What do *you* do with yourself in London, Walter? Don't you miss the stables and the fresh air?'

66

'A bit. I'd be lying if I said anything else and I won't lie to you, lad, ever. But I'm not as agile as I used to be so I couldn't have gone on in my old job for much longer. Your father had a chat to me about staying on as your helper and leaving the stables to younger fellows.'

'He never said a word to me about that. I'm sorry, Walter. You deserve better than caring for a crock like me.'

Walter came across to lay one hand on the younger man's shoulder. 'I think you need me more than the horses do now. And I care more about you than I do about the horses.'

Gil patted the hand, stood for a moment, then moved away, swallowing hard to hold back his emotions.

Walter held out a crumpled letter. 'You still haven't opened this.'

'Oh. I suppose I might as well see what it's about.' He slit it open, his left hand twitching inconveniently and making him slice through the top of the letter as well as the envelope. 'Can't even open a damned envelope properly,' he muttered.

'You'd do better if you moved more slowly.'

Gil shrugged and started to read. The letter was from a firm of lawyers in Swindon, representing Miss Alice Bennerden, who had sadly passed away two weeks previously. He stopped reading to frown at the letter. 'Who the hell is Alice Bennerden?'

'A distant relative of your grandmother's, so even more distantly connected to you. They were quite good friends when they were young. I remember Miss Alice when I was a lad and worked for your mother's family. She used to visit them occasionally. Then she had an accident, fell down some stone steps and hurt her spine. She wound up in a basket chair, poor lady, being wheeled around. She was only twenty when it happened, too.'

Gil continued reading his letter, exclaimed in surprise, read it all again then looked up at Walter. He had to try twice before he could get the words out. 'She's left me a house and an income. Look.' He held out the letter, his hand shaking.

Walter read it, then whistled softly. 'A house in Wiltshire, and that's a decent income, too.'

Gil buried his head in his hands for a moment or two, fighting the urge to weep. When he looked up at the old man, he said in a husky voice, 'This will set me free, Walter. My parents won't be able to haul me round specialists, or force me to stay in London or have dinner with their friends who all treat me as if I've become a halfwit.'

'They mean well.'

'I know. But I hate being pitied, and now that I've seen my last specialist, I need time to . . . I don't know . . . think about the future. I hadn't realised that I still had unrealistic hopes myself until Seaborne was utterly frank with me.'

He looked back at the letter, smiling slightly. 'This is a new kind of hope. I can't believe it's happened. Walter, will you come and live with me in Wiltshire?'

'Don't you want to see the house first before

you decide whether you're going to live there?'

'No. The lawyer says it's near Swindon, so maybe it's in the country. I hope so. I just want to get away from everyone for a while. I'm going to live there whatever the house is like, even if it's falling down about my ears. Will you come and work for me instead of my father?'

'Of course I'll come with you, lad. Try getting rid of me.'

'I don't want you as a groom, but as a . . . well, companion.'

'That'd be an honour, lad, but I'm not sure how your father will take that.'

'It won't matter. We can do what we want. If the house isn't in the country, I'll sell it and buy somewhere that is.'

Walter's face brightened. 'Maybe we can keep a horse or two. I'd not like to be without them.'

'You can have your horses. We'll need a pony trap to get around — unless I buy one of these newfangled motor cars.'

'Stinking things. Give me a horse any day.' He hesitated, before adding, 'You could still ride a quiet horse, you know.'

'I'm not riding a tame rocking horse.' Gil folded the letter and put it in his pocket, excitement rising in him. 'Let's go to Wiltshire now, this very afternoon. I don't want my father coming with me to see these lawyer chappies. I want to do everything myself from now on.'

'You should leave him a note explaining what's happened, though.'

He hesitated, then nodded. 'I suppose so. Will you pack for me while I write it, please? I shan't give Pa details, so he won't be able to pursue me.' He went off whistling.

It was the happiest the lad had looked since the accident. *Bless you, Alice Bennerden!* Walter thought. *My lad has a real chance of happiness now.*

4

When she sent the Christmas presents, Renie suggested to Nell in her letter that they ask Cliff if they could contact his family now to ask whether they'd heard from Mattie. After all, more than eighteen months had passed since they'd left Swindon.

In her reply Nell said Cliff wouldn't hear of it.

There's nothing I can do about it, Renie love, and I daren't write to them without his permission. He'd throw a fit, might even leave me.

We have to hope he'll change his mind next year, or that Mattie will somehow find us.

Sarah sends her love to her auntie. She's growing so quickly, you'll not recognise her when you see her in September. I reckon she'll be running about by then. Won't that be wonderful?

I'm so happy that you're going to spend your week's holiday with us. I know it's a long time away still, but it's something to look forward to. I think of it whenever I feel down and it cheers me up.

Work hard and make a good life for yourself.

Nell always finished her letters like that. Renie sighed and brought the paper up to her face, cuddling it against her cheek. She worried about her sister. What if Cliff hurt Nell? She wouldn't put it past him to thump her as some men did. She knew how short of money he kept her.

Renie didn't try to send money to her sister, though. She guessed he'd take that. But she did occasionally find some piece of clothing for her niece or sister on one of the market stalls. She was becoming an expert at finding bargains, yet thanks to her tips money, she was still able to save something each week.

Wouldn't Mattie stare to hear that? Her eldest sister had often told her off for spending any money she got as soon she laid hands on it. Pennies that had been. Her father had taken nearly everything she earned. Well, Renie was saving shillings now. Every single week. And they soon added up to pounds.

Having some money behind her made her feel safer when she walked the streets of London and didn't know a single face in the crowds.

In spite of being careful, she'd managed to buy herself some nice clothes second hand, real bargains, impossible to resist. No one would think she came from the country now. She took pride in looking smart when she went to church or out for a long walk on fine Sundays. She was waiting impatiently for the longer summer evenings when she could stay out for a while after work. She wanted to see so many of the famous places in London and you could stay out until half past eight on working nights or until dusk, whichever came first.

She'd made a list and was ticking the items off

one by one: the Tower of London, Westminster Abbey, Buckingham Palace headed it. She'd already seen those, but was going back to see them again. It'd take several visits to see Westminster Abbey properly. How wonderful it felt inside the old building. So much space, so much beautiful stonework.

Sometimes, if the weather was fine, she walked round Yew Tree Gardens after work, sighing over the poor yew trees, which were struggling to thrive. Their dark foliage wasn't all that cheering, but the flower beds always looked good. Someone took a lot of trouble to keep the garden neat and tidy, but she rarely saw hotel guests there, or the posh people who lived in the square. It was mainly nursemaids and servants who used it.

It was reading books that had made her realise she wanted to live in a village in the country, and a pretty one, too. Surely they weren't telling lies about what life was like in such places? That had become her secret dream, to live in a village where she knew everyone and they knew her. Not like London, where everyone you passed in the street was a stranger.

Was a village too much to ask? Why not? It didn't cost anything to dream. And ideally, of course, her sisters would live in the same village. How wonderful that would be!

She didn't know what she'd do for a job in such a place, though. She didn't want to work as a housemaid in a private home. You were like a slave when you did that, hardly allowed out of the house, even in your free time. She'd heard some of the women talking about it.

Other girls dreamt of marriage, and spoke of those dreams sometimes, but Renie remained adamant that she wasn't rushing into marriage. One day, perhaps, she might think of it. If she met a very special man. She had plenty of time before she need worry. She'd turn nineteen in August, and that was hardly on the shelf.

Since leaving Swindon, she'd grown up quickly. Strange how life changed you. She now understood how Mattie had had to grow up suddenly when their mother died and left her eldest daughter to bring up her half-sisters Renie and Nell.

People said dreams never came true, but Renie had already got herself a job in a big hotel, hadn't she? She'd achieved that dream.

If it was humanly possible, she'd make her other dream come true as well. She could be very determined when she wanted something, she'd found. She'd surprised herself since she came to London.

★ ★ ★

Walter wasn't stupid enough to think things would be easy for the lad, even with an inheritance. Life never was. But he was sure Gil would have a much better chance of happiness away from his father. The lad had a good heart and that was what mattered. Walter just hoped he'd be spared long enough to see him on his way.

He went to check the train timetables in the

master's *Bradshaw* to find one for Swindon, where Miss Bennerden's lawyer was. The railway guide got heavier each year, he thought — must be over a thousand pages in this edition. Still, you could usually rely on it for train times.

Once he'd done that, he went to finish the packing. He'd be glad to get back to the country. He didn't enjoy city life, any more than his lad did.

The door of the bedroom banged open and Gil came in smiling. 'It's just starting to sink in, Walter. I'm free now, I really am. I can go to hell in my own way.'

Walter had had enough of this sort of talk and said sharply, 'Or you can find something worthwhile to do with your life and stop feeling sorry for yourself.'

Gil gaped at him, shocked by these rough words, but Walter wasn't smoothing things over.

'You've pitied yourself for long enough now, my lad. There are lots of folk worse off than you, but every time anyone reminds you of that, you go glassy-eyed. Once you've claimed this inheritance, I shall expect you to take a hold of things. I'll not stay with you if you turn to alcohol or sit in a corner feeling sorry for yourself — or even if you laze around doing nothing useful.'

He folded his arms and stared at Gil, not meaning a word of it — as if he could leave his lad — but trying to look as if he would carry out this threat.

Gil sank down on the bed and began to fiddle with the counterpane. 'I have been feeling sorry for myself. I know I have. But I couldn't seem to pull myself out of it. You're right, though. I'm very lucky and I promise you, Walter, I won't waste this chance.'

That was more like it, Walter thought, hiding his relief.

★ ★ ★

Miss Bennerden's lawyers, Perryworth and Mortlake, had rooms just off Regent Street, in the centre of Swindon. When they got off the train, Gil took a chance and simply turned up without an appointment.

Walter waited outside in the cab, chatting to the driver, while the horse stood patiently under an old blanket because it was a chilly day.

Gil didn't care that it was cold and blowy. He was warmed by hope today. The clerk greeted him with a flattering amount of fuss as soon as he gave his name.

'I'll let Mr Mortlake know you're here, Mr Rycroft. He'll be delighted to see you.'

He returned almost immediately. 'Mr Mortlake will be free in five minutes.'

'Is there a hotel in Swindon you could recommend? My man's outside with the luggage. I could send him off to book a room.'

'Won't you be staying at Oakdene House, sir?'

That hadn't occurred to Gil. 'I don't know anything about my inheritance. I'd assumed there were formalities to complete before I could take possession.'

With a fatherly smile, the clerk said, 'Mr

Mortlake will explain it all and I'll let your man know to wait. I'm sure the cab driver won't mind.'

Mr Mortlake was a thin gentleman of about fifty with a bald head, large nose and dark eyes. He resembled an amiable eagle, Gil thought, but there was a shrewdness to his eyes that said he was no one's fool.

He came across his office to greet the heir, shaking hands and smiling. 'I'm delighted to meet you, Mr Rycroft, delighted. Do take a seat.'

Gil's arm chose that time to twitch itself out of his pocket and he clutched it with a mutter of annoyance.

But Mr Mortlake's shrewd gaze betrayed neither pity nor disgust, just a calm interest. 'Must be annoying.'

'It is.'

'Miss Bennerden had a twitch in the left side of her face after the accident. People who knew her soon got used to it, but some found it disconcerting at first. People round here are very friendly, you'll find, even more so in the country than in the town itself.'

Gil realised the man was offering comfort — and what he'd said *was* comforting. Strange that a complete stranger could do that for him. 'Is that where the house is, in the country? I'm afraid I know nothing of Miss Bennerden, except that she was a distant connection of my grandmother and had had a bad accident.'

'Yes. Very bad. It left her in pain and unable to walk without help. She was a fine lady, a sad loss to us all, and will be greatly missed in her village.

77

She didn't let her own problems stop her helping others. I admired her greatly.'

'Do you know why she made me her heir?'

'She didn't leave everything to you, so you're not the sole heir. There are several other bequests to people she knew and loved, people she felt needed a little help. But she wanted you to receive yours first and understand its implications before other announcements were made.'

'I see. But that still doesn't explain why she chose me. We'd never even met.'

The lawyer paused, as if to consider his next words. 'She'd always kept in touch with your grandmother and even after Mrs Rycroft died, she still corresponded with another lady who lives near your father's country estate. So Miss Bennerden knew what was happening to your family and . . . ' He hesitated. 'Well, she knew how difficult things had become for you. She understood what that was like better than anyone else could, I'm sure.'

'You mean, she was sorry for me.' Gil heard how flat and ungracious his voice sounded, couldn't help it.

'In one sense, yes. But mainly, she felt your problems would give you a better understanding of the troubles of others. She asks that you use the money she's left you not only to help yourself but to help those in need.'

Gil didn't know what to say. He wasn't ungrateful, far from it, but he hated that being a cripple was the reason for his legacy. As for playing the benefactor, he hadn't a clue how to set about that. He'd feel a fool even trying, he was sure.

'It's a lot to take in and you're looking tired, Mr Rycroft, if you don't mind me saying so. I have some papers for you to sign, then if you wish, you can go straight to Oakdene.'

'I'd like that.'

'Unfortunately I can't accompany you because I have another appointment within the hour and then a social engagement this evening which means a lot to my wife. I'll visit you tomorrow afternoon at Oakdene, however, and go through the details of your own and the other bequests then.'

He pushed some papers across to Gil, who read them carefully, then signed them because they seemed straightforward enough, and also because this man wouldn't try to cheat anyone, he was sure.

Mr Mortlake put the papers into a folder, then got up and walked round the desk, ready to show his guest out.

'I hope I haven't sounded . . . ungrateful.'

'You've sounded worn out.' He patted Gil's shoulder. 'Things will seem much better in the morning. Mrs Tibbins, the housekeeper, will see that you're looked after for tonight. You'll need to take a train to Wootton Bassett, then another cab out to the house. Don't forget, Oakdene House in the village of Pypard West.'

The cabbie touched the brim of his bowler hat and, once his passenger was safely inside, pulled the blanket off the horse and climbed back into the driving seat. When he told it to walk on, it moved gently through the busy town to the station.

After another train ride, it was a relief to find a cab waiting at the station. 'Do you know where Oakdene House is?'

'Yes, sir. I've took folk out there a few times.'

It sounded more like *oi've* and *toimes* to Gil, a gentle burr of an accent he found vaguely soothing.

Thank goodness his journey was nearing an end! He leant his head against the side of the cab and shivered. At this time of year, it grew cold quickly as the day waned. The lawyer was right. He was utterly exhausted. Was it only this morning he'd been to see yet another specialist doctor? It felt as if that had happened to another person in another world.

He saw Walter watching him and smiled to show he was all right, then closed his eyes for a moment or two.

In spite of the cold, he felt himself dozing off. He blinked his eyes and tried to keep alert, but simply couldn't manage it. Ah, what did it matter? He had a house of his own, where he could surely do as he pleased. He could sleep all day, if he chose. Refuse to see people, if he didn't want bothering.

Or pull himself together and do something worthwhile. If Miss Alice Bennerden could overcome her physical problems, then he could too, and —

'Mr Gil, wake up. We're here.'

He started awake, stared round unable to work out where he was, then realised that he was in a cab and it had stopped moving. 'Sorry.'

'I nearly dozed off myself,' Walter said. 'It's been a long, eventful day, hasn't it?'

'It has. And I think you should always call me Gil from now on.'

Walter gave him a shrewd sideways glance. 'Well, I will then, Gil. Except when your father's around. No use stirring up trouble you don't need, and he'd take exception.'

'Even then,' Gil said firmly.

They got out, and before the luggage was unloaded, both of them took a good look at the front of the house. It was square, built of stone, looking about a hundred years old. A neat, plain dwelling, suitable for a gentleman. The main entrance had a small portico over it, with two windows on either side. There were three storeys, but the third was the attics and had dormer windows set in the roof.

'It's a nice gentleman's house, that is.' Walter turned to help the cab driver unload the luggage.

'My father would consider it small and undistinguished.' Gil paid the driver and moved forward, insisting he could carry his own suitcase.

In all this time no one had come to the door to see who had arrived, so Gil banged the knocker sharply, waited, then banged it again, harder.

Still no one came.

He and Walter exchanged puzzled glances.

'Mr Mortlake wouldn't have sent us here today if there were no staff. I remember distinctly him saying the housekeeper, Mrs Tibbins, would look after us.' Gil tried the door and it opened easily, so after a moment's hesitation, he led the way inside. After all, it was his own house, wasn't it? 'We'll leave our bags here and see if anyone is around.'

'Don't rush. Let's look at it.'

'I don't feel as if it's mine yet.' But he couldn't resist peeping into the rooms off the hall, finding them well furnished, with fires laid but not lit. It was cold and Gil couldn't help shivering.

Hearing sounds of movement to the rear of the hall, he called out, 'Is anyone there?'

The baize-covered door to the servants' quarters opened to reveal a middle-aged woman, wearing her outdoor clothes. She had an unflattering felt hat jammed down on her head, with a big hatpin stuck through the back of it, and was staring at him in shock. 'Who are you?'

'I'm the new owner, Gilbert Rycroft. And you are?'

'If you're the new owner, why isn't Mr Mortlake with you?' She turned her head to call, 'Cyril, come here quick!'

Running footsteps then a burly man joined her. He too was wearing outdoor clothing.

'This gentleman just let himself in. He says he's the new owner.'

Another scowl greeted the newcomers. 'Can you prove that?' He studied them and added a belated, 'Sir.'

Gil told himself they were right to be careful. As he moved across the hall, he tried to pull out the letter Mr Mortlake had given him. But of course, his left arm jerked awkwardly and it fell to the floor. He bent to pick it up then held it out. 'Here.'

They both stared at his arm and nodded, as if they knew about his problems. 'No need for the papers, sir,' the woman said.

'Miss Bennerden told us you had a bad arm,' Cyril added.

This time they both spoke more politely, but still coolly, Gil thought, as if they didn't welcome his arrival.

'You'll forgive us for being careful, I'm sure, sir. Come into the kitchen. It's a lot warmer there.'

He followed her, stopping to frown and look at her questioningly as he saw bundles and boxes by the door. Someone was clearly moving out.

'Cyril and I were taking our things outside.'

'Are you Mrs Tibbins?'

'No, sir. She broke her leg two days ago and they took her to stay at her daughter's over Swindon way. I'm Mary. I was the head house-maid. Cyril's my husband. He was the gardener.'

Was? Gil wondered. What did that mean? Why were they leaving?

Footsteps clattered down the kitchen stairs and a young woman of about twenty stopped on the bottom step, staring from one to the other, open-mouthed. She too had a bundle, but hers was wrapped in what looked like an old sheet.

'There's just me and Cyril here now, and Lizzie, who's the maid of all work.' Mary glanced at her husband, as if for support, and added, 'And I'm sorry, sir, but we're leaving today. Cook's already gone.'

For a moment her words didn't sink in, then Gil asked, 'Does Mr Mortlake know about this?'

'No, sir. We'll send him a letter tomorrow.'

'Why are you leaving?'

'I don't want to talk about it, sir. Only we've made up our minds and you'll not change them. Some things aren't right, whatever the lawyers say.'

'I don't understand.'

'Ask Mr Mortlake. He'll understand when he gets the letter. Me an' my Cyril have another job to go to.' She glanced at her husband and jerked her head towards the door.

Their expressions were definitely not friendly yet Gil couldn't think what he'd done to upset them. 'It would only be fair to tell me why you're leaving.'

'It's not my place. Come along, Lizzie.'

As the girl hesitated, looking as if she didn't want to go, Walter stepped forward. 'Surely you don't have to leave just because they do, lass? We'll still need help in the house, so you'll still have a job.'

'Lizzie!' Mary's voice was sharp.

Still the girl hesitated, looking from Gil to Walter, then she set down her bundles as if something she'd seen reassured her. 'Mam needs my money, you know she does, Mary. And *I* haven't got another job to go to.'

She looked pleadingly at Walter. 'I'll need to get my trunk off the cart, though.'

'I'll help you.' He followed her outside, having to wait a few seconds at the door for a scowling Cyril to get out of their way.

'That girl will regret this,' Mary told Gil. 'No one in the village is happy about you inheriting when others deserve it more. And they won't be happy about her staying. That's all I'll say.'

She turned and went out to join her husband, leaving Gil even more puzzled. Who else deserved the money? There were other, smaller legacies still to be announced, but Miss Bennerden hadn't wanted those people informed till he was here. And it was surely her right to leave her money as she chose?

He rubbed his forehead. It was aching and he was desperately thirsty. He turned with relief as Walter and the girl came back, carrying a battered trunk which they set next to the bundle she'd left by the stairs. 'Thank you for staying, Lizzie. We're in great need of your help. I'm Walter Bilham, by the way.'

'Pleased to meet you.' She looked back at Gil. 'It's the money, sir. Mam's desperate for it since Dad run off. Only . . . Miss Bennerden used to pay me weekly and let me take the money home. I should have asked before I got my trunk, only I'm all of a maze today. Can you please pay me weekly as well? If you can't, I'll have to look for another job.'

'Of course I can. When is your next money due?'

'Today, sir. Mam and the kids won't have enough to eat if I don't get paid.'

Gil saw an opportunity of becoming a philanthropist immediately, which would no doubt please the ghost of Miss Bennerden if she was keeping an eye on him. 'I'll give you the wages at once.'

Her expression brightened. 'Oh, thank you, sir.

If I can only get the money for Mam, I shan't care what them in the village say about me. It fair breaks my heart to see the little 'uns go hungry.'

'How much?'

'Five shillin' a week, sir.'

It seemed a pitifully small amount. He fumbled in his pocket and pulled out his change purse, selecting three half-crown pieces and holding them out to her. 'Here.'

She took two of them, leaving the third coin on his palm. 'It's too much, sir. I don't get seven shillings and sixpence a week.'

'You do now. You just got a rise for your loyalty.' He could see Walter nodding approvingly.

'Oh, sir.' She clapped one hand to her mouth and blinked her eyes, but a few tears escaped. 'It'll be such a big help to Mam.'

He pressed the other coin into her hand and said gently, 'You can run home tomorrow morning and give your mother the money.'

'Thank you, sir.' She mopped her eyes then pulled a pinafore out of the bundle and tied it round herself. 'Right. What shall I do first?'

'Can you please make us all a cup of tea, you included, Lizzie? Then perhaps you can tell me what's going on. I have no idea why people are angry with me.'

He'd lost all desire to sleep, but his bad leg was aching furiously, so he limped across to the big kitchen table and sat down.

'They said you had a gimpy leg and a bad arm, sir. Did you have an accident like Miss Bennerden?'

Somehow he wasn't offended by her question.

'Yes, a riding accident.'

'Must have been a bad one. Still, you've got the house and all, haven't you? So you'll be all right.'

Walter grinned at him from the other side of the room and Gil knew what he was thinking. The girl was right. Suddenly he knew he would manage better, thanks to a kind lady. Whatever happened from now on, Miss Bennerden had given him a chance to do something useful with his life. Like helping Lizzie and her family. That might not be exciting but it was important.

He had felt so useless!

Leaning back in his chair, he watched Lizzie make a cup of tea, her movements quick and sure.

Walter came to sit next to him. 'Nice big kitchen, this. Where did the cook go, Lizzie?'

'She went to work for Mr Chapman as well. He must have got some money, because even though he has a big house, it used to be just Ben as helped him out and Mrs Kendey to scrub and wash for him twice a week.'

She quickly produced a pot of tea and found them some stale bread, which she toasted and offered with a new jar of jam. 'Sorry, sir. They took the butter and stuff that'd go bad with them. They wasn't meaning to steal anything, but no one likes to see good food go to waste.'

'You'll need to eat too,' Walter pointed out.

'Ooh, it wouldn't be right to eat with the master!'

'It would if I say so,' Gil told her. 'Sit down, Lizzie. I won't eat anything till you do.'

He waited till she was finishing her second cup of tea, after three slices of toast and jam. 'I'd be really grateful if you'd tell me why people are so upset with me, Lizzie. I need to know.'

'Well . . . it's because of Mr Chapman, sir, Mr Duncan Chapman. He lives in the village and he's a relative of Miss Bennerden as well. He did a lot for her after he come to live here, a few years ago. She got very frail towards the end, poor lady.'

'What did he do?'

'I think he helped her with her money. He said she always promised to make him her heir.'

That didn't sound like the woman Mr Mortlake had talked about. It suddenly occurred to Gil that anybody could say what they wanted about a dead woman, with no chance of being contradicted. 'Did *you* hear your mistress say she'd make him her heir?'

She frowned. 'Well, I didn't hear her myself, but then, she wouldn't talk about such things to me, would she? I suppose Mary must have heard her say it or she wouldn't be so angry now. Mary and Cyril have gone to work for Mr Chapman as well. He lives the other side of the village in his uncle's house. Bit tumbledown it is for a gentleman, even if it is big. Mary and Cook won't like that. They're snickety-pickety about keeping things just so.'

He hid a smile at her turn of phrase. If she had many made-up words like that, he was going to enjoy chatting to her. 'The lawyer didn't say anything about Miss Bennerden having other relatives. I must ask him when he comes tomorrow afternoon.'

Gil drained his cup and suddenly felt too exhausted to do more. 'I know it's early, but it's been a very long day. I think I should go to bed. Can you show us to the bedrooms, Lizzie?'

She bounced to her feet, young, graceful and full of energy. He couldn't help feeling envious, but then he glanced round and it reminded him how lucky he was. *No more feeling sorry for yourself, Gil, my lad!*

'They didn't get anything ready for you, sir, but I can easy make up beds if you decide which rooms you want.'

Walter went over to the back door. 'It's getting dark now. Let me just lock up before we go upstairs. Better to be safe than sorry. You'll have to show me where all the doors are, Lizzie.'

She looked at him in surprise. 'Oh, I don't think anyone from our village would come and steal anything, Mr Bilham. We don't usually bother to lock up at all.'

'I'm afraid us townies feel better if doors are locked at night, so you and I will go round all the outside doors before we go upstairs to sort out bedrooms for Mr Rycroft and myself.' He looked across at Gil. 'Wait for me here, lad, while I make everything safe. Your leg must be aching.'

'Thank you. It is.'

Gil smiled as he heard Walter insisting on shooting the bolts on all the outside doors as well as turning the keys in the locks. He even went round checking the windows in every downstairs room, finding several of the old-fashioned sash windows that weren't locked.

89

It was annoying to be so feeble that an older man had more energy. It was about time Gil started doing more, even if it did make his leg ache. He'd have to go back to London to see the man recommended by Seaborne, so that he knew which exercises would help him most. And he'd see the bootmaker, too. However bad the built-up shoe looked, if it made him limp less, perhaps his hip wouldn't hurt so much.

When Walter and Lizzie came back, she found them all candlesticks, since the house didn't have gas lighting, then led the way upstairs.

'Are there no oil lamps?' Gil asked.

'Yes, sir, but Cyril usually sees to those and he didn't clean and fill them this morning. He was too busy packing up. I could get the fancy lamps from the sitting room, only they're hard to carry round.'

'We'll make do with candles tonight, then.'

The bedrooms looked as comfortable as the downstairs rooms, filled with old-fashioned furniture but of good quality. The one where Alice Bennerden had slept pleased Gil and he opted to use it. Lizzie bustled around, finding clean sheets and making up the beds. Then she hesitated. 'I'll just take her clothes out of the drawers and lay them on one of the other beds, shall I? It won't take me long.'

'We'll help you,' Gil said.

When that was done, Walter said he'd sleep next door, if Gil didn't mind the liberty. 'Just to be within call if you need me.'

'I shan't need you, but you deserve a comfortable room after all you've done for me. I don't consider it a liberty but a right. Thank you, Walter.'

'I'll bring you up some water to wash in, shall I, sir?'

'That would be lovely.'

'We've got warm water still in the tank, though it's not hot now. It won't take me long.'

While she was gone, Walter unpacked Gil's things.

'It's a strange welcome,' Gil said.

'It's a nice house, though, and I like the looks of that lass.'

It was a relief when his two helpers stopped fussing and left him alone. Gil undressed slowly, enjoyed a leisurely washdown with the lace-trimmed facecloth, and got into bed, sighing with relief.

Although his bad leg was aching furiously, he wasn't going to take a sleeping powder, because they always left him dopey in the mornings.

He felt quite sure he'd need all his wits about him for a while.

Why were people so angry about Chapman not inheriting? Why had Miss Bennerden not left the money to the fellow if he'd been helping her?

Well, whatever Chapman had or had not done, Gil wasn't going to give up his inheritance. He needed it.

Besides, Miss Bennerden didn't sound like an unfair sort of person. She must have had a very good reason to cut Chapman out of the will.

I'm home, he thought as he snuggled down. I have my own home now.

91

5

Gil woke with a start, his heart pounding as he realised what had disturbed him: the sound of breaking glass.

He got out of bed and went to look out of the window, but could see no sign of anyone near the house.

There was a knock on his bedroom door. 'Gil?'

'Come in, Walter.'

'Are you all right?'

'Yes. Did you hear it too?'

'I did, sir, and cursed myself to think we don't have anything to defend ourselves with. I wonder if there are any guns in the house.'

'I shouldn't think so. An elderly spinster would hardly collect guns, and she wouldn't be the hunting type anyway, not if she was a friend of my grandmother's.'

'I'll go and take a look downstairs, see if anyone's broken in. There's enough moonlight to find my way. I don't want to show them where I am by carrying a lighted candle.'

'I'll come with you. No, don't argue. This is a case of two being safer than one.'

When they went out on to the landing, they saw something white at the end of it, then it moved towards them, to reveal Lizzie, in a floor-length nightdress with a darker shawl clutched tightly round her shoulders.

'We're going to look round. Do you want to

come with us?' Gil whispered.

She answered very quietly too. 'Yes, please, sir. I don't like being on my own up there in the attics. I've never slep' on my own in my whole life before.'

They heard no sounds from below as they crept down the stairs. The broken window was in the front sitting room, as they'd thought. The floor near it was covered by shards of glass which gleamed in the moonlight, but the hole wasn't big enough for anyone to climb through.

'Good thing we locked up,' Walter said in a low voice.

On the floor near the window was a brick with some paper tied round it.

'Looks like a message to me.' Walter glanced down. 'I've got my shoes on, you two are wearing slippers, so I'll get that brick, then we can see what they want.'

'We could light a candle in the hall to read it,' Lizzie volunteered. 'We always leave matches and candles there. No one will be able to see what we're doing.'

'Good idea. You light some candles for us, lass. You know where things are kept.'

The message was short but to the point, printed in big black letters in pencil.

GO AWAY
YORE NOT WANTID HERE

'We'll keep this to show to the police. Is there a village policeman, Lizzie?'

'Yes, sir, but . . . ' she hesitated, then finished

in a rush, 'he's Mary's cousin, and I don't think he'll do anything to upset her or the others in the village.'

'He'll have to take action if a crime has been committed. It's his job.'

She didn't contradict him, but she looked unconvinced.

'We'll do our best to keep you out of it, lass,' Walter said soothingly.

She sighed and looked at him. 'How will you do that if I'm working here?'

'Do you want to leave?' Gil asked. 'If you do, I'll give you enough money to tide you over till you find another job.'

She looked from one man to the other. 'You're that kind!' She seemed surprised by it. 'I don't want to leave. I never did, but *they* said I had to. I like working here, with good food and clean clothes and all. Mam was desperate when they told her I had to leave. All of a tozz-wozz, she was, for days.'

'Well, we're very happy to have you stay.' Gil looked at the time on the big grandfather clock with a gleaming brass trim around the dial that stood in the hall. It was just after midnight.

'Do you think they'll come back, sir?' Lizzie looked round nervously.

'I doubt it. They didn't try to break in this time. I think they just wanted to upset us.'

'We might as well go to bed, then,' Walter said. 'I agree with you, lad. They've sent their message and that's probably it for tonight.'

Gil picked up the piece of paper and put it in his pocket.

Walter patted Lizzie's shoulder. 'Thank you for staying, lass. Your mother's not the only one who needs your help. Two men on their own would have trouble finding anything in a strange house. We'll get some other help for you as soon as we can.'

'Mrs Turvey would come back, sir. She does the scrubbing and she didn't want to stop working here, neither.'

'Can you let her know she's still wanted? And perhaps she can come in every day.'

'Yes, sir. She lives near Mam.'

'Then you can see her after you take your mother her money.' Gil had a sudden idea. 'Tell Mrs Turvey I'll pay her an extra shilling a day. Just as I'll continue to pay you higher wages. Walter and I value your loyalty.'

She drew in a breath of surprise. 'That'll mean a lot to Mrs Turvey, more work and more money for it.'

A shilling, Gil thought as he lay on his bed. One shilling a day would mean a lot. He hadn't realised. Why had he not realised? Because he'd been spoilt rotten and selfish, that's why.

He couldn't get back to sleep, his thoughts were in such a confused tangle, but one thing had become clear: the independence which money gave meant a lot to him — not just the comfort but the purpose in life, the ability to help others.

Why hadn't Miss Bennerden left the money to this Chapman fellow if he was a relative? Did the lawyer know?

There wouldn't just be trouble in the village,

Gil thought with a wry smile. He'd have trouble with his father, who would try to tell him what to do with his inheritance. But fortunately his father had no power over him now.

And no one else was going to tell him what to do, either. He might limp, he might have a stupid, useless arm, but he could still stand firm against blackmail and bullying, couldn't he?

'I won't let you down, Alice Bennerden,' he whispered into the darkness and sighed with relief as he felt himself slipping gently towards sleep.

★ ★ ★

In spite of his disturbed night, Gil woke up early. Outside, birds were making occasional soft noises in the dimness of the false dawn.

He was in his own home!

Yawning hugely, he snuggled down for a few minutes, but the lighter it became, the more he wanted to be up and doing.

He heard footsteps coming down the attic stairs. If that was Lizzie starting work without anyone telling her what to do, she was a good, honest lass.

Someone stirred in the bedroom next to his. Walter. So they were all three awake.

Gil swung his legs out of bed and looked for his dressing gown, then realised he'd not brought it with him. He must send for his clothes from home — no, his family's house wasn't his home any longer.

But if he sent for his clothes, he'd have to tell

them where he was. He wanted to settle in a little before he faced his father.

Someone knocked on the door. 'Come in, Walter.'

'You're awake, then?'

'Yes. Too excited to sleep.'

'I'll get dressed, then go down and get you a cup of tea. Once there's some hot water, I can bring it up for you to shave.'

Gil couldn't bear to wait around for others to fetch and carry. 'I could get a cup of tea myself. If I come down, that'll save some running about.'

Walter nodded. 'I've been thinking. We can't expect that girl to run the whole house, even with a daily cleaner. We need a cook, a garden lad, all sorts of help — and quickly.'

'Lizzie's a good lass.'

'Yes. You did right to raise her wages. I remember going hungry as a child.'

'Did you really?'

'Oh yes.' Walter's eyes grew blind with memories for a few seconds, then he smiled and went to get dressed.

Gil did the same, feeling excited and happy.

In the kitchen Lizzie had just got the black lead out and was about to clean the cooking range.

'It won't hurt to leave the black leading for a day or two,' Walter said. 'Just get the stove lit and some tea brewed. We won't wait for the water in the cistern to heat up. If you boil a kettleful, we can shave before breakfast.'

Walter was studying the kitchen and its amenities. 'We could do with gas here, couldn't we?'

'It goes past the village, sir, but no one here

can afford to have it connected,' she volunteered.

'Well, we'll look into that,' Gil said. 'It'd make all our lives easier.'

She looked doubtful. 'I've heard tell it's dangerous.'

'Not if you treat it properly,' Walter said. 'We had it in London. I know what to do and I'll show you.'

She smiled in relief. 'That'd be good.'

All the time she was talking, her hands were busy, first lighting the fire, then filling the kettle, Gil noticed. He'd never have been aware of that sort of thing before the accident. He'd only paid attention to his own needs in those days. 'As soon as we've eaten, you can nip over to your mother's with the money and ask Mrs Turvey to come back.'

She beamed at him. 'Thank you, sir.'

'Any other people in the village looking for work?' Walter asked. 'We need someone to do the cooking. We shan't mind if they can't do fancy stuff.'

Lizzie stood thinking, head on one side. 'There's Madge Hilton. She lost her husband two weeks ago and she's got to move out of the tied cottage. She's a good cook, everyone says. Only she's got her daughter to think of.'

'When you go and see your mother, ask Mrs Hilton to come and see us,' Gil said. 'I told you yesterday — we're desperate for help. If the daughter's old enough, she can live here too and help around the place.'

'Will it upset Mrs Hilton to go against the village?' Walter asked.

Lizzie smiled. 'Madge would go against the King himself if she thought she was in the right. She's very plain-speaking. But the daughter's . . .' She hesitated. 'Amy's grown-up but she's slow-thinking. Madge won't put her in the workhouse, though, whatever anyone says.'

'Is the daughter violent?'

'Bless you, no. Amy wouldn't hurt a fly. She's terrified of anyone she doesn't know, and of some she does know, too. There are village lads as torment her if they get the chance. It's not right, but Mr Chapman just laughs about it.'

'What's it got to do with him?'

'He's sort of taken over in the village, acting like he's squire.'

'Has he, now.' The more Gil heard, the less he liked the sound of Chapman. Fancy laughing when people tormented someone.

★ ★ ★

By ten o'clock Lizzie was back from her mother's with a very thin woman whose eyes were red and swollen, as if she'd been crying. She was holding the hand of a young woman taller than she was, a shambling, shapeless creature, who was half hiding behind her mother.

As Gil sought for the right way to conduct an interview for a cook, a task his mother and the housekeeper had always undertaken, Madge took over. 'Lizzie says you're looking for a cook, sir.'

'Yes. You must know that the others have left, and why.'

'Everyone knows. He wants to tell us how to think, that Mr Chapman does, but I make up my own mind about people. I might as well say at the start that I can't do fancy cooking, sir, though if you bought me a cookery book, I dare say I could learn some new dishes, yes and enjoy doing it, too. And I don't mind helping out anywhere to start off with. You'll be at sixes and sevens for a while.'

'What about your daughter?'

'Amy can do simple jobs, like filling the wood boxes and bringing up your hot water. She's very strong and I don't let her sit around idle. It just takes her longer to learn new things.'

'Then she could work for her keep.'

'Oh, sir!' Her lips wobbled for a minute, then she nodded. 'I've got my own furniture. Can I use that in my room? Farmer says he'll store it for me in his barn, but I don't want insects getting into my mattresses and bed linen.'

'Of course you can. And put the rest in our attics here.'

She had to breathe deeply and was clearly near tears. 'You're kind, sir. Like Miss Bennerden was.' Madge nodded as if that settled something. 'If you still want me, I'll be happy to work for you.'

He beamed at her. 'I do want you . . . Cook.'

She smiled back, relaxing visibly. 'Is that my new title?'

'It is indeed.'

So they had a cook and a general helper now, Gil thought, feeling pleased with himself.

He went upstairs after the interview, and as he

100

looked out of his bedroom window, he saw Madge stop just beyond the vegetable garden at the side, thinking herself out of sight. She indulged in a short, sharp bout of weeping against her daughter's shoulder and the girl wasn't too stupid to offer her comfort, patting her mother and holding her close.

Gil felt a lump in his throat at the sight of that.

After a few moments, Madge scrubbed her face, kissed her daughter's cheek and took hold of her hand, then hurried off through the woods to pack up her home.

How quickly poor people could lose everything. How little it took to help them. He was getting a series of rapid lessons about this.

After he'd shaved and washed, Gil decided to go through his new home room by room. He wanted to fix the layout in his mind and learn what each room had been used for. He was relieved that Walter left him to do that on his own, while he helped Lizzie.

Oh, the peace of the place! No sounds of traffic, just birdsong and the sound of the wind.

And yet, even in this peaceful village, someone had thrown a brick through his window last night. Would they do it again tonight? Or something worse?

Lizzie had cleared up the broken glass this morning and Walter had nailed a plank across the broken window. But the message carried by the brick was burnt into Gil's brain.

Who didn't want him here?

There was one obvious answer.

101

Mr Mortlake arrived at Oakdene at two-thirty in the afternoon, by which time Gil knew every curling line and flower on the patterned carpet in the sitting room. He wasn't sure why he felt so apprehensive, but he did. He couldn't settle to anything and was reduced to pacing slowly up and down the room, trying to avoid treading on certain parts of the pattern in the carpet to distract himself.

Walter showed the lawyer in, and after Gil had shaken Mr Mortlake's hand, he said, 'Stay with us, Walter.'

Mr Mortlake looked at him in surprise.

'Walter is like an honorary uncle and I'm not going to hide that any longer,' Gil explained. 'He's known me since I was a child and he's far more than a servant to me. If it wasn't for him, I don't know what I'd have done during the past few months.'

'You're lucky to have a friend like that.'

'Yes, I am.'

When they were all seated, the lawyer asked, 'And how are you settling in? I'm sure Mrs Tibbins has made you comfortable.'

Gil explained the changed situation and saw the shock on the other man's face.

'I can't believe this has happened in a village like Pypard West. The people here have always seemed so friendly.'

'It all seems to be connected to a Mr Duncan Chapman.'

'*What?*'

'You know him, obviously.'

'Yes.'

'I gather he's a distant relative of Miss Bennerden.'

'*He* says he is, and he certainly knows about her mother's family, more than she knew herself. However, *I* haven't been able to trace the connection and I have tried, believe me.'

Another pause, as the lawyer bit his lip, seeming uncertain whether to continue or not. 'And . . . ?' Gil prompted.

'She took his word for that at first and treated him like a nephew, but she lived to regret it.'

'Oh?' Gil waited.

'This must go no further, because I have no proof, but I fear he stole items from this house, presumably because he was short of money. She wouldn't have him prosecuted, though she refused to see him after that. Earlier on, he'd tried to persuade her to let him help her with her money, though what sort of financial skill a penniless man has to offer, I cannot think. I was honoured that she refused his help and continued to place her trust in me.'

Gil didn't like the sound of all this.

Mr Mortlake sighed. 'She was a dear lady, the kindest imaginable. Over the years, she was cheated once or twice because if there was doubt, she preferred to trust people. And I must admit that more often than not, her trust worked miracles and brought out the best in people. In the case of Duncan Chapman, it didn't and that upset her greatly.'

'I wish I'd known her.'

'I think she'd have been pleased with you, Mr Rycroft.'

He was a bit surprised at this compliment. 'How can you tell? You don't know me.'

'I pride myself on my ability to judge people, and have rarely been wrong. Besides, from what you've told me, you've already started helping others less fortunate than yourself. She would have approved of the way you're treating your servants.'

Gil shrugged and changed the subject, embarrassed by the unaccustomed praise. 'Well, I've certainly had no experience in dealing with money, so I hope you'll continue to act as my lawyer and help me with the financial side of things, as you did her.'

'I'd be honoured to do so, Mr Rycroft.'

'Did she leave Chapman anything?'

'No. She cut him out of her will completely and left a letter with me in case he tried to go to court over it.'

Walter cleared his throat and when they looked at him said, 'He can't be short of money now, not if he's taken on three new servants.'

'That puzzles me, I must admit. The fellow's been living from hand to mouth for a while and still has debts that haven't been cleared.' Mortlake shook his head. 'Ah well, he's lost out now, so we'll forget about him.'

It would be rather difficult to forget about a man who lived in the same village and who had already set people against you, Gil thought. But that was his business, not his lawyer's.

Mr Mortlake took out some papers. 'Let us

turn to a happier subject: the bequests. There are quite a few smaller legacies. I have the list here. Miss Bennerden wished you to see these people, Mr Rycroft, and tell them of their good fortune in person, rather than me sending them a letter. Most of them live in the village or nearby. She thought it would be a good way for you to meet people in the neighbourhood.'

He took out some keys. 'There is a safe place in the house, where Miss Alice kept her more valuable items, silverware and one or two pieces of jewellery. Let me show it to you.'

He led the way down to the wine cellar, which had a locked door to one side. Beyond the door were more bottles of wine and two casks, labelled 'Port' and 'Sherry' respectively. He moved the cask of sherry forward and it rolled easily, together with what at first appeared to be a solid section of wall but then opened to reveal a recess behind it, about five foot high, with shelves and double doors.

When the doors were opened, they revealed bundles wrapped in green baize and boxes of various sizes, all fairly small.

'I'll leave you to go through these at your leisure,' Mr Mortlake said. 'I just wanted to make sure you knew how to open the secure cupboard. I've included a complete list of the contents in the papers I shall leave with you.'

He showed them how to close the cupboard by treading on a spring which sent the cask and wooden 'wall' behind it rolling back into place. 'A very simple device, but effective, installed by the first owner. Miss Bennerden didn't like to leave all her valuables in the bank because sometimes she'd enjoy using them. Every now and then she'd invite people to dinner and bring some of these things out, including her mother's jewellery, which I presume you'll give to your wife one day.'

Gil couldn't imagine himself marrying, but didn't spoil the moment by saying so.

When the lawyer had left, Gil beamed at Walter. 'Isn't it wonderful?'

'It is, lad. It is. See that you deserve it all.'

'Don't give in to this, you mean?' He indicated his arm with a grimace. 'I can't promise not to fret now and then. It's been such a big change. As to me marrying, I doubt any woman will want a man with this.'

'You have other attributes that will more than make up for that.'

'The money, you mean? I don't want a wife who's marrying me for my money, thank you very much.'

'You're still a good-looking young man. People will like you for yourself.'

Gil grimaced. 'I shall stay single, Walter. I've decided on that.'

He didn't challenge the disbelieving expression on the other man's face or tell him the main reason why. Since the accident Gil hadn't felt the need for a woman, something he'd experienced regularly before. He very much feared he was now unable to father a child.

But he wasn't going to tell anyone about that, not even a doctor. A man had his pride.

6

'You ought to write to your father,' Walter told Gil. 'He'll be upset that you didn't tell him exactly where you were going and why. Don't make it worse.'

'I suppose I'll have to let him know my address. I need my clothes and things sending. But he'll come haring down to tell me what to do, you know he will.'

'And he won't be able to make you do it, will he? So you can afford to be kind to him.'

'*Me*? Kind to *him*?'

'Yes, lad. He doesn't know how to change his ways, but you do.'

Which left Gil thoughtful.

★ ★ ★

And of course, his father turned up two days later, without warning, driven there in a motor car, bringing some of Gil's things. The first anyone knew about the visit was when Lizzie answered the door and was scolded for not inviting Mr and Mrs Rycroft straight in.

Gil wasn't having the girl treated like that, not after the hard work she'd been putting in so cheerfully. He hurried out into the hall. 'Ah, Mother. Father. You should have let us know you were coming. And how is Lizzie supposed to know who you are when she's never met you, Father?'

107

As he went to kiss his mother's cheek, he winked at Lizzie, who flashed him a grateful look as she took his father's coat and hat, then waited for Gil to help his mother out of her wrap. She was wearing a very fashionable tailor-made costume in a soft grey, with a straight, narrow skirt just clear of the ground. On her head she wore a silk-covered toque, decorated with a big bow of dark-blue ribbon, rather than one of the huge hats decorated with flowers that she usually favoured. Round her neck was a long scarf, which she handed to Gil. She couldn't have needed the scarf to keep her hat on because the car was a Daimler with enclosed seating for the passengers.

He had intended to take his parents into the sitting room for a chat before they did the inevitable tour of the house, but his father started walking up and down the hall, throwing open the doors without waiting for an invitation to explore.

'Come and sit down before you look round, Father,' he said at last, hoping he sounded firm.

His mother linked her arm in his and murmured, 'If we go into your drawing room, he'll soon follow.'

'I'd rather look round first and see what we've got,' his father said.

We? Did his father think this house was family property? As Gil opened his mouth to protest that assumption, his mother intervened.

'I'm longing for a cup of tea, Bertram dear.'

'I'm sure Lizzie will be bringing us a tea tray.' Gil gave in to his mother's tugging on his arm, hoping Walter would check that the tray was perfectly presented.

They went into the sitting room, and to his relief, his father did follow them a few seconds later, muttering something about this being an old-fashioned sort of place.

Gil made sure his mother was comfortably seated, took his usual chair and indicated the other to his father.

'How much did the old lady leave you, Gil?'

'Enough to live on comfortably.'

'How much?'

'Bertram, dear, it's not your business.'

'He's my son, ain't he? He doesn't know much about money and he's going to need my help to look after it. So of course I need to know what we're dealing with.'

His father always barked orders. Gil hadn't realised how much he hated that till he was free to run his own house peacefully, without anyone shouting at others who didn't dare shout back, like servants and youngest sons. He was about to refuse to give details, when his mother spoke in a much sharper voice.

'Bertram!'

His father harrumphed and fell quiet.

Gil hid a smile. Occasionally his mother spoke in that firm tone, without adding 'dear', and it generally stopped whatever his father was doing. Mostly, though, she coaxed his father into doing as she wanted before he became too outrageous. Gil had never thought about it much, just accepted that. Now, he watched her tactics with more interest.

'I think the exact details of my legacy are my own business,' he said at last when he saw her looking at him as if to tell him to speak. 'And I'm sure I'll be quite capable of managing it, with the lawyer's help.'

'As the person who's been supporting you for twenty-six years, I still think I've a right to know,' his father snapped.

'If you feel I need to repay you, then send an account to my lawyer.'

It was his turn to be gently reprimanded by his mother.

'Gil, dear.'

He took a deep breath and said more quietly, 'I'll give you a general idea, Father, but the details are private. From what the lawyer says, after paying the expenses of running this house, I'll have about four times what my old allowance was, which will be more than enough to manage on in the country. I will not, of course, need an allowance from you now, though I'm grateful for your support over the years.'

His mother nodded approvingly at this more conciliatory speech.

His father let out a low whistle. 'As much as that, eh?'

'Yes. Miss Bennerden was very generous.'

There was a knock on the door and Lizzie came in, carrying a tray with a plate of scones, butter and jam on it, followed by Walter with a tray of tea-making equipment. He gave the maid an encouraging nod, as if reminding her to speak.

'Cook's sorry she can't offer you better than

this, Mrs Rycroft, but our other cook left without giving notice. Mrs Hilton has only just taken over the kitchen, so she's not had time to settle in yet.'

'I'm grateful for a cup of tea and the scones look very light.'

'They're delicious, ma'am.' Lizzie bobbed an awkward curtsey and left.

Mrs Rycroft smiled at Walter. 'I'm glad you're still with my son.'

'Walter has become my . . . um, general factotum,' Gil said.

'I need to tender my resignation to you, Mr Rycroft, if you don't mind,' Walter put in diplomatically.

'Yes. Yes, of course. Let's consider that done immediately. I'll send you the money for the wages you're owed. Booth will take over my stables. You trained him well. Gil will need an older head to advise him here, I'm sure.'

Walter nodded and left the room.

It felt like another hurdle overcome to Gil.

More silence as his father took a cup of tea from his wife, sipping appreciatively. 'Well, the new cook can make a good cup of tea. I'll say that for her.'

'Yes, delicious. And I'm glad to see you looking more like your old self than you have since the accident, Gil dear,' his mother said. 'I'm so pleased for you about this inheritance.'

His father handed her his cup for a refill. 'How much do you think the house is worth?'

'I don't know and it doesn't matter, because I don't intend to sell it.'

'You can't hide away, boy. You need to come out and face the world again.'

'I'm not planning to hide away, but this is a lovely house in a beautiful part of England. I shall enjoy living here.'

'But it's miles away from anywhere. You'll surely want to live nearer your family?'

He didn't, had never got on particularly well with his brothers, but he wasn't cruel enough to say so to his parents. 'The truth is, I fell in love with Oakdene, so I'm planning to modernise it gradually and settle down here permanently.'

His father leant back, baffled. 'Well, that'll certainly keep you occupied, given the state it's in. But I still think you should live nearer home.'

'Bertram dear, this *is* Gil's home now.' His mother set down her empty cup. 'I'd love a tour of your house now, if that's all right with you, dear.'

'Of course. And if you have any suggestions for refurbishing it, I'll be happy to listen. I don't intend to spend much money at first, though. I need to see how I go on.'

Was this him talking? he wondered. He sounded so serious, unlike his former self. He sounded, he realised suddenly, grown-up. And about time too.

He listened to his mother's suggestions, surprised at how practical some of them were, and interrupted her to fetch a notebook.

'Women always know best about household details,' his father said complacently.

'I'll come down to stay for a few days next time your father's away and help you plan the furnishings,' she said. 'If you'll have me.'

'I'd love to have you and shall welcome your help with the house.'

Afterwards the two men walked round the outside of the house, and here Gil didn't mind listening to his father's advice.

'It looks pretty sound, structurally. What happened to that window? You'll have to repaint the frame.'

'It got broken.' Gil hurried along to the side door.

'This is rotten and will need replacing,' his father said. 'Not worth repainting.'

The poor state of the door distracted him from asking Gil how the window had got broken, thank goodness.

'You'll have to keep an eye on this side of the house. Gets all the weather, I should think. The woodwork will need painting more often.'

Gil had never thought about that sort of thing and looked at the house with new eyes. He felt ashamed of how focused he'd been on horses and hunting, how he'd never earned any money. His parents had pretended he was going to set up a stud and breed sound riding horses for children, but he hadn't even tried to get started.

After listening to the horse he'd killed giving out muffled groans as it struggled to cope with the pain — horses were such stoic animals — Gil hadn't felt he deserved to ride one again. Which was foolish. He'd need a couple of horses, at least one of them suitable for a trap. Or maybe . . . maybe he really would buy a motor car. He could look into that.

Excitement filled him. Something different. He'd learn about cars. He wondered if he'd be able to drive one. It might be fun.

When he and his father went back inside the house, Walter came in to offer a light luncheon. 'Not what you're used to, Mrs Rycroft, but Mrs Hilton can provide sandwiches and an apple pie with cream. Our own apples, too.'

'We shall be delighted to take luncheon here.'

When the car came to collect them at three o'clock, Gil breathed a sigh of relief. As he handed his mother into it, she whispered, 'Not too bad, eh? I'll send the rest of your things down.'

'You're smiling,' Walter said as Gil came back into the house.

'It went better than I expected with Father, thanks mainly to Mother. I hadn't really noticed before how much she controls him.'

'She's a very clever woman, your mother is. We servants have always admired her. Yet she never raises her voice, not to anyone. But you held firm against your father today, too. I was pleased to see that.'

'It gives you heart, having a house of your own. We'll have to make a start on the job of telling people about the legacies tomorrow. I was going to do that today.'

'I thought we were going into London to see about exercises and special footwear tomorrow?'

'Oh, yes. The day after, then.' Gil smiled at his friend. 'It's good to have plenty to do. I'm not the sort to sit around and read books.'

Walter found it necessary to blow his nose

vigorously at that comment. He didn't say anything, but he patted his lad's hand a couple of times.

* * *

Going up to London wasn't easy without a vehicle to drive them to Wootton Bassett Station. Lizzie said the landlord of the Gaudy Pheasant had a gig he hired out, so Walter went into the village to see if it was free.

He came back furious, because the landlord said it'd been hired already. 'I asked him how about tomorrow and he said it was hired then, as well. I asked about every day this week, same answer.'

'Giving us the cold shoulder, eh? Did you get any hint about why?'

'No. When I asked outright, he said he was a busy man and hadn't time to chat.'

'Let's ask Lizzie and Mrs Hilton if they know of any other vehicle for hire,' Walter said. 'Perhaps in Bassett — that's what the locals call Wootton Bassett.'

Gil looked at his leg ruefully. 'I can't walk into Bassett, and I doubt you can, either.'

Walter shot a quick glance sideways.

'I've noticed that you're not as spry as you used to be, and you get breathless if you have to do too much.'

Silence, then, 'Well, I am seventy-six, you know.'

Gil was surprised. 'I didn't realise you were that old.'

115

Walter shrugged. 'You don't tell an employer how old you are, in case he sacks you.'

'Father would never have sacked you.'

'He might have found me easier duties, and I didn't want the humiliation of that in a place where I'd run the stables.'

'Well, your age makes no difference to your job here. Let's ask Cook if she knows anyone with a vehicle to hire.'

Mrs Hilton said bluntly, 'No one will hire to you, sir. They're afraid of the others in the village refusing to deal with them if they do.'

'I don't understand.'

'Chapman. Most of them will come round once they get to know you, but it'll take time.'

Lizzie cleared her throat. 'We could send my brother Don into Wootton Bassett, sir. It's only about three miles. He can walk it easy. And no one will dare pick on him for going, because he's a big lad for his age and knows how to look after himself.'

'I'll pay him for his trouble. Five shillings, do you think?'

She went bright pink. 'Oooh, thank you, sir. That'll be lovely. Mam will be that pleased! He hasn't been able to find steady work, let alone get into a trade, which she was hoping for till she found out you have to pay for that.'

Young Don was happy to walk three miles to the nearest town for that generous payment and set off at once.

'We need to buy a horse and trap straight away,' Walter said. 'I'll start looking round for one as soon as we get back. In the meantime we can perhaps hire one by the week from a livery stable in Bassett.'

★ ★ ★

After the freshness of the Wiltshire countryside, London seemed dirtier and busier than ever. They took a motor cab to the shoemaker Mr Seaborne had recommended and Gil watched in fascination as the driver manipulated the gear lever and brakes.

The shoemaker studied Gil's foot and leg with calm interest and made him walk up and down, first in his shoes, then barefoot.

'I'll make you one pair to start off with,' he decided. 'If they're comfortable, we'll give you your own cast and then you need only send me word when you want new shoes. I'll furnish you with a list of the styles we make. The first pair will be ready next week, but I'll need you to try them on this time.'

'Can't it be sooner?' Gil pleaded.

The man shook his head. 'I have a queue, sir. I'm sorry to keep you waiting, but it's only fair to take customers as they come. I could work more quickly, but good apprentices are hard to find, so I've not got as much help as I'd like.'

That made Gil think about Lizzie's lively younger brother. She said Don could only find temporary jobs and was longing to be old enough to join the army, which upset her mother.

'Would you be able to house a country lad?' he asked.

117

The shoemaker looked at him. 'You know someone?'

'I think so. Our maid's brother seems a bright lad. I'd pay his premium for him.'

'I'll give him a week's trial. It's what I always do. They have to be able to get on with customers, you see, because people get upset about their problems. Bring him along with you when you pick up the shoes and we'll see what he looks like. But I warn you, I'll send him back if he isn't suitable.'

They shook hands on this.

The man who would provide Gil with exercises to help his leg, and possibly his arm, was equally busy, but agreed, just this once, to give up part of his lunch hour to get his new patient started. His assistant could finish the session off.

Afterwards, Gil looked at Walter with a wry smile. 'I'm aching after all that stretching and all I really want now is to go home. Strange, isn't it? I already think of Oakdene as home.'

'That's a good thing. Everyone needs a home.'

As they stood on the pavement, trying to hail a cab, one stopped next to them and a woman poked her head out of the window. 'It *is* you, Gil Rycroft.'

He looked at her in puzzlement for a few seconds, then realised who she was. 'Julia! My goodness, how you've changed! Your hair's so short.'

She patted it and smiled. 'It's called 'bobbed'. I had it done in Paris the first time. It's more popular there than here, though some of my friends have had their hair cut short since I did, because it's much easier to manage than all those pads and false pieces of hair.'

'It suits you.'

'Thank you. I heard about the accident. I'm so sorry, Gil. I know what an outdoor type you are.'

He nodded, swallowing hard. Sympathy from her was particularly hard to bear. He could remember dancing with her, spinning round and round, the pair of them giddy with laughter.

'Have you eaten? No? Then come and have a late lunch with me at the Ritz,' she coaxed. 'You can tell me what you're doing with yourself.'

He hesitated. He'd once made a fool of himself over Julia and had no intention of reigniting that flame.

She seemed to sense his hesitation and said brightly, 'Don't be silly. That soppy stuff was all over and done with a long time ago. But we're still good friends, surely?'

'Of course we are.'

She looked beyond him to Walter. Gil hesitated, wondering what to do about his friend during lunch, but as usual, the matter was taken out of his hands. 'I'll ride to the hotel with you and Miss Gardiner, if that's all right, then find myself somewhere else to eat. I don't know if you remember me, miss, but — '

Julia smiled. 'Oh, yes. I remember you very clearly, Walter Bilham. The best groom there ever was, my father used to say.'

'He tried to get me to work for him often enough.'

'Are you working for Gil, now?'

'Sort of — '

'He's my friend and general factotum,' Gil interrupted. 'No one else would live with me and put up with my moods.'

'You mean, you're doing something unorthodox? I thought the day would never come,' she teased.

Once they were seated in the restaurant, Julia said simply, 'How are you managing, Gil? The truth, mind.'

'Not well at first, but I'm getting used to it now. I've had a bit of good luck, for a change.' He explained about his inheritance.

'Jolly good show! Best thing that could have happened to you, getting out from under your father's eagle gaze. I thought he'd have got you married to Amelia Frensham by now.'

'I couldn't. Not that I'm not fond of her, but it'd be like marrying my sister.'

'No other woman on the horizon?'

He looked at her warily.

She gave a trill of laughter. 'Not me, you fool. I don't want to marry anyone. I'm financially independent too, thanks to my grandmother, and I've found a purpose in life . . . I've joined the Women's Social and Political Union.'

'The Suffragettes!'

She grimaced. 'I do wish the *Daily Mail* hadn't coined that silly word. It's how people think of us nowadays. They just don't take our purpose seriously.'

'I doubt they ever will.'

Her face grew fierce. 'You're wrong. We're very determined and our numbers are growing all the time. Women of all classes, too. Now that we've become more forceful, surely we're proving that we won't stop demanding our rights.' She cocked her head on one side. 'Where do *you* stand about votes for women, Gil?'

'I've never really thought about it.'

'Then it's about time you did. Is your mother as intelligent as your father?'

'Far more intelligent.'

'Then why does he have the vote and not her?'

Gil stared at her. He hadn't thought of it that way. Hadn't thought about anything very seriously before his accident. 'Why indeed?'

She patted his hand. 'Maybe there's hope for you yet, my lad. Now, tell me where exactly this Oakdene of yours is.'

'Near Wootton Bassett, which is south-west of Swindon.'

She clapped her hands together. 'I have a friend who lives near there. Jane Walvin. Do you remember her? Wears spectacles.'

'Oh, yes. Rather plain.'

'There you go again. Being pretty isn't the only important thing for a woman, you know. Jane does a lot of work for women whom other people despise, and I admire her greatly.'

'Fallen women, you mean?'

'They didn't fall; they were pushed, many of them raped and then cast out by their families. I give Jane money sometimes and help place the women she takes in when I can. If you need housemaids, she could probably find you one. It wouldn't hurt to try, would it?'

Gil felt uncomfortable to hear Julia talking so openly about something that wasn't usually discussed by ladies. He didn't know what to say.

She glared at him. 'I expect you think women who get raped are asking for it. That's what their families usually say. Even my father does. Only they weren't asking for it. Most of the ones she's helped have been battered and bruised by their attackers as they fought back. Is that asking for it?'

Her eyes were glowing with fervour and he had never admired her more. He wished he could be so forceful and determined.

'You said you needed more staff, Gil. Do you or don't you?'

'I do.'

'Then I'll come down and help you find some.'

'I don't know what I need yet — a housekeeper first of all, I suppose. Then it'll be up to her. You probably don't have anyone suitable for that sort of position.'

'Do you think it's only young women who get attacked? We'll see if we can find you a house-keeper. I'll come down to Wiltshire the day after tomorrow.'

What had he got himself into? But he could never say no to Julia. And if she was right about these women, well, Miss Bennerden would approve of him helping them, he was sure.

In an effort to take the scowl from her face, he said, 'I'm thinking of buying a car, too.'

'That'll give your father a purple fit.'

He smiled. 'Don't you believe it. Even he sees the benefits of motor cars. He came to see my new house in one.'

'Good for him. *My* father won't go near them.

You must definitely buy one.'

'I don't know if I could manage to drive with this.' He gestured to his left arm.

'You could hire a mechanic to drive you round and look after the motor car. In fact, now I come to think of it, I know someone who might suit.'

'I can find my own mechanic,' he said hastily.

'Why bother when I know a good one? He's the brother of a friend in the WSPU. We cross all class boundaries, you know. I'll see if Horry's still looking for a job and send him down to talk to you. He's got a big scar across his face from an accident in his youth, and some people are stupid enough to think that prevents him from being a good chauffeur. But he's mad about cars. He can also drive a horse and trap, of course.'

Gil gave up trying to hold out against her. 'OK. Send him to see me.'

Julia had always been a managing sort of female, he thought as they said goodbye, but now she had a new maturity and confidence. Was this due to being active in the WSPU? Or just because she was older? It made her even more attractive in some ways, but he couldn't have lived with a female like her.

Although Gil's leg was aching badly as he and Walter set off for the station, it didn't seem to matter quite so much. Spending time with Julia had cheered him up.

7

The following day Gil made a start on visiting the people in and around the village who had been left something in Miss Bennerden's will. He had a letter from her for each person to whom she'd left money.

He was more than a little nervous, worried they'd be rude to him, but it had to be done. He didn't intend to let his benefactress down.

Lizzie assured him that the first person on the list lived only a few minutes' away, on this side of the village, if you went by the short cut. He felt he could cope with walking there and back, and had been told to exercise his bad leg more, though only gently at first. He'd do anything, anything at all, to improve the way he walked.

She took him to the start of the path, which was concealed in a corner of the garden, then went back to the house.

Gil saw that it was the path Cook had gone down after her interview with him. The short cut was used mainly by servants going from Oakdene to the village or by lads bringing deliveries from the village.

They had to push through a scratchy opening in the hedge. 'This needs a proper gate,' he said as he brushed twigs and leaves from his jacket.

According to the list he'd been given, Mrs Jane Wyndham was an impoverished widow, living in Rosybank Cottage behind the church.

That was all he knew about her.

His first surprise was to find that the church was small and modern, built of red brick, with plain windows that were decorated only by narrow, coloured panels of glass round the edges. Its door was padlocked. A notice said that services were held here on alternate Sundays, also at Christmas and Easter.

There was no house attached to the church and the few graves in the small churchyard had very simple markers, poorer people's graves, except for one with a marble plinth and a newly erected headstone.

He guessed this was where his benefactress was buried and couldn't resist going to pay his respects, reading the neatly chiselled words aloud.

Here lies Alice Mary Bennerden
taken in the 72nd year of her life
A lady of great kindness
who will be sadly missed
by all who knew her

They must have worked quickly to get the inscription finished. There were cherubs carved in each upper corner of the headstone and roses in the lower corners. The carvings were exquisite. Such skilled work took time. Had she arranged for her own headstone in advance? She seemed to have organised everything else before she died.

He bowed his head and said a short prayer, then added silent thanks for her legacy, before walking out of the churchyard and across to the cottage.

The door was opened before he got there and a tall woman, very thin and dressed in threadbare black, stood looking at him.

'Mrs Wyndham?'

'Yes.'

'I'm Gilbert Rycroft, the new owner of Oakdene.'

'You had to be. You're the only newcomer to the village.' She made no attempt to invite him in and her expression was definitely disapproving.

'I have a message from Miss Bennerden, which she asked me to deliver personally.'

'Oh.' After a moment's hesitation, she stepped back. 'You'd better come in, then. You can sit on that chair. It should hold you.'

At over six feet, he felt like Gulliver in Lilliput, a giant among midgets. The tiny front room, clearly the only downstairs room apart from the kitchen, was full of furniture, which looked as if it'd come from a larger house. Ornaments and knick-knacks jostled each other for space on bookshelves, occasional tables and the mantelpiece.

His hostess sat down opposite him and folded her hands neatly in her lap, giving him no help to start a conversation.

'Miss Bennerden has left bequests to several people in the village and you're one of them. She asked that I deliver the information and a letter personally to each of them.'

'Well, it's good that you're doing as she asked, I suppose.'

He held out the letter with his right hand. 'Here's your letter. Your bequest is — '

He broke off as she blinked furiously at the sight of her name on the envelope. A tear rolled down her cheek and she brushed it quickly away with one lined, age-spotted hand. The other hand trembled as it held the letter.

'She was a good woman, Miss Bennerden. None better.'

'I only wish I'd known her.'

Mrs Wyndham looked at him in surprise. 'But surely . . . They said . . . You *must* have met her!'

'No, never. She was a friend of my grandmother, a very good friend, I'm told.'

'Then why did she leave everything to you, if she'd never met you?'

'I don't know. I can only be grateful.'

His hostess was still frowning. 'You don't look like a liar.'

He was baffled by her reactions. 'I'm not lying. Why should I be?'

'But Mr Chapman said — ' She broke off and pressed her lips firmly together, then took a paper knife and slit open the envelope with great care.

Chapman again, he thought. And now it sounded as if the fellow had been spreading lies about him. Damn him!

As Mrs Wyndham read the letter, tears began to fall in earnest and she fumbled in vain for a handkerchief.

Gil took out his own and thrust it into her hand.

She used the square of neatly pressed cotton,

then had to use it again as tears continued to fall.

'So kind, so very kind of her.' She blew her nose hard and managed to stop weeping. Only then did she realise what a mess she'd made of Gil's handkerchief. 'Oh. I'm sorry.'

'It's all right. I was happy to be of service.'

'I will, of course, wash and iron the handkerchief for you.'

'Thank you. Perhaps you could bring it up to Oakdene one afternoon and take tea with me? I don't know anyone in the village yet and I'd like to hear more about Miss Bennerden.'

She inclined her head in acceptance.

He thought she would probably come to visit him, hoped she would, but didn't press the point. 'Have you finished reading the letter?'

'Yes.'

'I'm to tell you that she's left you two hundred pounds, and her hope is that this will make your life more comfortable. And she asks if you will be so kind as to help me to dispose of her clothes. She said you were to keep any which pleased you and give the others to deserving women. She didn't like to think of good clothes going to waste.'

'Nor do I.' She glanced down at her own threadbare garments.

'As a man, I feel a little reluctant even to touch Miss Bennerden's things, so they're just lying on one of the spare beds. I'll leave dealing with them until you can help me, if you don't mind.'

There was another nod and the handkerchief was used to mop a final tear, then Mrs Wyndham looked at him without her former hostility. 'Have you hurt your foot, Mr Rycroft? You were limping as you came along the street.'

'I was involved in a riding accident last year and damaged my leg and arm.' As if to prove this, his left arm jerked in the sudden way it had and he clasped it to his body with his right hand. 'Sorry. I have trouble controlling my left arm now. It looks foolish when it jerks, but it doesn't hurt any more.'

'That's not what — '

He wondered what she had been going to say. What else had Chapman been saying about him? He didn't pursue the point because he wanted to keep the mood pleasant. 'Um, about the money. It can be paid to you in any way you wish, in banknotes or else paid into your savings bank account by Miss Bennerden's lawyer in Swindon. If you'll let me know how you want it delivered, I'll make the necessary arrangements.'

'I don't know. Perhaps I could collect the money from your lawyer's office — oh my, such a large amount! — then the lawyer's clerk could accompany me to my savings bank in Swindon? What do you think?'

'Very sensible.'

She gave him a genuine smile this time. 'I wonder if you'd like a cup of tea, Mr Rycroft?'

'I'd love one.'

'I won't be a minute. The kettle is always on the boil.'

He heard crockery rattling in the nearby kitchen, then a kettle whistling. After that she came back to stand in the doorway. 'It's just brewing.'

'Thank you. I am rather thirsty.'

'I believe you've hired Madge Hilton to cook for you, and you took in Amy as well.'

'Yes. Mrs Hilton has taken over in difficult circumstances. And her daughter makes herself useful. She's a pleasant lass, always smiling.'

Mrs Wyndham opened her mouth, closed it as if changing her mind about speaking, then blurted out, 'He was wrong about you.'

Gil looked at her in puzzlement but she didn't explain, just vanished into the kitchen. It must be Duncan Chapman again. He hoped people would make up their own minds about him, as Mrs Wyndham had just done, instead of listening to lies.

He and Chapman would no doubt meet eventually, because it was a small village, but Gil didn't see why *he* should make the effort. After all, Chapman had no legacy coming to him, so there was no obligation to visit him.

Only after consuming two cups of weak tea did Gil feel it right to take his leave. His leg was aching from the walk here, but he felt he'd acquitted himself well.

He hoped the built-up shoe would make walking easier. He hated being penned indoors or limited to short strolls round the garden.

He must buy a trap, a couple of horses *and* a motor car as quickly as possible, then he could get out and about. How wonderful that he could afford that!

★　★　★

Gil met Duncan Chapman for the first time at the village church. Walter nudged him into going and insisted on driving him there in the hired trap.

'I'll be waiting here after the service,' he said as he tied up the placid little mare supplied by the livery stables.

Gil turned towards the church, horrified to find a fringe of people along the path, all staring at him. He would have liked to turn back, but wasn't going to give them the satisfaction of seeing him turn tail.

Even as he watched, a fashionably dressed man of about forty detached himself from the crowd and came towards him.

'You're not wanted here,' the fellow said loudly. 'People who cheat old ladies out of their fortunes are the scum of the earth.'

For a moment Gil wondered how to respond to that, then he remembered his mother's gentle hauteur. 'Dear me, how do you know anything about me when we've never met?'

'You came here a couple of times.'

'I didn't.'

'I say differently.'

Gil shrugged. 'What you say is irrelevant. I'm speaking the truth. Kindly move out of my way and let me go inside to worship my Maker.'

For a moment Duncan hesitated, then Mrs Wyndham moved out of the crowd to walk along the path towards them and Chapman stepped back.

'I'm glad to see you attending church, Mr Rycroft,' she said loudly. 'I shall call tomorrow morning to start carrying out Miss Bennerden's

131

wishes, if that is convenient.'

'Certainly. I shall be glad of your help.' He tipped his hat to her and the group of ladies she'd been standing with.

A man stepped forward at the door. 'James Borton, sir, curate of this parish. You'll want the Oakdene pew. Please come this way.'

'Thank you.' Only when he'd sat down did Gil let himself sag. He hoped his nervousness hadn't shown. He was puzzled by the encounter. Why had that fellow claimed that he had met Miss Bennerden when he hadn't?

There were heavy footsteps and Chapman paused at the end of the pew to glare at him, then took the shorter pew at the front on the other side.

With much shuffling and fidgeting, everyone settled down and the curate went up to the plain wooden lectern.

Hymns were sung and Gil joined in automatically. During the sermon, his mind wandered and he had no idea what it was about. He presumed he'd stood and sat with the others, but he didn't remember doing it.

After the service was over, Chapman, who was sitting on the other side of the aisle at the front, pushed forward and led the way out.

Mrs Wyndham said loudly, 'He'd never have done that in Miss Bennerden's day. And I believe that under English law people are innocent until proved guilty. We have been judging Mr Rycroft without seeing the evidence and I for one regret doing that.'

She moved to the end of her pew and looked at Gil.

132

He suddenly realised she was waiting for him, so offered her his arm. She took it and didn't let go until they had left the church.

'I'll see you tomorrow morning, young man.'

'Thank you for your help today.'

'You're welcome.'

He watched her go. What a courageous person she was to go against the rest of the village! That made him feel even more ashamed of how he'd given in to adversity during the past year. Holding his head high, he went towards the trap, where Walter, who had sat at the rear of the church, was now sitting waiting for him.

The other man's anxiety showed in the restive way the horse moved to and fro, though his expression was calm.

Gil walked towards him. 'I can manage, thank you.' It was an effort but he did manage to get into the trap without help and sat very upright till they got home.

Walter smiled at him. 'Just keep calm and meet the people one by one, as you did today. You've clearly won over Mrs Wyndham.'

'I hope so. I admire her greatly. She's coming over in the morning to help sort out Miss Bennerden's clothes. I think I'll ask her advice about approaching the other beneficiaries. Oh, and when Lizzie comes back from visiting her family, could you ask her to see me? I want to talk to her about her brother and an apprenticeship.'

★ ★ ★

That evening it began to rain heavily, so they were surprised when someone hammered on the front door. Gil went to answer it and found a young man with a badly scarred face, carrying a battered carpet bag. He was soaking wet.

'I'm Horry Palmer, sir.'

Gil's mind went blank for a moment or two, then he remembered where he'd heard the name. 'Julia's protégé.'

'Yes, sir. Miss Gardiner said you needed a car and driver.'

'I do. I know nothing about motor cars.'

Wind rustled the trees and a flurry of light rain whispered around the house.

'Come inside. We'll discuss this later. It's going to pour down again soon. How did you get here?'

'Walked from the railway station in Wootton Bassett, sir.'

Gil saw pride warring with shame on his companion's face and guessed the man hadn't had the money for a cab. 'You must be tired and hungry, then. Walter and I are about to have our supper. Perhaps you'd join us?'

'Thank you, sir.' He looked beyond Gil.

'This is my friend Walter, who lives here with me.'

Horry turned his scarred side to the light and said bluntly, 'You don't mind my face, then?'

'Not at all. If you won't be bothered by my arm and my limp.'

The newcomer shook his head, his eyes over-bright.

Walter came to clap Horry on the shoulder. 'Few people are perfect, lad. It's not what's on

134

the outside, but what they're like inside them that I value most.'

Gil watched Horry relax visibly. Here was another person about to be helped by the wise old man.

As they ate, they talked about motor cars, what Gil needed, how much he could afford to spend. One thing soon became clear: Horry knew what he was talking about.

He asked a few questions, then said, 'I know a fellow in London who has a car for sale. It's not new, but it's a good runner. It's a Talbot 4T, with a side-valve engine, transmission brakes at the rear and — '

Gil laughed and held up one hand. 'I don't understand a word of that, but I trust you, Horry. I'm going up to London next week to try on my special shoes. Could we look at it then?'

Horry looked at him in surprise. 'How can you trust me when you hardly know me?'

'First, Julia vouches for you. Second, you have an honest face.'

'Oh. Well. Thank you. I'll write to him and arrange to see the car.'

Walter smiled benignly at them both. 'That's good. Now, Gil, we'd better find Horry somewhere to sleep. Lizzie will know where to put him, but there are those rooms over the stables. Maybe he'll be best there, if they're in good condition. We'll go out and look at them tomorrow morning.'

'I could help out in any way you need till we get a car,' Horry volunteered.

'Then your first job will be to clean out and

set up your living quarters,' Walter said. 'Those rooms are sound but they haven't been used for a while.'

Once they'd sent Horry off with Lizzie, Gil looked at his friend. 'Isn't it wonderful how things are falling into place?'

'Perfect.' Walter clapped one hand to his chest and grimaced.

'Are you all right?'

'Just a touch of indigestion. It's happened a couple of times lately. I'll have to be more careful what I eat.'

As he got ready for bed, excitement filled Gil. He was going to buy a motor car, he had happy news for several people in the village, and tomorrow he'd talk to Lizzie about her brother.

It was good to feel useful again. No, not again. He'd not been much use to anyone but himself before.

★ ★ ★

Julia came to visit two days later, bringing the housekeeper she'd found for Gil, as she'd said in a letter. The woman was so colourless, he was surprised she'd been the target of any man's lusts. It was her reddened eyes that made him agree to hire her and the way her hands twisted together in her apron.

'Why do men do it?' he muttered to Julia afterwards. 'It's not hard to woo a woman with kindness.'

'Some men enjoy frightening people.' She patted his arm. 'Thank goodness for ones like you, Gil.'

136

That was as may be. It was one thing not to assault women, but he was at the other extreme. The thought of being impotent was just as hard to bear as the physical disabilities had been. Would he grow used to that, too? Would he become a crusty old bachelor?

Once Julia had been driven away, Gil handed the woman over to Lizzie and Madge to show her around the house, and he and Walter went into the sitting room.

'She might be all right as a housekeeper, but she's a quiet one and you're never sure what to think with that sort,' Walter said.

'Maybe she'll cheer up once she's settled in.'

Gil tried to chat to his new housekeeper, but she answered only in monosyllables, so in the end he gave up the attempt.

Walter met with the same sort of response.

But Gil overheard Lizzie and Cook talking a few days later, saying she gave them the shivers, so quietly did she move around the house.

'You shouldn't have let Miss Gardiner push you into hiring her,' Walter said. 'You should choose your staff by how you feel about them. The rest of us get on well, more like a family. She doesn't fit in.'

'I can hardly sack the poor woman. She seems to do her job competently. I think I need a woman to hire people like housekeepers. Maybe I should ask my mother to do that sort of thing for me in future.'

'And maybe you should learn to do things for yourself.'

'You could help with that sort of thing,

though. You're a good judge of people.'

'I won't always be around to help.'

Gil looked at him in horror. 'Aren't you feeling well?'

'I'm well past my threescore years and ten. Living on borrowed time, some would say.'

Gil shuddered. 'Don't talk like that.'

'Don't put blinkers on. Look at the world as it is.' He waited for this to sink in, then added in a more cheerful tone, 'Now, how about you go and see the rest of the beneficiaries? I reckon they've been waiting long enough to hear the good news.'

★ ★ ★

On his way to the next person on his list, Gil encountered Duncan Chapman in the village and had to stop because the other man deliberately barred his path.

'I was coming to see you,' Chapman said.

'It's not convenient just now. I'm on my way to see someone.'

A sneer curved Chapman's fleshy lips. 'Another beneficiary?'

Gil didn't like his tone. 'None of your business.'

'It ought to be.' He raised his voice. 'If it weren't for you, I'd be the one sitting at Oakdene now.'

'I beg your pardon?'

'You heard me. I don't know how you got round the old lady, but people in these parts don't appreciate you getting Oakdene by trickery.'

Gil raised his own voice to match, realising

138

Chapman was performing for an audience, presumably people in nearby houses or the village shop. 'I'd never even met Miss Bennerden and I don't appreciate your insinuations. If you keep making them, you'll be hearing from my lawyer. Slander, they call it.'

'It's not slander when it's the simple truth.'

'I'm quite prepared to take the matter to court.' He hadn't meant to, had decided to ignore it, but Chapman wouldn't let the matter drop.

'Oh, yes. Very easy for you to do that when you have all her money.'

Gil tried to step round him, but Chapman moved more quickly to block his path.

'You'll regret it.' This time he spoke in a low voice.

'Please get out of my way,' Gil said loudly.

Chapman raised his voice again. 'Not till I've had my say. Does it make you feel good to play Lord Bountiful and tell people what they've been left?'

'I'm doing as Miss Bennerden asked.'

'What has she left me, then? I'm not prepared to wait any longer to find out.'

'Nothing.'

Chapman's previously ruddy face turned white. 'I don't believe you. I'm a relative. She *couldn't* have ignored me completely.'

'She hasn't left you anything. You should ask Mr Mortlake, if you don't believe it. He can also tell you that I had nothing whatsoever to do with Miss Bennerden's will.'

This time, when Chapman tried to stop him moving on, Gil pushed him aside and started walking down the street.

But the other caught up with him and grabbed him by the injured arm. 'Don't you treat me like that.'

They were saved by the village policeman, who moved across from the other side of the street, clearing his throat and looking embarrassed. 'Now, gentlemen, if you please. Let's not have any arguing and shouting.'

'He's the one causing trouble,' Chapman said at once.

Gil turned to the policeman. 'I was accosted by this fellow who is preventing me from going about my business.' He turned and walked off, wishing he could stride away instead of limping slowly.

Behind him he heard clearly, 'It's not worth it, sir. No arguments can change a will.'

'I'm not so sure about that. People should stand up for what's right.'

Gil stopped and turned round, meeting such a look of hatred from Chapman that for the first time he wondered whether the other man's threats should be taken seriously.

It might have been foolish, but the very next day he went into Swindon and visited Mr Mortlake, making an extremely simple will in which he left everything he owned to his mother, and if she predeceased him, his second brother, Jonathon. Under no circumstances was Chapman going to get his hands on Oakdene.

He didn't tell Walter what he was doing, because the old man had come down with a cold.

Gil had probably been needlessly concerned. This was England and the twentieth century. People didn't kill others because they were upset at not being left any money.

But still, doing this gave him peace of mind.

* * *

The new housekeeper asked to speak to Gil after she'd been there a week.

'I'm sorry to disappoint you, sir, but I can't settle in this house. It's so far away from everywhere, and when I go into the village, people won't chat to me.'

She didn't say that was because Chapman was still stirring up trouble, didn't need to.

'Oh. Well, where do you want to go?'

'Back to the home, if you please. I felt safer there and I had company.'

He hoped he'd hidden his relief at this, but of course, it left him with the problem of finding another housekeeper. Or did it?

'Why don't we just find another maid?' he suggested to Walter the evening after he'd taken the housekeeper back to the home. 'We don't need a fancy housekeeper as well as Madge, surely? She's proving to be a very capable woman.'

'Copping out?' Walter asked.

'No. Just trying to create a peaceful home and life.'

'You'll never be truly peaceful here till you've sorted things out in the village.'

'First I'm going to London to pick up my new

141

shoes, buy a car and take Don up to meet the shoemaker.'

★ ★ ★

The visit to London went well. Horry accompanied Gil instead of Walter, so that he could show Gil the motor car. He kept an eye on young Don, who had never ridden on a train before, his mother being too poor to afford outings.

The bootmaker fitted the new shoes very carefully, checking the most minute details, then sat back on his heels and looked up at Gil. 'Try walking in them.'

Gil moved across the room, then back. It was so much more comfortable, and he beamed at the bootmaker. 'Wonderful.'

'I pride myself on making a difference.'

'Could you make me another couple of pairs, and maybe some boots for winter?'

The man rolled his eyes. 'You'll have to wait your turn. I'm as busy as ever.'

'Perhaps you should talk to Don about an apprenticeship, then. He's waiting outside.'

To everyone's delight, the bootmaker pronounced Don a 'likely lad' and agreed to give him a month's trial, after which they would sign apprenticeship papers, with Gil paying the fees.

'I won't let you down, Mr Rycroft,' the boy whispered as they got ready to leave.

'Don't let yourself down.'

Chapman might sneer about playing Lord Bountiful, but Gil found helping people very satisfying indeed.

They went on from the bootmaker to see the new motor car.

Here, Horry took charge, clambering all over it, sliding underneath, and driving it up and down the road.

'What do you think?' Gil asked him when he pulled up again, setting the big handbrake on carefully. Horry might talk about the mechanics of it, but Gil liked the comfort of the leather seats and the way the spokes on the wheels spun so fast as the car was driven along that they turned into a blur.

'Time you came for a ride, sir.'

When they were out on the road, he drove up a hill, parking to test the handbrake, then said earnestly as they made their way back, 'I don't think you'd go wrong buying it, and you'd not have to wait for delivery. He'll let us drive it away today. We can motor home, if that's all right with you?'

'It's fine with me. I brought the money in case.'

He handed over the money and gave himself up to the pleasure of spinning along the roads.

All was right with his little world.

1912

8

At the beginning of January Renie was summoned to see Mrs Tolson as soon as she was free.
The housekeeper was considerate enough not to
take away a waitress during a busy period.

Renie went as soon as the lunchtime rush died
down, knocking on the housekeeper's door and
waiting.

'Come!'

Inside, Mrs Tolson was sitting behind her
desk, smiling, thank goodness, so Renie knew
she wasn't in trouble.

'Sit down, Irene.'

'Thank you, ma'am.'

'We've been watching you over the past few
months. You've picked things up very quickly
and you're a hard worker.'

Renie couldn't help beaming at this praise.

'Mr Greaves and I were wondering whether
you want to stay here as a waitress till you marry,
or whether you'd be interested in making a
career in our hotels. You know that the Carling
family owns several?'

'Yes, ma'am.' She paused, puzzled. 'I don't
know what you mean, exactly.'

'We have to move with the times. At the
moment we have women who work in the office,
but who know little about the day-to-day work in
the rest of the hotel, and we have women who
work in housekeeping or, like you, in waitressing,

147

but who don't know about office work. Mr Greaves and I wondered if you'd like to learn about other areas, then learn office work as well. I've seen how you love books, so perhaps you'd be able to handle the paperwork. You've been going through those books in the staff sitting room very quickly, I gather.'

It took a moment or two for this to sink in. 'Office work! I thought only men did that, except for lady typists. And I don't know how to typewrite.'

'Men have done the clerical work until now, but women are doing a lot of different jobs these days. The thing is, there are times in hotels when a lady guest needs to speak to another woman about some problem. And there are more ladies travelling on their own these days, too, so we've been considering this for a while. Mr Greaves is very forward-thinking, for all he's not a young man.'

Renie tried to appear calm and efficient, but couldn't help bursting out with, 'Ooh, that sounds marvellous, Mrs Tolson.'

It won her a smile. 'What about marriage? Some of the women who work here are courting and only working till they marry.' She sat watching, head on one side.

They always asked younger women that. Renie wondered suddenly if they asked the men too, something that hadn't occurred to her before. Then she realised the housekeeper was still waiting for an answer. 'I don't want to get married, Mrs Tolson. My sister did and . . . well, I've seen how unhappy she is. Anyway, I don't have a young man.' The lads were a bit too cheeky for her in London. She wasn't going to risk being forced as Nell had been. Cliff had even had the cheek to blame Nell for expecting a baby after doing *that* to her.

'Then would you like to try our idea? It'd mean working in other areas: doing the bedrooms for a while, learning to type and do simple accounts, all sorts of things. You'd lose the extra tips money but you'd be earning a higher wage once you were fully trained, and I think you'd find the working conditions more pleasant too.'

'I'd *love* to try it.' Renie had thought all jobs were boring, and you just had to put up with that in order to earn your daily bread. But this one actually sounded interesting.

'Good. Say nothing to the others. I'll announce it when I'm ready to move you.'

* * *

It caused a sensation when the other women were told that Renie was going to work in housekeeping, then move to the office. Some of the older women, who'd been there some years, didn't try to hide their jealousy. One of them stopped talking to her and there was less help offered when they were rushed. There were even a couple of nasty tricks played, which upset her.

'You're mad to do it,' Daff said. 'You'll lose your tips and you'll lose your friends, too.'

Renie had already begun to realise that. 'But I'll have a chance to do something more

149

interesting with my life. And I'll earn more later.'

'But you'll be making beds and emptying chamber pots. Ugh. I wouldn't like a job doing that, not unless I was desperate.'

If you'd lived in Willow Court, Renie thought, you'd be quite used to filth. You could always wash yourself when you'd finished, after all. Anyway, if suffragettes could chain themselves to railings and get arrested, could suffer through hunger strikes, all to win votes for women, she could surely put up with these small cruelties to do a job that was a new thing for women. She read about the suffragettes avidly in newspapers and greatly admired them, but knew she couldn't have been that brave.

When she changed to cleaning the guests' rooms, the other cleaners were suspicious of her and unhelpful. If it hadn't been for Miss Pilkins keeping an eye on her, they too would have played nasty tricks on her.

When Miss Pilkins found her crying over her work one day, she sat down on the bed and patted it. 'Sit beside me and tell me what's wrong, Irene.'

'No one speaks to me and they don't help me. It's not going to work, Miss Pilkins. It just . . . isn't. Maybe you should have chosen one of them to do this.'

'If any of the others had been suitable, they'd be working in waitressing now to learn about that area, then being trained as an assistant to the manager instead of you. But they're not suitable, even though they're older. They're good workers or they'd not be employed here, but they

150

don't think beyond their daily routine.'

She winked. '*They* don't take an interest in what the suffragettes are doing or think about women getting the vote.'

Renie looked at her, worried this was going to turn into a reprimand.

'I admire them too,' Miss Pilkins said quietly. 'But if we're wise we won't tell others how we feel. You can do this, Irene, I know you can.'

'But I'm only eighteen. What do I know of the world?'

'You know how to learn. That's why you were chosen. Mr Greaves wants to have the training of you before you get set in your ways. You're a quick-thinking young woman who reacts well in an emergency. That's important, too. You saved us a lot of trouble when you helped Mrs Thompson a few weeks ago. That wasn't part of your job, but you brought back her dog and calmed her down. She turned to you, even though more senior men were available, because she felt more comfortable with another woman.'

She stood up. 'Get on with your work now. I'm going to speak to the others.'

Renie couldn't see how that would help, but when she heard footsteps and saw the other two maids on this floor going towards the stairs, then heard voices in the stairwell, she realised Miss Pilkins had actually pulled all the other housemaids away from their work to attend a meeting.

Something hard and hurting inside her eased a little at this gesture of support. Even if it didn't help, it made her feel better, not so much alone.

151

She set to work on the room, determined to do her very best and prove they'd been right to trust her.

* * *

Miss Pilkins had informed Mrs Tolson of the problem and what she intended to do about it. They'd agreed not to tell Mr Greaves yet. He hadn't been well lately, so they tried not to worry him about details, especially during the busy Christmas period.

She waited until all the housekeeping staff except Irene were gathered in the staff sitting room, then rapped on a table for their attention.

'I'm going to be blunt today. The management has chosen to give Irene Fuller a chance at a new type of job and that's upsetting some of you.'

Mutters greeted this, but they avoided looking her in the eye.

'You no doubt think someone who's been here longer should have been chosen for the new job, but I'm afraid Irene was considered the most suitable.'

She looked round, ignoring the scowls. 'Among the reasons are that she hasn't yet got any fixed ideas about how things should be done in the hotel. But also, she's a clever girl — you've all seen how voraciously she reads — and she's a quick learner. Mr Greaves, Mrs Tolson and I have made our decision for this experiment. If Irene left now — and don't pretend you're not trying to drive her away — we'd not choose anyone else here but would look in one of the other hotels for someone suitable and bring that person in over your heads.'

She paused, then said bluntly, 'I will add two things. First, if Irene succeeds, she opens an opportunity for young women that wasn't there before. You should all welcome that. Second, I shall sack anyone who plays nasty tricks on her — and no, she didn't tell me about those. I have eyes in my head and I know how our housekeeping system works.'

As someone tried to call out, she held up one hand to stop them. 'I'm not going to discuss it with you further. Either you want to work here or you don't. Make up your minds, because if you don't let Irene have her chance, you'll be the one who leaves, not her. Now, get back to your work, please.'

She waited till they'd all gone, then let out her breath in a long sigh. She'd risen through the housekeeping ranks herself, knew that most of the women who worked here didn't have what it took to do a thinking job and also that it'd been dinned into them that some jobs were only for men.

It was a hard path doing something different, as she herself knew. From now on, the open hostility and nasty tricks would end — Miss Pilkins was pretty sure of that — but the resentment would still simmer beneath the surface.

Irene would definitely earn her promotion. It would be hard, but it could be the making of her, young as she was.

★　★　★

153

It was very lonely, Renie found, doing something different from everyone else, something they resented. Oh, the others had stopped playing tricks on her, would even help if she asked, but they never started a conversation with her while working and didn't include her in their fun.

Daff was the only one who was unchanged by it all, but then Daff was such a cheerful person, it took a lot to upset her.

'Rather you than me,' she said frankly when they went out for a walk on the Sunday. 'You'll be going into the office later. Ugh! I'd hate to work with the men all day. They'll try to treat you like a skivvy. Look at how they talk to us, even the youngest waiter, who's not much more than a silly lad! All except Mr Greaves, that is. He's lovely to everyone.'

'I won't let them be rude to me.'

'You can't say no to bosses.'

'Mrs Tolson will tell them what my duties are and I'll be answerable to her, so they won't be my bosses.' She hoped she was right in this, because she didn't like the way one of the younger men in the office had started eyeing her.

'Mrs Tolson won't be around all the time. You're even having a rough time with the *women* you work with. It'll be worse with men. Think I haven't heard you crying at night after everyone's gone to sleep?'

'Oh, no! Do you suppose anyone else has heard me?'

'If they have, they've not said so.'

Renie did a lot of thinking after that conversation, but she still wanted to seize this opportunity.

154

In March she was feeling upset so wrote to ask Nell's advice about whether it was worth trying to better herself, even though it wasn't easy. She didn't go into detail because she didn't want to upset Nell.

Her sister wrote back to say how proud their mother and Mattie would be of her and she must certainly keep trying, whatever the difficulties.

They never mentioned their father in their letters, or even considered trying to contact him. Renie hoped she'd never see him again.

But this month marked two years since they'd fled from Swindon so Nell said she would wait till he was in a good mood and then ask her husband about trying to contact his family, in the hope that Mattie had been in touch.

But in her next letter, she said Cliff had again refused to contact them. Tears came into Renie's eyes as she read that. What if Mattie was trying to contact them? What if they never found their eldest sister again?

She tried to talk herself into a better mood. Concentrate on the job in hand. She was coping, wasn't she? She had September to look forward to, when she'd have a whole week's holiday. She'd already arranged to spend it with Nell. Where else would she go?

If it was still hard going at work, they could discuss Renie's problems then. Nell always had such wise advice. Of course, Cliff would be there, but he'd be out all day at work and half the evenings as well, because he was still going to the pub, Nell said. So there wasn't much Cliff could do to spoil her time with her sister.

It made you think, though. Even if you were careful about getting married, men could change, couldn't they? Once they'd got what they wanted, most went their own sweet way, using their wives as servants.

Well, that's what it seemed like to Renie, anyway. She had two eyes in her head and knew what she'd seen in her own family and in the neighbours' families. Except for one young couple who lived nearby, she remembered suddenly. They'd married and had two little children and still looked at each other so lovingly, it brought tears to your eyes to see them.

Most people weren't that lucky.

★ ★ ★

As the weeks passed, Renie was tempted many times to abandon her new job. She wasn't saving nearly as much money because of not getting a share of the tips, but worst of all, she was lonely. She went to the sitting room each evening out of pride and sat with the others, reading a book. If Daff was there, her friend still talked to her, which made her feel a bit better.

Every now and then, Miss Pilkins would take Renie off the floor for a day or two to sit beside her and learn about the paperwork. Estimates for new bed linen and towels, not to mention keeping track of a myriad small items like soap. The lists of what was needed had to be submitted to Mr Greaves' assistant in charge of accounts, and they had to be accurate to the penny, which wasn't always easy.

Miss Pilkins wasn't good at figures, as she freely admitted, and it took her a lot of hard work to keep her accounts and balance sheets in order.

Renie found she enjoyed doing the accounts and could speed things up for her supervisor. That was a surprise because she'd never enjoyed arithmetic at school. But accounts were different. They were real, as arithmetic problems had never been.

She enjoyed writing numbers neatly in the long columns, proud of her penmanship, practising on odd pages that Mr Greaves provided, which had a few figures crossed out neatly at the top. She loved to see the way the money balanced out at the bottom.

Such big sums of money! So many details to get right! It was even more complicated running a big hotel than she'd expected.

Her love affair with accounts continued when she went back to the catering side. This time it was Miss Green who took her through the tea shop accounts and, when she picked that up quite quickly, said grudgingly that she could see she had little to teach Irene.

After that Miss Green was a bit friendlier to her. It was as if the new assistant had passed some sort of test.

Next Renie was passed to Monsieur Leduc, who ran the restaurant, but before she started, Mrs Tolson said she needed smarter clothes now. They found her a very attractive skirt and jacket, dark grey with black braid round the hem and jacket edges. There were also three white blouses. And she was told to pull her hair back into a severe bun at the nape of her neck. Wisps came out, of course, because her hair was fine and slightly wavy, but she tucked them in again whenever she noticed.

All these clothes had to be paid for, but as they were second hand, they weren't as expensive as Renie had feared. Apparently some people left clothes behind in their hotel rooms — either intentionally or by mistake, no one knew which — and they didn't bother to send for them. Imagine having so many clothes you could lose some and not care, perhaps not even notice! She moved some of her well-worn old clothing up to her trunk in the attic.

Renie hardly recognised herself in the mirror the first morning she wore the new outfit. Looking so smart gave her confidence. When she went into the staff dining room, everyone fell silent and stared at her.

'You look lovely,' Daff said loudly.

'Thank you.'

Another girl said, 'I like the shape of that skirt.'

Most of them gave Renie dirty looks, though.

She was so nervous, she couldn't eat her breakfast. When she pushed her food to the side of her plate and set down her knife and fork, Daff whispered, 'Aren't you feeling well?'

Her voice came out as a croak. 'I'm too nervous.'

'I would be too, if I had to deal with His Majesty.' She rolled her eyes. Mr Leduc was universally feared by the waitresses, for his scorn and his loud voice, his complaints and his tendency to tip a plate of food on the floor if they disturbed the food on it, and tell the waitress to carry it properly next time.

Renie got to his office ten minutes early. She didn't know whether to go back and wait until the exact time he'd specified, or whether to stay outside. In the end she stayed, because she was terrified of something making her late if she left the area.

As it turned out, he seemed to sense that she was there because he poked his head out of the door and stared at her. 'Why did you not knock, Miss Fuller?'

'I'm too early.'

He shrugged. 'Come in. Punctuality is, at least, a proper start.' He went to sit behind his desk and studied her. 'You are a good girl?'

She gaped at him, then drew herself up. 'If you mean what I think, yes, I am.'

'I 'ave not seen you flirting, that I will admit. See that you continue to behave yourself when you work with the men. I will not allow flirting in my area.'

'Then I'd be obliged if you'd tell your cooks and waiters the same thing. We girls have trouble with them.'

He became thoughtful. 'It is natural for men to look.'

'And touch?'

His eyes narrowed. 'They do that?'

'Yes.'

'That is too much. I do not believe in women

159

working as waitresses, but since the 'otel chooses to do this, I shall speak to my staff about you. You will 'ave no trouble in my area.'

'Thank you, Mr Leduc.'

'You will call me 'Monsieur'. It is the French for 'mister'. Just 'Monsieur'.'

'Very well. Could you say it again, please? I'd only read it in books till I came to the Rathleigh and I said it wrong in my head.' She listened and repeated the word after him till he nodded.

'*Bien.* You 'ave it perfectly correct now.'

'Thank you, monsieur.'

'Today you stay with me. You follow be'ind me, or you stand where I tell you, and you watch. Very carefully, you watch. Nothing more yet. You are to learn first 'ow the restaurants and kitchens operate.'

'Yes, monsieur.'

It was a long, tiring day. And to her embarrassment, she had to explain to him when she had to go to the lavatory because he allowed her no time for this. He didn't seem embarrassed by it, but when she came back, he said, 'I will give you five minutes every two hours to attend to your needs. Also, you will be provided with lunch and a cup of English tea or of coffee, as you prefer, whenever I myself take refreshment. Is that satisfactory?'

'Yes. Thank you very much, monsieur.'

That was only one of the embarrassing things about working in a man's world. The men still looked at her. They might have been warned not to say anything or touch her, but they still looked at her in ways that made her feel uncomfortable, as if she had no clothes on.

She couldn't let this continue, so practised in front of a mirror to get the right expression on her face for dealing with them. She managed a cool, scornful look similar to one she'd seen a young lady use in the café when a flashy gentleman, who was trying to flirt with her, said something that made her draw herself upright and stop talking to him.

It wasn't going to be easy working with Monsieur, though. He wanted you to be perfect in everything.

The trouble was, *he* seemed never to make a mistake.

9

Two weeks later when Renie was on the way back to the hotel after a brisk walk on her afternoon off, she noticed a man sitting in Yew Tree Gardens with his face turned up to the spring sunshine. It wasn't really warm today, but she too was enjoying the brightness, which took her mind off her worries about her sister, so she smiled sympathetically.

It was his smile that attracted her and the way he was enjoying the same simple pleasure she did. Then she couldn't help noticing how handsome he was, a bit older than her, but still not all that old. From his clothing, he was a gentleman, so would never look twice at her. If he was a customer at the hotel, she shouldn't be staring at him. Or was he a customer? She had a feeling she'd seen him before in the gardens, in the distance. Perhaps he lived nearby.

She looked away and saw a flower bed filled with tulips. It was so pretty, she went across to admire it. She loved flowers, always had. Their colours seemed so much more alive than the same colours in magazines or dress materials. There had been few flowers in her life in Swindon, and even fewer in Lancashire.

They had vases of flowers in the hotel, but she preferred the ones in gardens. They looked happier, somehow, and would surely last longer.

As she turned to continue her walk, the man

stood up and started off towards an older man, who had come along the street. She saw that the younger man was walking with a limp and there was something wrong with his arm, too. He must have been in an accident, poor fellow.

But if you were rich, that wouldn't make half as much difference to your life as it would if you were poor. He'd not lose everything.

Suddenly she heard a newsboy calling out shrilly, followed by cries and shouts. She turned to see what had made the regular newsboy behave like that in front of the Rathleigh, because he surely knew better.

Only this time the doorman didn't come out to chase him away and he continued to yell.

People in the street and park had turned to see what was going on and those closer began making their way towards the lad.

The words he was shouting and those on his poster sank in and she too gasped.

TITANIC DISASTER
GREAT LOSS OF LIFE

'The *Titanic*'s sunk!' yelled a man hurrying past.

She was shocked rigid. It was a brand-new ship and she'd heard guests talking about it, seen it in the newspapers. How could a brand-new ship sink?

And, oh dear! Miss Cholmondley-Berne had been sailing on it. She was a dear old lady, a regular customer who always tipped well and was liked by the staff.

Renie was so upset to think of her drowning, she didn't look where she was going and bumped into someone. It took her only a few seconds to realise it was the man she'd been watching. She had to steady him because she'd hit him hard and caught him off balance. 'I'm so sorry, sir! I wasn't watching where I was going.'

'I'm all right. Are you?'

'Oh yes, I'm fine. I was just upset about the news.'

He turned to look towards the news seller and called to the older man, who was now a few paces away. 'Walter, could you get me a paper? I don't want to risk myself among those crowds.'

The older man went off and Renie lingered, wanting to see what the newspaper said. She looked at her companion uncertainly. If he seemed annoyed that she was still there, she'd move on. But instead he spoke to her.

'Do you want to hear more about the *Titanic*, too?'

'If you don't mind, sir. One of our favourite customers from the hotel was sailing on it.'

His face went suddenly white. 'Dear God, my eldest brother was on it, too. How could I possibly have forgotten that? Not only him, but his wife and two little children.'

Her heart went out to him. 'All the passengers can't have died, surely?'

'I pray not. They do carry lifeboats on those big ships. It depends how quickly it sank, I suppose.' He watched his friend join the queue and wait for a newspaper.

He spoke to Renie again, but absently, as if his

164

thoughts were elsewhere and he was only being polite. 'What do you do at the hotel?'

'I'm assistant to the housekeeper. It's a new sort of job, to help our lady customers.'

'What they call a *new woman*, are you, eh?'

She smiled. She'd read that phrase but no one she knew had ever used it about her. Still, she liked the idea. 'I hope so. As much as I can be. Times are changing, aren't they?'

The older man returned just then and her companion stopped trying to smile and make conversation.

The two of them studied the front page of the newspaper, looking upset, searching for a certain name: Rycroft. From what they said, the younger man was called Gil. Short for Gilbert, probably. And if he had the same surname as his brother, it was Rycroft. The other was called Walter. They didn't seem to want her to leave, so she waited, standing quietly next to them. She tried to work out what had happened as she listened to their exclamations and comments.

'It says the early reports which stated that all the people on board had been saved were wrong,' Gil said.

Their heads bent closer to the newspaper.

'Oh, no! It's now believed that two-thirds of the passengers and crew have been lost!' Gil stopped reading for a moment. 'That's shocking. Surely they had enough lifeboats for all? It was a modern, well-found ship. Everyone was proud of it. My brother was excited to be going on its first voyage, said it would be an experience of a lifetime.'

'They can't have had enough lifeboats if they've lost so many people,' Walter said. 'Or else it happened too quickly.'

'We must pray that Robert and his family were among the survivors. Poor Harriet! And those two little girls! What must they have gone through!'

Renie laid one hand on his arm without thinking. 'I'm so sorry, sir. I hope they'll be all right.'

She shouldn't have touched a stranger like that, but she could see how upset he was.

He patted her hand before she took it away, as if he found her sympathy comforting.

She knew better than to linger and pester a gentleman, let alone a person facing such a terrible family tragedy. 'Thank you, sir. I appreciate you letting me know more.'

'Good luck with your new job.'

Even in his distress, he'd tried to be kind to her. What a nice man! Pity the hotel guests weren't all like him.

* * *

Gil watched her go and admitted to himself that when she'd touched him, for the first time — the very first time since his accident — he'd felt a twinge of desire. And he hadn't been imagining it, because it was the last thing he'd expected after hearing such news.

He didn't even know her name, but she was pretty and fresh-looking, with a lively, intelligent expression. Any man would find her attractive.

In the past, he'd usually gone for pretty faces and soft, plump bodies, never mind whether the women were stupid, but this woman was . . . different somehow.

Anyone could tell that she wasn't a loose woman, so he could do nothing about his feelings. He didn't believe in corrupting innocent young women, even if they were from the lower classes, whom some men of his acquaintance considered fair game.

He'd enjoyed hearing her speak, too, a slower, gentler accent than you normally heard in London. Come to think of it, she sounded as if she was from Wiltshire, but with something else in her voice, as if she'd lived elsewhere.

He'd probably never see her again, but he was deeply grateful to her for wakening his senses. It gave him hope that one day he might feel himself a proper man again, even be able to marry and have children. Was that possible? Dare he hope?

What was the old saying? *One swallow does not a summer make.* He mustn't get his hopes too high. But still . . .

Then he remembered his eldest brother Robert, who had children, two delightful little daughters. Gil dismissed his own problems, which were minor matters. Robert and his family had been on the *Titanic*, might even have been killed.

Please, God, let them all have got off the ship safely!

'We'd better visit my parents, Walter, and catch a later train back to Swindon. They might need me.' He didn't always visit them when he came to London, because they always found something to nag him about, couldn't seem to believe that he was happy living at Oakdene House. But this was a time for families to stick together.

He found his mother at home, trying and failing to keep a stiff upper lip. She fell into Gil's arms and for the first time he found himself in the comforting, supporting role with her.

'They must be safe. They must be. They can't be dead. Not my lovely boy! Not those little girls.' She sobbed against his chest.

'We must hope for the best, pray for them.' Such trite words, but what else could he say? He felt so helpless.

'Your father's gone to the club to see if he can find out more there.' She mopped her eyes again. 'I don't know why he thinks he will. He should have stayed home to comfort me, be with me, in case we . . . heard something.'

Gil could guess exactly why his father had gone out. His father couldn't cope with sadness and tears, even in a minor way. And now, with a family tragedy possible, he wouldn't know how to deal with a wife in such distress.

'You won't leave me, Gil, will you?' she begged. 'Not till we know?'

'Of course I won't.'

In the end, he sent Walter to buy a few things they needed and used his old clothes from the attic, sharing some of them with Walter. His mother wanted him with her at all times and clung tightly to his hand every time the parlourmaid brought in the latest edition of a newspaper.

168

He realised in mild surprise that his parents had probably never faced anything so disastrous. They'd had a pleasant, uneventful life and hadn't lost a child, as so many families did. His own accident had been the worst they'd faced.

If Gil hadn't learnt the hard way to cope with problems, he'd be no use to them now. Strange to be thankful for that. He knew now that you could face major upsets in life and continue. They had yet to learn that.

But perhaps Robert and his family would be all right. After all, a third of the people on board the ship had survived, so there was a fairly good chance Robert might have been among the lucky ones.

Not as good a chance that all four of them had survived, though. He shivered. What a dreadful thought.

*　*　*

Renie hurried round to the rear of the hotel and went in by the employees' entrance. She found the staff upset by the tragedy, stopping in small groups to discuss it and share the latest news. She didn't join in these conversations, but nodded occasionally or muttered, 'Mmm' or 'Terrible'.

It seemed that several of their regular customers had been on the ship. That wasn't like having family on it, though. She felt sorry about the customers in a vague way, but she felt far more sorry for that poor young man whose brother had been involved. She remembered his

169

surname, would check the lists of deaths that would surely be published in the newspapers to see if anyone called Rycroft was on it.

It was none of her business, but she couldn't help being interested. Gil was such a good-looking man, and so kind. Very different from her brother-in-law Cliff, or the men who sometimes pestered her at the markets. She'd have liked to get to know Gil.

There she went again, daydreaming like an idiot. A gentleman like that wouldn't even look twice at a girl like her, and even if he did, he'd not marry her, even if she wanted to get married, which she didn't. At least most of the time she thought she didn't . . .

But still . . .

'Oh, Irene, there you are.'

She turned. 'Yes, Mrs Tolson?'

'Could you please stay in the foyer and keep an eye open for lady customers who might need soothing.'

Renie did that, and was able to provide cups of tea and encouragement to keep their hopes up to two elderly ladies, whose nephew was on the *Titanic*, and later to the wife of a regular customer who had also sailed on that ship.

It was a strange sort of day at the hotel. Customers were upset by the sinking of the *Titanic*, even when they didn't have friends or relatives involved. Staff were upset too. New editions of each newspaper were rushed in and snatched from the counter before their purchase could be noted against the room numbers.

In the end, Mr Greaves sent a message round

170

to all staff to stay calm, and they tried, they really did. But it was such a terrible tragedy that the smallest thing would set some of the women off weeping.

Mrs Tolson came to find her later. 'You've done well today, Irene. Mr Greaves saw you help those old ladies and was very pleased about how you did it. They needed a woman, not a man, at a time like that.'

'Thank you. I was glad I could help them.'

'Once this fuss is over and done with, we'll be moving you into the office for a while.' She smiled as she added, 'And you'll have a new title from now on — 'housekeeper's assistant'. We'll raise your wages to go with that. You've worked very hard, and both Mr Greaves and I are proud of you. Young as you are, you're doing just what he wanted.'

When she was alone, Renie couldn't help beaming. She had tried her hardest not to let them down. She'd paid for her new status in loneliness and less money, but now she was about to get her reward. Housekeeper's assistant! How grand that sounded. Nell would be so pleased.

*   *   *

The news came to the Rycrofts at last and it was very bad. Gil's father was at his club, his brother Jonathon was at home in Tonbridge Wells, where his wife had inherited a house. As second son, Jonathon had become a lawyer and had joined his wife's uncle's practice. In fact, it had been a very useful marriage in several ways and Jonathon was doing very well for himself. He was now awaiting the birth of his first child.

When the butler brought the telegram in to Gil's mother, she took it with a hand that trembled and dismissed him with a mutter.

She sat staring at the telegram for so long, Gil took her hand. 'Shall I open it for you, Mother?'

Nodding, she passed it to him, then clasped her hands together so tightly her knuckles showed white.

He opened it and read it first, feeling sick with sadness. There was no way to soften the news but he hated to say the words.

'It's bad, isn't it?' she said.

'Yes. Very bad.' He took her hand. 'We've lost three of them, Mother: Robert, Harriet and little Jennifer.'

He half expected her to scream or fall into hysterics, but instead she sat very still, rocking slightly, staring blindly towards a patch of sunlight on the carpet, her hand limp in his.

'Mother? Are you all right?'

She turned slowly to look at him. 'No. I'm . . . frozen. I can't seem to think beyond the news. What must we do? Tell me what to do.'

This was so unlike her. She normally knew exactly what to do. Gil spoke gently. 'I think I should go and fetch Father from the club, then we'll decide together what to do next. Don't forget there's little Elizabeth, on her own in New York.'

'Poor thing. Someone will have to go and fetch her, I suppose.'

'You and Father, presumably. Harriet's parents are in India.' He waited a moment then asked, 'Will you be all right if I go and fetch Father now? I don't think we should send a servant or even a note. Not for this.'

'Send for my maid first, then go,' she said. 'You're right. Bertram has to be told in person. And I . . . must change into my blacks.' She pressed her hand against her mouth as if to hold in her anguish, but tears spilt from her eyes and ran down over her fingers.

At the club Gil had a word with Peterson, who was a sort of glorified butler and ran the place. When he explained why he'd come, there was no question of finding someone to sign him in. Peterson himself took him to his father, who was sitting in his usual armchair, hidden behind a newspaper.

But though it was late in the morning, only one page had been turned and his father was staring blankly at the nearby window. He didn't put the newspaper down until Gil said, 'I need to speak to you, Father. There's . . . news. Bad news, I'm afraid.'

He waited until his father had carefully folded up the newspaper, then told him, not going into details, or asking what to do.

His father's face was expressionless, but it began to flush, turning a sort of purplish red. He smelt of port, early as it was to be drinking, and he kept pressing a hand against his chest. 'Indigestion.'

Gil waited, but his father continued to sit there, saying nothing, just frowning and continuing to press one hand against his chest.

'We need to go home,' he said at last. 'Mother will need you.'

'Mmmh.' His father tried to stand up and fell back. His eyes rolled up and he slumped in his chair.

Gil shouted for help and Peterson came running, taking in the situation at a glance.

'I'll send for a doctor. There's one nearby we've used before.'

It seemed a long time till the doctor came, though it was only minutes. Gil loosened his father's tie and removed the stiff winged collar, making soothing murmurs. He didn't know what else to do and was glad to stand back and let the doctor examine his father.

The doctor shook his head and whispered, 'It's a seizure. Not much you can do but nurse him and hope for the best.'

Gil looked at him in shock.

'It's in God's hands whether he'll survive or not. Take him home and I'll send a nurse round to your house.'

'Thank you.' Gil turned and found that the redoubtable Peterson had already borrowed a carriage from another member and arranged for two men to carry Mr Rycroft out to it.

Gil followed, tipped them all for their trouble and asked if the two men could come with him to do the same service at the other end of the journey, after which they could ride back in the carriage.

He sat crowded on one seat with them, watching his father's still body on the other. He made sure the unconscious man didn't roll off, but that was all he could do.

At the house, he flung the front door open and hurried inside, relieved to find Walter coming across the hall towards him. Gil whispered what had happened and left Walter to show the two men carrying his father up to his bedroom.

His mother's maid opened the door of her bedroom. 'She's lying down in her dressing room, Mr Gil.'

'I need to see her.'

'But — '

He pushed past the maid and went across to tell his mother what had happened. To his relief, the dreadful frozen expression was replaced at once by a more alert look.

'I'll organise his bedroom,' she said. 'Please get Rawson to send for our own doctor and thank the men who carried him up.'

After that there was little Gil could do but wait while others tended his father.

'I'm glad you're here,' she told her son. 'You'll stay, won't you? Till we're sure . . . what's going to happen.'

'Of course I will.'

He didn't sleep well. The night was disturbed by voices, doors being closed quietly, though not quietly enough that you didn't know someone was moving around.

The first day or two were the most dangerous time after a seizure, everyone said. Gil could only doze and hope for the best.

His parents had never shown any sign of loving one another, until now.

In April, Renie received a letter from her sister. It was passed to her in the evening when she was sitting with the others after their meal. She'd been worried because she hadn't heard from Nell for a couple of weeks, but she'd been so busy the past week that she hadn't found time to write and ask her sister if something was wrong.

She was relieved to see the letter, but it felt very light, with only one sheet of paper in it. This had happened a time or two before when little Sarah was sick, or the minister's wife wasn't well. Mrs Garrett had helped Nell when they first moved to Milnrow, so if she needed help in turn, Nell always helped out. Cliff grumbled about that, but her sister would never turn away from a friend in need.

The handwriting was shaky and there was what looked like a tear stain on the address. Her heart clenched. It was bad news, she was sure. What could have happened? Was Nell ill?

She hesitated, because she usually liked to open her letters in private, but she couldn't bear to wait. Inside was less than a page of writing and not only was the ink blotchy in places but the paper was blistered. Nell had definitely been crying when she wrote this.

Dearest Renie,

I have sad news to tell you and no way to soften the blow.

Over two weeks ago there was a gas explosion in our house and it killed Cliff and

Sarah. I was out at the shops at the time, so I escaped.

I've buried them both and am trying to pull myself together, but I can't help weeping for my darling child.

I don't know what I'm going to do with myself, but for the time being I'm staying with the Garretts. They've been very kind to me, but nothing really helps.

I'm all right for money because Cliff had taken out insurance on our lives.

Don't try to come up to Lancashire to see me. I mean that. I won't be staying here much longer. I'll let you know where I go when I figure it out myself. I just know I have to get away.

Nell

Renie burst into tears, weeping wildly and rocking to and fro. After a moment's shocked silence, one of the other women came to sit beside her, then held her as she continued to sob. A circle gathered round them.

'What's wrong? Tell us what's wrong.'

She couldn't speak for weeping, and the next thing she knew, Miss Pilkins was there.

'Come with me, Renie.'

They tugged her to her feet and someone picked up the letter and gave it to Miss Pilkins. Renie let them take her where they wanted. She kept seeing her little niece's face, remembering the cuddles and fun they'd had.

It was a while before she could calm down. She realised she was in Miss Pilkins' bedroom, next to the dormitory, and Maud was there with them.

'What's wrong, Renie?'

She tried to put it into words and couldn't. 'It's in the letter.'

'Is this what you're looking for?' Miss Pilkins held out a crumpled piece of paper.

She nodded. 'Read it.' Then she pressed her hand to her mouth and tried to keep her anguish in.

Little Sarah was dead.

She couldn't seem to get past that thought. Her lovely little niece. How could Nell face that? How could God let such a terrible thing happen to an innocent child?

'Dear heaven! How terrible!'

Miss Pilkins passed the letter to Maud, who gasped and said in a choked voice, 'I read about that accident in the paper, only I didn't know it was Renie's sister. Oh, my dear girl, how can we help?'

Renie could only stare at them, feeling blank, unable to think clearly.

'She needs some time to be quiet. We'll move her to the sickroom. Is that all right, dear?'

It was a moment or two before the words sank in, then she realised that they were offering her a chance to be alone, so Renie nodded. 'Yes. Thank you.'

They moved her things, brought her cocoa, fussed over her. But it didn't help the pain. She kept thinking of Nell, wanting to be with her sister. Only she couldn't be, because Nell was moving and might not even be there if Renie went up to Milnrow.

All she could do was write a letter. Not till she'd calmed down, though. And even then it'd be hard. What comfort could you offer at a time like this?

'You're very kind,' she said at last. 'But I need to be by myself now, to try to . . . take it in.'

'Of course. And don't bother if you're late for work in the morning. I'll explain.'

But she shook her head. 'I'd rather go to work. If I sit here, I'll just weep. I'll write to my sister after breakfast, though, before I start. Would that be all right?'

'Yes, of course. I'll make sure someone fetches your breakfast to you here and some writing paper, too.'

Then they were gone.

But the pain wouldn't go. Or the deep sorrow.

Little Sarah was dead and Nell was all alone in the world, with no one to comfort her.

Renie was alone, too. This tragedy had made her feel utterly helpless.

It wasn't until the following morning that she really considered the fact that Cliff was dead. She didn't feel any sorrow for him, only a vague regret that anyone should die in such a terrible way. She couldn't help being glad her sister was free of his petty, carping ways.

She remembered all too clearly how the gas stove had sometimes gone out for no reason for the whole time they'd been living in that slum. He'd refused point-blank to 'pay good money' to have it mended. There must have been a fault and . . . She sat down on the edge of the bed, feeling sick. Was it . . . could the explosion have been because of that?

It must have been. The stove was the only thing that used gas in that mean little house.

She wasn't going to waste any more sympathy on Cliff. It was all his fault. She'd keep her sympathy for her poor sister and her dear little niece.

After Renie had written a long, loving letter to Nell, weeping as she wrote, she went to work, conscious of her swollen eyes. It was a while before she realised how gently the men in the hotel were treating her this morning.

They should have been kind before. People should always be kind to one another, because you never knew when fate would take away someone you loved. She'd lost her own mother when she was young and been brought up mainly by Mattie.

She didn't even know where Mattie was now.

She wanted to see Nell and hug her close. Oh, how much she wanted to be with her at this sad time!

A little later, she stopped writing to stare into space as it occurred to her that if Nell had the insurance money and Renie had her savings, perhaps they could open a little shop or run a boarding house, or make some sort of new life together.

She stared round. She no longer enjoyed working at the Rathleigh. She was on edge every minute because of the way Judson stared at her and sometimes crept up behind her.

It was then that she remembered Gilbert

Rycroft. He'd said he would help her and somehow she knew he'd meant it. He might limp and have trouble with his arm, but he was very good-looking and had such a warm smile. She didn't know when she'd taken to someone so quickly.

Oh, she was terrible. How could she daydream about a man when her sister was facing a tragedy?

Once she heard from Nell again, she'd suggest them setting up home together, then she'd ask Gilbert Rycroft for advice. A gentleman was bound to know more about starting a business than they did.

The thought of being with her sister again was the only comfort during a very sad time.

10

Over the next few days the newspapers continued to publish the latest information and it was even worse than anyone had expected. Renie was shocked to learn that about fifteen hundred people had died, an unthinkable number, and only seven hundred or so had been rescued.

She kept her eyes open and at last found a crumpled newspaper, left by a guest, which gave a list of passengers who had survived, stopping with a gasp at the name: *Elizabeth Rycroft, aged 6 years.* That poor little child! What must she have gone through?

She continued down the list, but no other Rycrofts were mentioned. Her heart sank. Surely the rest of the young family hadn't been lost?

Next she scanned the names of those definitely killed and found the surname she was looking for at once: *Robert Rycroft, 36, of London; Harriet Rycroft, 29, wife of Robert; Jennifer Rycroft, 3, daughter of Robert and Harriet.*

Oh, that poor family! How must they be feeling? She knew how bad she'd felt when she heard about Nell's tragedy and little Sarah's death. *Agonised* was the first word that sprang to mind. And another word she'd read in books: *bereft.* She'd had to look it up in a dictionary to find what it meant and wasn't even sure how to pronounce it.

She bent her head to say a prayer for all the

182

people who'd lost loved ones in the disaster, and made a special mention of the Rycrofts. It was all she could think to do. She didn't know anything about the family, except that Gil Rycroft was a kind young man, but they must be devastated by losing three members of the family at once. Anyone would.

This reminded her of how she'd lost touch with her sister Mattie. That still upset her, but it wasn't likely that Mattie was dead. Her sister had always been very healthy. Renie had that comfort at least. She still had hope.

One day, surely, they'd all three be reunited.

* * *

Renie started work in the office the very next week. She felt excited at the thought of learning new skills, but that excitement quickly faded, because they sat her in a corner and gave her simple tasks to do, checking lists of supplies, fetching office supplies for the male clerks or making tea.

The latter job made the office boy smirk at her and complain about the cup of tea she'd given him.

She guessed this was really his job and wasn't going to be bullied by a mere lad, so leant forward and said in a low voice, 'Any more cheek from you, young man, and I'll trip up and spill hot tea all over you *accidentally*. Don't think I won't do it, either. And my name is Miss Fuller to you, spoken politely. Is that clear?'

Their eyes met and he tried to outstare her,

but didn't succeed. She only had to summon up the anger she was feeling about her treatment here and she could outstare King George himself.

She found the week's work so dull and slow she began to wonder if it was worth it and felt very downhearted. She was learning nothing and no one in the office spoke to her unless they had to.

On Friday afternoon, even though he was sitting nearby, the assistant bookkeeper sent the office boy across the room to tell Renie that Mrs Tolson wished to see her.

The housekeeper greeted her with a smile. 'Do sit down, Irene. How is it going? What have you learnt this week?'

Then the tears came and she couldn't help sobbing. She'd had such high hopes of this new job, but the men weren't going to let her work with them as an equal, they'd shown that very clearly.

Mrs Tolson waited until she'd finished weeping and said in a bracing tone, 'Let that be the only time you weep over those fools.'

Renie stared at her in shock. This was the last thing she'd expected to hear. 'What do you mean?'

'The ones in that office are assistant clerks. It's where they train the new office boys. The older men won't rise any higher, and they know it, so they're jealous of anyone who seems to be looked on favourably by Mr Greaves or the owners. It must gall them when that person is a woman.'

'Oh.'

'Bear with it for another week. If I intervene too soon, they can say they were just letting you settle in. But what I would ask you to do is keep a list of all the tasks you perform, a complete list of every single task. Bring it to me on Thursday after work. Armed with that, I shall consult Mr Greaves.'

'Oh.'

'It never does to react in anger. You are far less likely to make your point. Learn patience, Irene. Learn endurance. You're going to need both many times during the coming years. When women do something different, there are always obstacles deliberately thrown in their way.'

Renie mopped her eyes and was pleased to find she'd completely lost the desire to weep.

'Now, you have one morning still to work this week, then you can enjoy your weekend. Are you and Daff going anywhere?'

'Just to the markets. I like to pick up bargains there.'

'So do I, when I can find the time. I buy things for my cousin sometimes. Her husband is very stingy with her.'

'So was my sister's husband.'

'That's why I have never married.'

Was that the choice you had to make? Renie wondered. You either married and put up with unfair treatment in order to have a husband and family, or you didn't marry at all. Surely not all men were mean? But the two marriages she'd experienced at close hand, her mother's and her sister's, had been extremely unhappy.

185

She wasn't going to put up with that sort of life, even for the sake of having children. But she didn't want to live her life alone. Perhaps if she could find Mattie, they could live together. Mattie was past the age of marrying.

Seeing her eldest sister again was something to hope for.

* * *

Gil's father made it through the night, and in the morning his mother joined Gil for breakfast as they waited for the doctor's visit.

'*You* will have to go to New York to fetch Elizabeth back, Gil.'

He looked at her in shock. 'Me? But I thought you wanted me here to help with Father.'

'That child's need is greater than mine, I realised that during the night. Who else is there to fetch her but you? Jonathon's wife is expecting her first child any day now, so your brother can't go. Harriet's closest family are in South Africa. And besides, Elizabeth is our only grandchild, while Harriet's parents have several others, so I feel *we* should be the ones to look after her from now on.'

'But I don't know anything about little girls.'

'Of course you don't. You'll naturally take a nursemaid with you.'

He still didn't like the idea, but his mother's voice had cracked on the last few words and he could see how close she was to breaking down. She'd been very brave; he could be no less brave. He took a deep breath. 'Very well. I'll do that.'

186

'Thank you. I'll make sure you have plenty of money to cover your expenses. No, I insist! You need your own money for your house now.'

After he left her, he went to look for Walter. 'We have to go to New York to fetch my niece Elizabeth. And as soon as possible.'

Walter looked at him in dismay, then shook his head. 'I don't think I can, lad.'

'What do you mean?'

'I've been tiring quickly lately, so I went to see a fancy London doctor. He says it's my heart. Well, at my age, you expect something to start going wrong, don't you? He advises me to lead a quiet life.'

Gil looked at him in dismay. 'You should have said something sooner. We'd have made things easier for you.'

'I said it when it had to be faced. I wanted to continue without people fussing over me for as long as I could.' He paused to think. 'Why don't you take Horry with you to New York? He's an intelligent young fellow.'

'I need a woman, too, to look after Elizabeth.'

'Take Lizzie. She's from a large family, so she'll know how to look after a little girl. You won't want a starchy nurse telling her not to cry. I've seen them when folk visited at your parents', telling children not to cry when they fell off a horse, stopping them *feeling* things.'

He sighed. 'Us poorer folk live more normal lives, I reckon. We don't have to keep those stiff upper lips. That little girl has a right to cry as much as she needs. She's lost everyone, must be feeling desperate. I hope someone is looking after her over in New York, treating her kindly.'

'You're right. Lizzie and Horry it is, then.'

Walter clapped his shoulder. 'Good lad. I'm proud of you.'

Things happened so quickly after that, Gil didn't feel he stopped to take a breath until he and his two helpers got on the ship. They were lucky that one was due to leave in two days' time. Walter helped Horry obtain more clothes and Mrs Rycroft's London housekeeper took charge of Lizzie's clothing needs.

If truth be told, Lizzie's joy in her new clothes cheered Gil up. His father was making only slow progress and would probably be unable to walk or speak properly again. He knew how that felt. He was full of admiration for his mother. After the first shock, Louisa Rycroft had become calmly supportive, spending a lot of time with her husband. It was to her that his father's eyes always turned, and she seemed to guess what he needed when he couldn't fit words together.

Even the thought of her little granddaughter didn't seem important to his mother now that she'd handed that task over to her son. She was concentrating only on her husband's recovery and welfare. Their love had never been demonstrated in public, but it showed clearly now.

He wished he could find someone to love. It must be . . . nice not to be alone.

He didn't have a passport, nor did his two helpers, but the shipping agent assured him that it wasn't obligatory, though there was talk of it becoming obligatory in a year or two if you wanted to re-enter the United Kingdom.

'You're only visiting New York and because of the ... ahem ... tragedy, I'm sure they won't fuss about such details at either end.'

The voyage passed peacefully, with only one day of blustery weather. Some of the passengers were seasick, but Gil found he was a good sailor, as were Horry and Lizzie.

There were people on the ship on the same errand as Gil, some of them going only to identify loved ones' bodies and bury them, so there wasn't the usual round of dining and entertainment.

During the daytime Gil avoided the other passengers as much as he could without being impolite, and spent a lot of time standing by the rail, staring into the distance. His thoughts often turned to his eldest brother. Robert had been ten years older than Gil, so they had never been close. He had looked up to Robert, though. His brother was a popular fellow, who had enjoyed life, found everything easy. He'd been in the school teams for every sport he took up, then had gone to university for a time.

But as he had little taste for studying, he left after a year and came home to learn to manage the family estate, which, as eldest son, he would inherit one day. The trouble was he'd clashed with his father and the estate manager about what should be done, so when he'd met and married Harriet, he'd gone to live in the house she'd inherited from her grandmother.

Now, Robert would never come home to Merriton House, and he'd not left a son to carry

189

on the family name.

Gil supposed the estate would go to Jonathon, the middle brother.

Gil had no desire to inherit Merriton, which was quite a large house and needed rather a lot of renovations. He'd heard his father complaining about that. He enjoyed his quiet life in Wiltshire, with a house that was smaller and somehow friendlier. He was starting to get on better with people in the village, though Chapman was still a thorn in his flesh.

It was good, Gil found, to have this time to come to terms with his sad errand, and most of the other passengers left him in peace.

From time to time, he saw Horry and Lizzie out on the lower deck. They seemed always to be talking and smiling, either together or with other younger people. He envied them that ease.

And then suddenly they were in New York, and he had to take charge of the situation once more.

Elizabeth, he found, had been placed in a boarding school for little girls, which had volunteered to take her.

As soon as they'd settled into the hotel, he took Lizzie with him and they went to find his niece. Horry said he'd go out and look at American motor cars, if no one needed him.

★ ★ ★

On her second Friday working in the office, Renie was again asked to report to Mrs Tolson. This time she found Mr Greaves sitting with the

190

housekeeper, and they had her notes about what she'd been doing in front of them.

Mr Greaves shared in the questioning about her first two weeks, and after she'd finished, he gave her one of his twinkling smiles. 'Be prepared to work much harder next week, young Irene.'

'Yes, sir.' She wondered what he and Mrs Tolson were planning, but they gave her no hint, only dismissed her and told her to enjoy her weekend.

She found it rather lonely. Daff was on weekend duty, no one else wanted to go out with her, so Renie was left to her own devices. She didn't go to the markets because she didn't need anything and the weather was showery, so she could only nip out during fine spells to walk round Yew Tree Gardens and admire the flowers, then stay in the staff sitting room and read.

A young man tried to get into conversation with her on one of her outings, but she'd had enough of men this week and gave him short shrift.

She stopped to watch two children playing, which reminded her of her poor little niece, who hadn't had anywhere like these gardens to take the air and enjoy herself.

She also thought about Gil Rycroft and wondered what he was doing, how he and his family were coping with their loss.

Then it began to rain again, so she went back inside to read her book.

She hoped Mr Greaves would be able to do something about her job. She didn't mind working hard, but she hated to be bored now that she'd experienced a more interesting sort of work.

★ ★ ★

On the Monday, Mr Greaves walked into the big office mid morning. He moved slowly round the room, looking at what each person was doing.

The assistant bookkeeper, who was in charge of organising Renie's work, hesitated, then called across to her, 'Miss Fuller, will you kindly go and — '

Mr Greaves said quietly, 'Not now, Wetherfield. I wish to see what everyone is doing.' He said nothing, but as he moved, the tension in the room rose and even the pens seemed to be scratching more quietly across the pages as if they too were holding their breaths.

He moved to Renie's desk last of all. 'What are you doing today, Miss Fuller?'

'Copying these lists, Mr Greaves.'

He stood very still, not saying a word, but frowning.

Just when she thought she'd burst with keeping quiet, Mr Greaves said, '*Copying?* That is a job for the office boy, not for the housekeeper's assistant. Who set you this task?'

She stared down at her page, hating to be the one to land someone in trouble, however much they deserved it.

'Wetherfield?'

The head clerk got up and hurried across.

'We are training Miss Fuller to help our lady

192

customers, not to assist the office boy.'

'Sorry, sir. I must have, um, mistaken the reason for her being here.'

'No, Wetherfield. You did not. I explained the reasons to you myself.' He looked round the room and raised his voice. 'And in case any of you think Miss Fuller came running to complain to me, I can assure you she didn't. Other people have eyes in their heads and do not approve of wasting staff's time — time for which their employers are paying. I move all round the hotel. I do not just sit in my office all day.'

He let his words sink in, then added sharply, 'We will continue this discussion in my office.' He turned to the office boy. 'You need not accompany us, Fitch.' He gestured to Renie to come with them.

Flushing with embarrassment she stood up, waiting for the men to lead the way out, since they were senior to her.

Mr Greaves held back, so the rest of them did too. 'After you, Miss Fuller. We do still practise good manners here, I hope.'

They stood in a semicircle in front of his desk. The session was gently conducted, but by the end of it, the men had been guided into putting together a plan for training Renie properly.

Mr Greaves ended by saying, 'I will just say this: Chef didn't approve of what we're doing, but by the end of Miss Fuller's time with him, he did admit that she was intelligent and picked things up quickly. And even he could see that it will be useful to have a woman who understands the working of our hotel available to deal with our lady customers, as well as to help Mrs Tolson in any way that is needed. It is our customers' welfare we should be thinking of here, not our own, or even Miss Fuller's. We are all here to make our customers' stay at the Rathleigh as pleasant as possible.'

Renie was sure she must be scarlet, her cheeks felt so hot.

'My dear young lady, this has been very difficult for you and I'm delighted at your self-control. Please take half an hour to compose yourself. Gentlemen, stay with me.'

When she'd left the room, he said more sharply than usual, 'If she was your sister or aunt or cousin, how would you feel about the way she's been treated?'

Silence greeted his words.

'There is another thing to bear in mind. I very much fear that we are moving towards a war with Germany.'

Some of them looked at him in shock, some nodded as if they too had come to the same conclusion.

'If that happens, we shall need well-trained young women to take the place of the men who leave to fight for their country, some of whom will not return. But whatever happens, we shall keep the Rathleigh running and serve our customers as best we can. Always think several years ahead, gentlemen. It is forward-thinking people who make progress in the business world.'

He looked at them over his spectacles. 'If you have any questions, now is the time to ask.'

They shook their heads.

'Very well, then. That is all. I'm sure you won't let me down again. I trust Miss Fuller will be treated with courtesy from now on and taught about the hotel business properly. And let us all pray that war will be averted by those we have elected to govern our country.'

A chorus of voices said, 'Amen.'

★ ★ ★

After that intervention, Renie found herself so busy she felt like a spinning top. The weeks seemed to whiz past as she moved each week to assist clerks working in customer accounts, supplier accounts, stock keeping, wages, rosters — the list seemed endless.

One of the men who had been the most scornful said grudgingly at the end of her week with him, 'You're a quick learner, I'll grant you that, Miss Fuller.'

'Why should I not be?'

'My sister can't add two and seven.'

'I know men who can't add up, either.'

He didn't say anything in answer to that.

The men didn't become friendly, though, just polite and helpful when needed. She was still very much the outsider.

It was a lonely sort of life, both at work and during her leisure hours. She sometimes wondered if her new job was worth it.

But she was glad to be busy. It kept her mind off her sister. Most of the time, anyway.

11

Gil took a cab to the school where his niece was staying in New York and asked it to wait for him. He left Lizzie sitting in it, ready to join him inside.

He knocked on the door and explained his purpose to an elderly maid, who showed him into a small sitting room and went to fetch the headmistress.

Miss Needham was a stern-looking woman in her middle years, and Gil immediately took a dislike to her.

'You will need to find a suitable governess to look after Elizabeth on the way home,' she said. 'A man cannot care for a little girl. It would not be decent.'

'I've brought a nursemaid who understands children. And my niece is usually called Beth.'

Miss Needham looked down her nose at him. 'Surely you owe it to that child's parents to treat Elizabeth as a gentleman's daughter? She is of an age for a governess, not a nursemaid.'

'I owe it to her to love her, now that they can't. Could you please bring her to me?'

'I should prefer not to interrupt lessons. If you come back at four o'clock — '

Gil kept tight hold of his temper. 'I want to see Beth now, and if you don't produce her, I'll go round this place shouting her name till I find her.'

Miss Needham drew herself up. 'In that case,

if you're going to be ungrateful for what we've done — '

'I'm quite happy to pay you for your trouble.'

'I shall send the bill to your hotel.'

So much for philanthropy, he thought.

Shortly afterwards, a younger woman with a similarly stern expression brought his niece into the room.

The child was only six. She looked frail and terrified, and her eyes were reddened. His heart went out to her.

'Here is your uncle, Elizabeth.'

The little girl dropped him a sort of curtsey.

'Have you no word of greeting for him?'

Gil could control himself no longer. 'Thank you. If you'll have her things packed and send them to the hotel, we'll leave now.'

The teacher glared at him, hesitated, then left the room.

He waited till the door had closed behind her, then went to kneel and give Beth a hug. His parents had never cuddled him, but his nursemaid had and sometimes it had been the only thing that comforted him. The convulsive way his little niece clung to him told him he'd done the right thing.

He tried to stand up, but she whimpered and clung to him more tightly. 'Come on, darling. Let's go to the hotel.'

'Am I . . . coming back here?'

'No, never.'

She looked at him mutely, then buried her face in his chest, her whole body rigid. 'I'm sorry. I keep crying. I can't help it.'

197

'You can cry as much as you like when you get out of here, but let's walk out calmly, eh? We'll show them how brave Rycrofts can be.' He stood up and wiped her eyes with his handkerchief, dabbed at his own, then led the way outside.

In the cab, Lizzie was waiting. She started to stretch out her arms to the child, but Gil shook his head, and to his relief, she understood what he was saying. He kept hold of Beth's hand as they sat down, then introduced Lizzie to her.

'They're very strict in there,' he said by way of explanation. 'Beth knows we aren't like that.'

Lizzie looked at him, then the little girl. 'Children need love,' she said simply.

'I agree.' He turned to his niece, who was sitting next to him, pressing close and clutching his hand. 'Lizzie has come all the way from England to look after you. You'll like her. She has little brothers and sisters so knows how to play lots of games.'

'My name's Elizabeth too, only everyone calls me Lizzie,' the maid volunteered.

That caught the child's attention and she stared at the young woman. 'Why do they call you that?'

'Because my grandma was called Elizabeth.'

'Didn't you tell them at the school you were usually called Beth?' Gil asked.

'Yes, but Miss Needham said it was vulgar to shorten names.'

He couldn't believe how unkind those women had been to a child who had lost so much. Lizzie's soft, cheerful voice interrupted his dark thoughts.

'We've brought you a lovely doll. I'll give her

198

to you when we get back to the hotel.'

Tears welled in Beth's eyes. 'I had a doll, but she drowned like Mummy and Daddy and Jennifer. They fell into the water when the boat rocked about. I nearly fell in too, but a man grabbed me and put me in another boat. I haven't got any toys left now.'

There was silence while the two adults looked at one another.

'There will be some of your toys at home still. We'll send for them.' Gil's throat was thick with a desire to weep for her. 'And we'll buy you some more tomorrow to play with.' He nearly added 'on the ship going back' but stopped himself in time. He was sure she wouldn't want to go back on a ship, but it was the only way to get home to England.

'Horry will be waiting for us at the hotel,' Lizzie said. 'He drives the car for your uncle. He got hurt and his face has a scar on, where the skin was torn, so he looks a bit fierce, but he's a really nice man.'

'Did you get hurt too?' Beth asked Gil. 'You were limping and your arm's funny.'

Only a child could say it so bluntly. But he found he preferred her openness. 'Yes, I got hurt when I fell off a horse, but most of me got better.'

She nodded, seeming to accept it as normal that people got hurt.

At the hotel they met Horry, who had been out looking at American cars and was full of what he'd seen. 'Have you ever ridden in a motor car, young lady?' he asked Beth.

She shook her head, shyer with him than with Lizzie.

'Then we'll have to arrange a ride for you and your uncle before we go back.'

'Lizzie too?'

'Of course.'

Gil felt relief run through him. That comment surely meant Beth had accepted Lizzie, which was so important. Well, how could anyone not accept such a cheerful young woman? She had been the perfect choice to help him with Beth.

★ ★ ★

They had a fairly trouble-free journey back to England. Beth clung alternately to Gil and to Lizzie, who shared a cabin with her. The child refused point-blank to go near the rail or even look at the water, if she could help it.

Gil didn't force her to do anything she didn't want. He was already growing to love his niece and wondered why he hadn't visited Robert and his wife more often — or why they hadn't tried to invite him, so that their children would know their relatives.

He found Lizzie sitting outside the cabin one evening after Beth had gone to sleep, so sat on the bench next to her.

'I wonder if you'd like to change jobs and look after Lizzie from now on?'

She looked surprised, but didn't hesitate. 'I'd love to, sir.'

'It'll mean more money too.'

'I'd do it for the same money. She's a lovely

child and my heart aches for her. A child shouldn't see her family drown.' She shivered.

'Thank you, but it's only fair that you have the usual pay for a nursemaid.' He saw her frowning and waited for her to speak.

'Won't your mother mind? Won't *she* want to choose the person to look after Beth?'

'I intend to look after my niece myself at Oakdene. And I don't think my mother will make a fuss, because she'll be too busy looking after my father.'

But Lizzie still looked doubtful.

'They'll have to take that child away from me by force.' He surprised himself by that, because he'd been hesitating about that decision. Now, it seemed, his heart had taken it for him. He already loved talking to Beth, taking care of her, helping her find her way in a puzzling and hurtful world. He understood how she felt, oh, he definitely did.

'Well, if I'm allowed, sir, I'd love to look after her.'

He knew Lizzie would do that well in all the ways which mattered. She was young for the job and his mother might try to make a fuss about hiring an ill-educated woman, but he was already sure that Lizzie's experience as part of a big family, as well as her cheerful attitude to life, would help the little girl to find happiness again. As he was finding happiness in things that had never interested him before, like children and motor cars and helping others.

When they reached the London house, it was to find that his father had been taken down to

Merriton House and his mother had left a message to bring little Elizabeth to them there.

Surely she should have known that the child was usually called Beth? She was the grandmother, after all, and she'd visited Robert regularly, because he was her favourite child.

'We'll stay here tonight,' he told the others. 'Then we'll go down to Oakdene. You'll like my house, Beth. When you're settled in there, I'll go and see my mother and father.'

He saw Lizzie and Horry exchange surprised glances, but pretended not to notice.

His mind was made up. He already loved Beth like a daughter. Just let them try to take her away from him!

* * *

Renie saw the man she'd met when the news of the *Titanic* sinking was announced, the one whose brother had been killed. He was getting out of a cab and going into a house on the other side of Yew Tree Gardens. He was holding the hand of a little girl, a child who looked frail and sad, and there were two other people with them.

Renie caught her breath. Could this be the one she'd read about in the newspaper, the one who'd survived? Her uncle must have gone to New York to fetch her.

She was sorry when the door closed on them. She'd have liked to find out what had happened.

Stop being a nosey parker, she told herself. *You've enough to do without taking on other people's troubles.*

Her lunch break was over. She had to go back into the office and face the men, who were always hoping to catch her out. She was tired of the struggle, but she wasn't going to let them drive her away, not when Mr Greaves and Mrs Tolson believed in her.

★ ★ ★

It was a week before Gil felt safe leaving Lizzie. At first the child had hovered near him from the moment she got up. But fortunately she took a liking to Walter, as well as Lizzie. The rest of his small staff were looking after her too, so she gradually started spending the occasional half-hour with them.

He explained to her that he had to go and see her grandmother to make arrangements to look after her from now on.

'She won't take me away from you, will she?'

He didn't dare make promises he might not be able to keep. 'I'll try very hard to keep you with me. But even if you have to go and live with her, I'll come and see you often.'

'I don't want to live with anyone else.'

He had already sent a telegram to his mother saying that he felt his niece needed some peace and quiet to help her recover from losing her family.

The reply was very brief. 'Bring her here for that.'

★ ★ ★

Before he could do anything about his mother, Gil was woken by shouts of 'Fire! Fire!' outside the house and got out of bed in such a hurry he staggered across the room and crashed into the tallboy, unable to save himself with his left arm. Cursing his stupid body, he dragged his dressing gown round himself and thrust his feet into his slippers.

On the landing he bumped into Madge and when he looked along the landing he saw Lizzie standing near the door of Beth's bedroom.

'Be ready to get Beth out of the house if it catches fire!' he called and ran awkwardly down the stairs.

Someone was hammering on the kitchen door. He yanked it open and found the stable lad there.

'Come quick, Mr Rycroft. The stables are on fire, sir. Mr Bilham and Mr Palmer are getting the horses out.'

Gil hurried across the yard. The horses were upset, but Walter's voice seemed to soothe them and they were persuaded to let him and Horry lead them out of the stables. They stood shivering at one side of the yard.

'Get a halter on them!' Walter yelled but the lad was already crossing to the two frightened animals.

'I need to get the car out,' Horry yelled.

But Gil grabbed hold of him and held on tight. 'You'll not manage it. The fire's spread to that area.'

'Stand back, lad,' Walter said. 'Lives are more important than machines.'

204

Horry was still poised as if to run, then he sagged and his shoulders slumped. 'We'd better all stand back. There isn't much petrol in it, luckily, but it's likely to explode.'

Even as he spoke, there was a whooshing sound and the car began to burn, upholstery and tyres ignited by the fierce flames.

'We can get another one,' Gil said quietly.

Horry just shook his head and dashed his sleeve against his eyes. 'I was fond of her,' he muttered.

'Can we stop the fire spreading to the rest of the outbuildings, at least?' Gil asked and watched Horry pull himself together.

'There aren't enough of us to form much of a bucket line. Best to let that end part burn and try to stop it spreading further along.' He ran to dip a bucket in the water barrel that caught rainwater from the stable roof and moved across to sling it against the leading edge of the flames.

Gil tried to do the same, but couldn't heft the bucket high enough. And Walter could only lift half-full buckets.

'Better stand back, sir, Walter. Me and the lad will do our best,' Horry said.

But it wasn't good enough and Gil watched helplessly as the wooden stable doors started burning. In a minute the hay store would catch light.

Suddenly there were yells and people came running along the short cut from the village, carrying empty buckets.

'We're the fire guards,' one man panted. 'Where's the water?'

Horry told him and almost before he'd finished speaking they'd formed a chain from the outside tap as well as the water barrel. Buckets were soon being passed from hand to hand. The group of men seemed to know what they were doing so Gil kept back, feeling bitter about being so useless.

It was touch and go for a while, but gradually the men's efforts stopped the fire from spreading to the hay store and they began to hurl water on the burning beams at one side of the stables.

It was nearly dawn before they'd got the blaze completely under control.

One of the men, unrecognisable with a blackened face, came up to Gil. 'Sorry we couldn't save that end part, sir. And I see you lost your motor car.'

He realised from the man's educated tone that it was the curate. 'I'm grateful you could save anything.'

'We have a village fire team. I got the idea in my last placement and it's paid off before, so the men take it seriously.' He wiped his forehead.

'I'd be happy to make a contribution to your funds, or buy you some equipment. You've saved me a lot of money and trouble today.'

'I hope you're insured.'

'Yes, of course. But if it hadn't been for you and your men, it could have been much worse.'

Madge came out of the kitchen. 'I've made a big pot of tea. Anyone thirsty?'

There were a few cheers at this.

'Come inside,' Gil said.

The curate smiled, his teeth shockingly white

against his smoke-blackened face. 'We're too dirty. If someone could bring it out?'

'I can help with that,' Walter said.

Gil found the tea trolley and was able to help get it over the threshold to the outside, then they placed two huge teapots, a monster milk jug and a big bowl of sugar on it. There were some mugs and Walter had another fistful dangling by their handles from his hands.

'Any biscuits?' Gil asked Madge.

'Plenty, if you don't mind me using them.'

'Use anything we've got.'

So the men stood around outside, eating and drinking, keeping an eye on the smouldering ruins.

'How did it start?' the curate asked. 'Was a lamp left burning?'

'Never!' Walter said. 'I've run stables for forty years and worked in them all my life. I'd never, ever leave a naked flame.'

'Then how could it have started? There was no lightning or anything like that.'

'Maybe it was that thing.' One of them pointed to the car.

'It damned well wasn't,' Horry said sharply. 'Once it's switched off there's nothing about it that *could* start a fire.'

The silence seemed to grow heavier, as men exchanged glances.

It was Walter who said it. 'That fire must have been set deliberately.'

'Who would do something like that?' Gil asked. Surely not even Chapman would go so far as to burn down stables, risk killing innocent animals — or even human beings?

'We've trampled all over the place,' one man said. 'If there was anything to show, any footprints or whatever, they'd be gone now.'

'Um . . . ' The curate hesitated, then said slowly, 'I read somewhere that if a fire's been lit with paraffin or petrol, you can still smell it afterwards.'

'Can you, now?' Gil put his mug down. 'We'd better go and check, then.'

They did find an area that smelt of petrol, and Horry said the square metal petrol cans used to fill the car had been moved.

'We need to call in the police,' the curate said.

But Gil had no faith in the village policeman. He felt the fire must have been set by Chapman, so he went to check what the fellow had been doing.

★ ★ ★

Gil and the curate led the small group of men back into the village. They went straight to Chapman's house and Gil hammered on the door.

No one answered, so he thumped it again with his clenched fist.

Still no answer.

'Let's look round the back.' He set off round the side of the house without waiting for an answer.

The back door was locked, and banging on it produced no response. No one could be seen through any of the windows.

'It looks as if he's out,' the curate said.

'Perhaps he didn't — '

'He's the only one in the village who'd have a motive.' Gil turned to study the garden. 'Let's look in that shed.'

There was no need to look for a key because the door was sagging on its hinges. It had to be pulled hard to open it.

He went inside and looked round, but could see no cans of paraffin.

'It must be someone else,' one of the villagers said, looking round nervously.

Gil wasn't giving up without checking everything. 'We might as well look inside all the outbuildings.'

They went from one ramshackle lean-to and shed to another. Nothing.

'We can't accuse a man without proof,' the curate said quietly.

'No. But I'm going to keep an eye on him from now on.'

'How will you do that when half the village are on his side, and will keep an eye on what you do?'

'I'll find a way. I have to.'

★   ★   ★

The next day someone banged on the front door of Oakdene, and when the new maid went to open it, Chapman thrust Mary to one side and stormed in.

'Where's your master?'

'I'll go and see if he's free.'

He pushed past her and yelled, 'Rycroft!

209

Come out and face me like a man, for once.'

Gil had been sitting in the room they called the library, lost in thought, trying to work out what to do next, when he heard someone yelling his name.

Puzzled, he got up and hurried towards the sound, astounded to find Chapman standing in the hall and Mary standing at the back as if ready to take flight.

'I didn't let him in, sir,' she said at once. 'He pushed past me.'

'Just as you pushed your way into my house,' Chapman shouted. 'How dare you search my outbuildings?'

'An arsonist had set fire to my stables.'

'What has that to do with me?'

'You're the only one in the village with a grudge against me.'

'You're even more of a fool than I thought, if that's what you believe. Most of the village has a grudge against you. They don't like people who trick old ladies and swindle others out of their inheritance.'

'You've never proved that you're related to Miss Bennerden, let alone that she intended to leave you her house.'

'Well, I can prove it now. You'll be hearing from my lawyer this very week, and even that villain Mortlake won't be able to deny me justice now. And if you set one foot on my property again, I'll sue you for trespass as well.'

He stabbed one finger as if intending to poke Gil in the chest, but someone grabbed him from behind.

'The door's this way, Chapman,' Horry said.

'Let go of me.'

The two men scuffled for a moment, but were evenly matched, and when Chapman pulled back, Horry let him.

'Standing behind others again, Rycroft,' Chapman sneered.

Gil opened his mouth to reply, but Horry spoke first.

'And you're attacking those who can't fight back. I've heard of you doing that more than once. A right old bully, you are. But you don't frighten me.'

Chapman gave him a dirty look. 'I won't forget those who've offended me when I take possession of this house.'

Horry let out a scornful snort and would have answered back if Gil hadn't spoken.

'Please leave my house, Chapman, and don't come here again.'

'I will be back — to take over my inheritance.'

Chapman strode out of the door, leaving it wide open behind him.

'He's a nasty bit of work, that one.' Horry went to close the door, then asked, 'Can he really take this house from you, sir?'

'I doubt it. Even if he did prove a relationship to Miss Bennerden, it'd be a distant one, and she left a will which stated her wishes very clearly. It's not as if he was a son of hers. Thank you for your help.'

'You helped me when I was desperate, sir. I'm happy to help you any time.'

Gil nodded and went back into his little

library to sit staring into space. Chapman's visit had left him with a feeling of apprehension. Why had the man spoken so confidently? And though Gil had been touched by Horry's support, even that had made him feel bitter about being unable to defend himself physically.

Every time he thought he was settling down and getting on with his life, something happened to upset his plans and disturb his peace. He was quite sure he hadn't heard the last from Chapman. The man must be mad to think he could take Oakdene away from Gil.

After a while he shook off the feelings of self-pity. He had Beth, didn't he? He was making friends in the area and no one had a better set of servants to help them.

He heard his niece's voice and hurried outside to find her. She grabbed his good arm and he began to run her to and fro, a game they'd invented together.

Then Lizzie came out of the wash house, pretending to be angry at Beth for hiding, which led to her and Gil both tickling the child till they were all laughing.

He didn't want Beth to forget her parents, but he did want her to be happy again. He'd never have believed it if anyone had told him how much he would enjoy having her around.

And that made him wish for more children to raise and cherish. So maybe he should look more seriously for a wife. It would certainly please his mother.

★ ★ ★

Once they'd got the area cleared up, Horry came to hunt him out with a determined expression on his face. 'If we bought another car, we could still drive to your parents' house and back in one day. That'd be better for Beth.'

Gil hadn't thought about a new car. 'And have you chosen the next one?' As if he didn't know which type Horry favoured.

'Yes, Mr Rycroft, I have. With your approval, of course. A Model T Ford. We both saw some in America and I've been reading about them in the newspapers, as I told you. They're very hardy machines, and reliable. Guess what. On May the thirteenth a man drove a Model T Ford right up to the summit of Ben Nevis.' He waited expectantly.

Gil didn't have to feign surprise. 'Right up to the top of the highest mountain in Britain?'

'Yes, sir. That shows how good a car it is. Isn't it amazing? Modern cars can do all sorts of things, sir. They're getting better every year.'

'Well, we must certainly have a look at a Model T Ford. Not that I shall want to drive up any mountains.'

Horry wasn't going to be diverted by even the mildest joke. 'There's a fellow selling them in Swindon.' He waited again and, when Gil didn't say anything, volunteered more information. 'He's Skurray. The man who told me thinks he's at Skurray's Mill, somewhere near Whale Bridge in Queen's Park.'

'We could go this afternoon.' Gil's mother had written again to say he was to bring Beth to her. He couldn't put off the confrontation much longer.

213

They drove into Bassett by trap, leaving it at the livery stables, then went into Swindon by train. From there they took a cab to Queen's Park. This was very tiring and made Gil miss the convenience of having his own motor car.

As the cab slowed down, Horry pointed excitedly. 'There! Look! He's got one standing outside.'

Gil studied it. 'It's smaller than I'd expected.'

'It seats four comfortably and has a hood that pulls up. And it would be better for the narrow country roads round Oakdene. After all, you don't have a big family to squeeze into it.'

Silence fell and Gil watched Horry stare avidly at the car. It was the sort of look other men reserved for a beautiful woman. 'Can you wait for us?' he asked the cab driver. 'I'll pay extra.'

'Happy to, sir.' He shot a disapproving glance at the car. 'Nasty, smelly things, they are. You'd be better off with a good horse.'

Gil didn't agree.

Mr Skurray himself came out and started chatting to Horry, who was already examining the car.

'You seem to know your stuff,' he said at last.

Gil didn't even try to join in the technical discussion. Where cars were concerned, Horry was in charge and they both knew it.

'We shall need to try it out,' Horry said after a while. 'Can't buy a car without seeing how it goes.'

'This one runs well, but the previous owner wasn't a careful driver and there are a few dents, so I'm afraid you'll have to wait for the next shipment to arrive from America before I can supply you with a new vehicle.'

'Oh, dear! I really need one now. Still, we can try this one. It won't be much different, will it?' Gil looked down at his arm with a sigh, wishing yet again that he could have a go at driving.

Horry drove them round the streets for a few minutes. 'How do you like it, sir?'

'I love it. Don't people stare, though?'

'She's worth staring at.' Horry patted the car as if it was alive. 'We wouldn't have to wait if we bought this one and it'd cost less.' He left the thought hanging between them, concentrating on driving.

'You'll be happy to drive it?'

Horry beamed at him. 'Oh, yes. And maintain it, too.'

'Then let's see if we can buy it.'

Mr Skurray was less sure. 'We-ell. You could have that one, I suppose. It hasn't been used much. What about the dents?'

Gil went back to walk round the vehicle. The dents were quite small. 'What do you think, Horry?'

'I think we should consider it, sir. But only if the price is right.' He nudged his employer as he spoke.

Gil wouldn't have thought of bargaining, had just been going to ask the price and pay it, so he closed his mouth and left it to Horry. He found himself paying a hundred and fifty pounds for a near new four-seater Touring car, instead of a hundred and ninety pounds, plus twenty-five shillings for a battery, to make starting easier, and fifty shillings each for three spare tyre tubes in case of punctures.

'It's a really modern car, better than the other,' Horry enthused. 'Look, it's got oil sidelights and acetylene headlamps. You'll be all right in this, even on a dark night.'

'Be careful going up steep hills, though,' the dealer warned. 'If your petrol is low, it'll all run to the back of the tank and your engine will stop firing.' He chuckled. 'You could get up the hill backwards, though.'

Gil didn't intend to wait until the fire insurance paid up. His need was too urgent. 'Very well, then. We'll take it. We shall need to go into Swindon to get the money out of the bank.' He took out his pocket watch. 'I think we just have time before the bank closes.'

It wasn't until they'd returned and paid for the car that he realised someone would have to drive the trap back to Oakdene from Bassett. Since he couldn't drive a motor car, it ought to be him, only he hadn't ridden or driven since his accident. Could he manage to drive the trap? Did he even want to try?

Horry seemed to read his mind. 'We could leave the horse and trap at the livery stables and I could take Walter into Bassett tomorrow to drive it home.'

Gil hesitated, then said, 'No. I'll have a go at driving it. If I think I can manage, you can follow me slowly in the car, in case anything goes wrong.'

'Yes, sir. Happy to. Dusty's a good horse, though. He'll go steadily. I'm sure you'll be all right.'

Gil's heart was pounding in his chest as he set off from Bassett, but as Horry had said, the horse was a quiet gelding and gave him no trouble. To his enormous relief, they didn't encounter many other vehicles or riders.

When he got to Oakdene House and drove round to the stables, he felt quite triumphant. Another step towards normality.

As he walked across towards the kitchen, a small figure shot out of the door and hurled herself at him, wrapping her arms round his legs.

'You've been gone a long time,' Beth said reproachfully. 'I wanted you.'

'I had to buy a car. Come and look at it.'

She went to stand with him and study the vehicle, head on one side. 'It's all right.'

'Tomorrow Horry will take us for a ride.'

'Lizzie too.'

'Lizzie too,' he agreed, as her little hand twisted in his. The hand was warm and soft. Love for her twisted more deeply into his heart every day.

No, he was definitely not giving Beth up to his mother. He couldn't send this vulnerable little girl back to those rigid ways of raising children.

★　★　★

Two days later, Gil set off for Merriton House, driven by Horry. Walter, Beth and Lizzie stood at the front door, waving them goodbye, and when he turned round for a final wave, Lizzie was tugging a reluctant child into the house.

It took them two hours to drive to his old

home, but that gave him time to get his thoughts and arguments in order.

He was let out at the front door and Horry very correctly drove round to the rear, where he would spend his time with the stable staff or in the servants' hall.

His mother joined him in the small drawing room, looking round in puzzlement. 'Where's the child?'

'Beth is still at Oakdene House.'

'But I have a governess here, ready to look after her.'

'I need to talk to you about her, but first, how's Father?'

'He's a lot better, but he wants me with him all the time. You must go up and say hello when we've finished our little chat about Elizabeth. Why have you left her at your house?'

'Robert and Harriet didn't call her Elizabeth. They called her Beth.'

She wrinkled her nose. 'Why do all my children shorten people's names? I didn't have you christened Gil, or your brother Jon.'

'Gil suits me, though. And about Beth . . . Look, Mother, you must have your hands full with Father. Don't tell me he's an easy patient, because I won't believe you.'

She smiled. 'I can manage him. And I do have a governess. The child won't be left to her own devices.'

'I'm sure you can manage Father but I've grown to love Beth and . . . I want to adopt her.' He saw the shock on her face. Before the accident this would never even have occurred to

218

him. He wondered if his mother had any idea how much he had changed over the past year. He doubted it.

She was quiet for a moment or two then said slowly, 'An unmarried man adopting a girl child? I could understand if it were a boy, but a girl needs a mother.' She frowned at him. 'Why, Gil?'

'Partly because I'm lonely but mostly because I've grown to love her. I've got a really good nursemaid to look after her, and of course, I'll find a governess once she's settled down a little. Not yet, though. I think she needs to enjoy the peace of the countryside first. She was in a terrible state when I found her in New York. They'd put her in a very strict school, where she wasn't even allowed to cry for her family.'

'Poor child!'

But his mother sounded as if she was saying this automatically, and she stole a quick glance at the clock as she spoke.

'I'm not at all sure you understand what you're doing, Gil.'

'Oh, but I do. And I warn you, Mother, I'm determined to adopt Beth. Nothing you can say or do will change my mind about that.'

She blinked at him in surprise, then looked thoughtful. 'It might be a good idea if you had a wife, then.'

'Well, I don't have one. I do have several women servants, though. Excellent people, all of them. One is employed as nursemaid to look after Beth.'

'Hmm. She's still only a servant. And after all,

there's nothing to stop you marrying and providing that child with a mother, is there?'

'Only the fact that I haven't met anyone I want to marry.'

She looked him firmly in the eye. 'I'll agree to you adopting little Elizabeth — '

'Beth!'

'Oh, very well, Beth, then. I'll agree to you adopting her and I'll support you if Harriet's family create a fuss. But I'll only do it if you give me your word to marry within the year.'

He gaped at her. This was the last thing he'd expected to hear. 'But I don't know any women — and look at me.' He tried to move his arm and for once it did what he wanted by twitching.

'They won't care about that. You're still a good-looking young man and you *are* a Rycroft, after all. You have a very nice house and adequate money to support a family in comfort. And if finding someone is all that worries you, I can introduce you to several suitable young women in London.'

He watched her fold her arms, with *that look* on her face, the look which meant she was determined to have her way.

'Give me two years,' he bargained desperately. 'I've still not got Oakdene House in order.'

Silence hung between them, then she said quietly, 'Eighteen months and not a day longer, Gil. And I want your word on that.'

He hesitated, but the thought of Beth being brought up by a strict governess made him add one more condition. 'Only if you let me choose my own wife.'

'She has to be respectable.'

'Of course. Would I let someone who wasn't look after the child?'

'Very well.' His mother held out her hand. 'Since your father can't do it, you and I will shake on the solemn bargain we've made.'

He did that, feeling as if fetters had settled round him, binding him tightly to the promise.

As his mother let go of his hand, she reached up to pat his cheek. 'You're a good boy, Gil. Any woman you marry should consider herself lucky to marry you.'

'I'm nearly twenty-seven now, hardly a boy.'

'No, you're not a boy since that accident. I'm proud of how you've coped.' She flushed as if embarrassed by giving him a compliment. 'Now that Elizabeth's future is settled, let's go and see your father.'

Gil felt relieved when he left Merriton House. He sat lost in thought, not seeing the countryside they drove through, relieved that Horry didn't try to chat.

Gil had achieved what he came for, but at what cost? Not even for Beth did he want to marry. As for bedding a woman, he shrank from the thought of that. How would he manage in bed with his stupid arm?

But if it was the only way to get Beth, he'd have to do it. Somehow. Though he needn't think about it seriously for a while, not till he'd settled his niece in at Oakdene, not to mention sorting out Chapman, who wasn't going to get away with burning down Gil's outbuildings.

Anyway, who knew what would happen in

eighteen months? Maybe he'd come up with a way to convince his mother to release him from his promise.

Only, what if she refused? He'd promised faithfully and a Rycroft never broke his word.

12

In September, Gil stopped to watch the bricklayer and his lad repointing the brickwork. He was gradually working his way through a list of renovations and improvements. The old house stood square and solid, but it did need a little work doing on the outside and more than a little modernising inside.

From an upstairs window came the cheerful sound of a child singing, accompanied on the piano by the governess. Miss Bramber was proving to be just what Gil had wanted, a kind, caring woman who didn't fuss if Beth got dirty. His mother thought the woman was too working class, but he admired the way Miss Bramber had fought to get an education, which the clergyman who'd provided her with glowing references had told him about.

He smiled as he listened. He thought he was doing quite well, raising *his* child. His mother was coming soon to visit them and he was going to ask her to release him from his promise to find a wife and marry. He didn't want anyone changing things and spoiling the happy atmosphere in his house.

The plumbing had been the first job he'd tackled, after discussing it with Walter. He didn't want Beth growing up with such primitive conditions. Besides, there could be health problems if people's waste wasn't disposed of properly.

There was no piped sewage system in the village, but he had made his own arrangements at Oakdene, with the help of a plumber from Swindon. There was plenty of room for a cesspit in the grounds, one far from the well used to water the garden.

He wasn't sure he trusted the well, but found he could pay to have the public water supply brought to the house and decided to do that, to the servants' delight. It really wasn't good enough to have washing water brought up to the bedrooms in ewers, or to go to the outhouse if you needed to relieve yourself.

He hated the thought of soiling the shiny blue and white chamber pot that sat in state under his bed for use during the night. He couldn't bring himself to use that, however hard it was raining. The thought of a maid he lived so closely with emptying it for him made him shudder.

He knew Walter had to use his chamber pot, because as his friend and mentor confessed, he got taken short at times. 'A sign of old age, lad.'

And to Gil's dismay, Walter was looking older. He was, after all, getting on for seventy-seven now. He carried his years lightly, but he got distinctly breathless if he had to exert himself, and he was much slower than he used to be.

Gil had a word with Horry about not letting Walter do any heavy work and hired a lad to help out generally, whether it was with the gardens or the stables or the motor car.

There were a lot of people in the village subsisting on part-time work, which upset him, but he couldn't invent jobs. He wasn't so rich he could spend his own money lavishly on creating work, not with the upkeep necessary for a beautiful old house.

Chapman stopped him in the village next time he went to take tea with Mrs Wyndham, who had become a friend of himself and Walter.

'Currying favour with the locals now, are you?' Chapman jeered. 'Inventing jobs when there aren't any.'

'I have nothing to say to you. And how you dare accuse *me* of that after the way you treated Mary and Cyril, hiring them then firing them within two months, I don't know. You should be ashamed of yourself.' They had never talked about the fire, but one day Gil would find out about it.

'If I'd received justice, I'd not have needed to do that. It was all your fault, smarming up to *my* cousin Alice and getting her to leave her money outside the family. You take advantage of being a cripple, you do, and play on it for pity. But you don't fool me. You're a conniving, thieving villain!'

'According to Mr Mortlake, Miss Bennerden was not your cousin.'

'What does that silly old fool know about anything?'

'He looked into it and could find no connection.'

'Well, there is one. And I'll get what I'm owed one day, see if I don't. I can wait when I want something. Your damned lawyer isn't the only one who can look for proof. Then watch out!'

Gil sighed as he watched Chapman stride

away. Here was the thorn in his flesh, the serpent in paradise. That man was still managing to keep some of the villagers on his side.

The mere sight of Chapman made Beth shrink closer to whoever she was with.

If only Chapman could be persuaded to sell his tumbledown house and move away from Pypard West, life would be so much more pleasant. Rumour had it that the place was in a very dilapidated state now, and that Chapman hadn't paid his bills for a while.

But still, some of the villagers looked at Gil as if they didn't trust him. And one or two of the local children jeered at Beth, who didn't go into the village on her own because of that.

What did Chapman hope to gain by fomenting hatred?

Well, life was never perfect, was it? Surely this trouble would gradually die down when Chapman realised he was never going to get anywhere with his spurious claims?

★　★　★

In late October, Gil's mother at last came to visit. He sent Horry to fetch her in the motor car, and as he was helping her down, she complimented Horry on driving carefully, not like some of the mad motorists she'd seen.

Horry grinned. 'I like to stay alive too, Mrs Rycroft. And I like the people I drive to be comfortable.' He tipped his cap to her and got back into the vehicle to take it round to the rear of the house.

Mrs Rycroft turned to her son. 'You're looking even better than last time I saw you. Life here seems to agree with you.'

Beth peeped at her from behind Gil.

'And is this Elizabeth? My goodness, you're growing. Come and give your grandmother a kiss, child.'

But Beth hung back until Gil said, 'We'll both come and kiss you, Ma.'

This diverted her, as he'd known it would.

'How many times have I told you boys not to call me Ma?' But her anger was feigned and she accepted his kiss, then let him lift Beth to kiss her too.

'Go back to Miss Bramber now, Beth. You can come down and have tea with us later this afternoon.'

His mother watched the child skip back into the house. 'She's looking a lot better.'

'Yes. But she still has nightmares and worries if I go away.'

His mother's eyes grew bright with tears. 'We all have nightmares about the *Titanic*, don't we? But we mustn't dwell on sad things. We can't change the past.'

When she was settled in the sitting room, she drank a cup of tea and commented on the work he'd had done to the house. Then she put her cup down and gave him *that look*. 'Time to talk, Gil.'

He didn't need telling what she wanted to talk about: him marrying. 'Now that you've seen how well Beth is doing, surely you can see I don't need a wife?'

'No, I can't. That child needs a woman who will stay with her, preferably a *lady*, born and bred. A governess can leave at any time. And you surely want children of your own?'

'Please, Mother, don't hold me to that promise.'

'I'm sorry, Gil, but it's for your own good. I want to see you leading a normal life, not living as a recluse.'

'I'm not living as a recluse. I have friends in the village and — '

'Friends of your own class?'

'One or two.'

'Do the better class families round here have any eligible young women?'

He couldn't lie to her, so contented himself with shaking his head.

'Then I shall expect you to spend next weekend at Merriton. Your father has recovered enough to enjoy social life again and I've invited a couple of other families.'

'Not Amelia Frensham!'

'No. She's engaged to be married. You missed out there. Pity. She'd have made such a suitable wife for you.'

'It'd be like marrying my sister. I couldn't . . . treat her like a wife.'

Cheeks a little pink, she said hastily, 'Next weekend, from Friday until Monday morning.'

'That's too long to be away from Beth.'

'You've assured me that the governess is an excellent woman, and there is Lizzie as well. I didn't expect it, but she sounds to be a very suitable nursemaid, young as she is.'

His mother fixed him with the stare that had

all her men folk agreeing to do what she wanted, and he could do nothing but agree to join her weekend house party.

Her voice softened. 'I know you find your arm embarrassing, but you're still a good-looking young man, and that built-up shoe really does help you walk more normally. You are more presentable than you realise.'

He shook his head but didn't protest.

She didn't raise the matter for the rest of her short visit, but concentrated on getting to know her granddaughter better and advising him on refurbishing the sitting room, which she said was too shabby for a gentleman's residence.

★   ★   ★

The following Friday morning he set off, driven by Horry, who had been coached by Walter on helping Gil look after his clothes and providing some of the services a gentleman needed.

'It isn't necessary, Walter. I'm quite capable of dealing with my own clothes and shaving myself.'

'It is necessary, lad, if only to please your parents.'

Gil hoped no one would realise how nervous he was. His parents gave no sign of noticing, and indeed, his father had his own problems since the seizure. One side of his mouth and one eye drooped slightly, and he couldn't move at more than a slow walk.

The other guests eyed Gil speculatively as he joined them in the drawing room. His heart sank as he saw who they were. Why hadn't he asked before? He knew them very well, with their hunting-mad sons and their horsey daughters.

He tried to do what was necessary, chatting about the weather, but falling silent when hunting or shooting was discussed because he'd lost his taste for killing animals he watched regularly from his windows.

When they gathered after dinner to entertain themselves, he even managed to sing a duet with Susannah Overill, though he knew he had a very ordinary voice. Hers was ordinary too, but well trained, so he thought they managed quite well.

He let out a sigh of relief when it was over and she smiled at him. 'Nervous?'

'I'm not a singer.'

'Nor am I. But Mama insists.'

He felt obliged to sit next to her on a sofa and saw his mother nodding approvingly, which tied his tongue in knots for a few moments.

'How is your niece?'

'Beth's recovering slowly, but she still has nightmares.'

'Poor little thing. But your mother says you have an excellent governess to look after her if she wakes.'

In fact, he went in to Beth himself if she began crying during the night and usually got there before Miss Bramber, whose only fault was that she was a very sound sleeper. But he didn't say that to Susannah. No doubt she'd let others bring up her children, as most ladies of his class did. How could he marry someone like that when he was discovering the joy of bringing up a young child?

Later he was obliged to sit and chat to Belinda Hillier, a very lively young woman whose brothers he'd known for most of his life. 'Thought you were engaged, Bel.'

'No. I ended it. He turned out to have several faults I really couldn't live with.'

He blinked at this frankness, but it explained why a lovely young woman had been dragged down to Merriton to meet a cripple like him.

'I'm going to be frank,' she said suddenly. 'I've met someone else, but my parents don't consider him suitable. So don't start thinking of courting me, Gil. It's David or no one for me.'

He tried not to let his relief show. 'No offence meant, but I wasn't going to start courting you. I don't really want to get married, only Ma made me promise.'

'Poor you. She's a terror when she decides on something. My mother's on a charity committee with her and if your mother decides to do something they all just say yes. Mother is terrified of upsetting her.'

When the guests had gone after what seemed a very long weekend, his mother questioned him.

'I can't see myself with either of them,' he said. 'A man has to be able to . . . ' He flushed, not knowing how to phrase it, but determined to make her understand his difficulties.

'Has to be able to bed a woman, do you mean?'

He nodded, feeling hot under the collar to be discussing this with a woman, and that the woman was his mother made it ten times worse.

She sat frowning, then asked bluntly, 'Can you

not bed a woman now?'

He shrugged. 'I think I can. But not . . . not women like that.'

'Like what?'

He shrugged. 'There has to be a spark, an attraction.' For some reason he had a vivid memory of the young woman from Yew Tree Gardens. Why did he keep remembering her after only one meeting? It was ridiculous. 'A willing body isn't enough for me, I'm afraid, Mother.'

'Hmm. Well, I shall keep trying until I find someone who does attract you. And I would be obliged if you would also look around and give these young women a fair chance. I shall not be . . . too fussy about her background if you find someone yourself. Given the circumstances.'

He started to speak, but she impaled him with that fierce gaze. 'I shall not give up on this, Gilbert, and nor must you. You've promised and I'm holding you to your word.'

His heart sank. For all his faults, he had never willingly broken a promise.

When he got home, he confided in Walter, who sat thoughtfully, then said, 'Your mother's right, really. You're too young to become a recluse and you're so wonderful with that child, it'd be sad if you didn't have children of your own.'

'But the ladies my mother produces don't attract me.'

'Someone will turn up.'

'I only have just over a year for that, so they'd better hurry.'

1913

13

Mr Greaves dropped down dead in his office one morning in February. His lady typist ran screaming for help, but it was too late. He was quite dead.

Everyone was shocked by this, because he was only sixty-four, but Mrs Tolson dealt firmly with any female member of staff who started to go into hysterics or used this as an excuse for neglecting her duties.

'Mr Greaves wouldn't want you to upset our customers,' she kept saying. 'He'd tell us to carry on as usual, and that's all we can do for him now. He made this hotel what it is, had been manager here since the beginning. A fine life's work.'

The deputy manager took charge, but he was near retirement, and when someone asked him if he was going to become manager now, he shook his head. 'I haven't announced it yet, but I shall be retiring quite soon. Don't worry, though. The Carlings always bear in mind the future needs of each hotel and they have several bright young men well trained and itching to take on a manager's job.'

The hotel didn't close for the funeral, but Mrs Tolson and the deputy manager attended it, together with a representative from each area of the hotel. And of course, Mr Maurice Carling and his wife both came to London from

Brighton for the occasion.

They were older than Mr Greaves had been and were showing their age, each needing a walking stick and moving very slowly. It was their son who was now in charge of everything.

Dennis Carling was solicitous of his parents, but very brisk and businesslike with the senior staff and clearly impatient to get the fuss over with.

After the funeral, it was no surprise when the Carlings announced over drinks and refreshments at the hotel that they were retiring completely from involvement with the hotels and leaving everything to 'dear Dennis'.

The staff went about their business as usual that day, not even allowed to wear black armbands, because it might upset the guests. Whatever happened, the guests must have a happy stay, or they might not come back again, and without guests there were no jobs.

There was much speculation at all levels about what would happen next, who would be appointed. No one could replace dear Mr Greaves, no one! And a sharp-tempered manager could make everyone's life a misery.

There were bound to be changes, there always were when a new man took over. What would they be? What would he be like?

Everyone was on edge.

★   ★   ★

Renie couldn't help noticing that Mrs Tolson came back to the hotel after the funeral looking worried, as if she'd heard bad news. Though the housekeeper said nothing, Renie accidentally overheard her telling Miss Pilkins that she was worried about one or two of the men Dennis Carling had marked for advancement and had mentioned in connection with the London Rathleigh. Apparently the final decision had not yet been taken.

'What do you mean?' Miss Pilkins asked.

'Some of the younger generation care more about money than people, but Mr Greaves made money by caring about people, both the employees and the guests. And yet they . . . '

She lowered her voice then and Renie didn't hear the rest of it. She wondered what else Mrs Tolson was confiding in her deputy.

Renie was extremely worried on her own account. Her job had been created by Mr Greaves, against the wishes of most of the senior staff. Would it be abolished now? Would she have to go back to being a waitress? Oh, she hoped not! She loved what she was doing and even enjoyed the accounting work she had taken on for Miss Pilkins, to that lady's relief.

When there was a whisper that the new manager had been chosen, she waited anxiously to find out who it was. No one knew anything for certain, not even where the rumour came from.

Mrs Tolson summoned Miss Pilkins and Renie into her office soon afterwards. 'Our new manager will be starting on Monday. You might have met him, Irene. I believe he worked at the Rochdale Rathleigh for a time.'

Renie looked at her in puzzlement. The only

one who'd worked there temporarily while she was there had been . . . No, it couldn't be that man. Please, no. Not *him*!

'It's Mr Ronald Judson, who is very well thought of by Mr Dennis Carling.' She stopped and looked at Renie, saying flatly, 'You don't like him.' It wasn't a question.

'It's not for me to like or dislike the manager.'

'I've worked with Judson before when he was younger. He was — ' She hesitated, then shook her head and didn't pursue the matter.

But she'd said enough. Renie lay awake for ages that night, worrying. Surely Judson wouldn't still be annoying the women staff, not if Dennis Carling thought well of him? Surely a manager wouldn't . . . couldn't . . . She shuddered at the memory of him grabbing her.

What if he hadn't changed? What if he still remembered her? As manager, he'd be in an ideal position to get his own back on her as he'd once threatened.

She might even lose her job completely. What would she do then? Not go back to Nell, that was sure. But she had her savings, so she'd be all right till she found another job, surely. Only . . . how did you find another job without references? Especially a good job, like the one she had here. There weren't many chances like this for women, especially younger women like her.

She had such a feeling of apprehension about this.

Mrs Tolson was frowning more than usual, too.

Mr Judson arrived soon afterwards, looking plumper than Renie remembered and wearing a very well-tailored suit. He sailed into the hotel like a king visiting his subjects. Renie tried to keep out of sight but the way he looked at one of the prettier maids hadn't changed. That fast sweep of the eyes up and down her body gave him away.

The senior staff were summoned to his office and the rest of the staff got on with their jobs, not stopping to gossip, working as hard as they could, in case he did an inspection of the hotel. Even the page boy wasn't whistling today.

A little later, Renie caught sight of Mrs Tolson walking back to her office, a grim expression on her face. When she was summoned to see her, Mrs Tolson said, 'He had a list of employees and questioned what you were doing.'

'Is he going to send me back to being a waitress?'

'I'm not sure what he's going to do. I just wanted to say . . . ' She lowered her voice. 'If you need references, I will provide them, whether Mr Judson agrees or not. You're a hard worker and I won't have you thrown on the street.'

'Thank you.'

'Better get about your duties now. What are you doing today?'

'Miss Pilkins wants to go over the accounts.'

Mrs Tolson's face relaxed into a near smile. 'She's excellent at her job, but is terrified of figures. It's a good thing she has you.'

Renie didn't meet Mr Judson face to face for a few days, though once or twice she felt as if someone was watching her. That was easy to do in a place with large plants and pieces of furniture strategically placed to make areas for guests to sit and talk.

She did the only thing she could: got on with her job and ignored the uneasy feeling.

The third day after Judson's arrival, a lady guest received a telephone call bringing bad news from home: her husband had died. As the telephone room was just off the hotel foyer, Renie was called to comfort the sobbing Mrs Wallace and did this to the best of her ability.

Mr Judson himself turned up to commiserate with the guest on her loss. His eyes were very sharp and assessing as the guest wept and clung to Renie's hand.

'Such a kind young lady,' Mrs Wallace said. 'If she could stay with me for a while . . . ?'

'Of course.' He turned to Renie. 'You know what to do?'

'Yes, sir. I've dealt with this sort of problem before.'

He nodded and turned back to Mrs Wallace. 'If you need any further help, don't hesitate to call me, my dear lady. We at the Rathleigh are completely at your service.'

Renie stayed with the distraught woman until her son arrived to escort her home.

Mr Judson came to show them out and Mrs Wallace stopped to say, 'I want to commend Miss Fuller, who has been a great comfort to me.'

Mr Judson stood next to Renie at the door of the hotel, then turned to her. 'Clearly you do your job properly.'

Relief flooded through her.

He gave her a wolfish smile. 'But I haven't forgotten how you behaved in Rochdale. You'd better start considering how much you want to keep the job, hadn't you?'

She watched him walk away, saw Mrs Tolson staring at them from across the foyer and hoped she hadn't betrayed her shock. And fear.

He had changed for the worse, seemed more powerful and more confident that he could do what he wanted.

But she didn't want to keep her job if it meant letting him have his way with her.

Mrs Tolson disappeared into her office and Renie went to tidy the room where she'd sat with Mrs Wallace.

Thank goodness she'd saved her money!

And thank goodness Mrs Tolson would give her a reference, whatever happened.

★ ★ ★

Gil was again summoned to attend a dinner party at his parents' house in London. His mother hadn't said what this was about, didn't need to. She'd be producing more women for him to meet. Where did she find them all?

He went up to town in the morning, taking Horry with him because Walter had a bad cold.

They left their luggage at the station and went to the shoemaker, whose place of work was nearby, to order some new shoes for Gil. After that they went on to the exercise specialist for a check-up.

'Your leg has improved,' the man said. 'We'll work out some more demanding exercises for you — but not too demanding. And we'll see if anything can help your arm.'

Gil wasn't optimistic about the arm, but was pleased to have his opinion about his leg confirmed.

As they came out into the street, he said, 'Let's go and have something to eat. I don't want to go to my mother's yet.'

Horry looked at him with a wry smile. 'It's only two days, sir.'

'It'll feel like two years.'

'Don't you want to marry?'

'Not unless I meet someone special. What about you?'

'I'd lose my job and I like working for you.'

Gil was pleased to hear that, but puzzled too. 'What made you think you'd lose your job? We could easily provide you with married quarters.'

'Oh. I thought people didn't like having married servants. Walter said so, anyway.'

'Walter's a bit old-fashioned. Don't let working for me hold you back if you want to get married.'

'Chance would be a fine thing. Who'd have me with this battered face?'

'All sorts of women would consider themselves fortunate.' And that was when Gil realised that this logic applied to him, too.

'It takes a rare sort of love,' Horry muttered.

'It happens, though.' And perhaps, Gil thought, it could even happen to him. But not if he rushed into a loveless marriage. If he hadn't met anyone by the time the eighteen months were up, he'd tell his mother he wasn't going to marry someone unless he thought they'd be happy together.

Something hard eased inside him at this decision.

'Well, it can't be put off any longer. Let's go and visit my parents.' They retrieved their suitcases from the left-luggage office and took a taxi to Yew Tree Gardens.

Horry looked out of the window disapprovingly. 'Couldn't they have chosen nicer trees than yews?'

Gil shrugged. 'I rather like the dark green.'

'I don't. Those trees remind me of churchyards and graves.'

The taxi came to a halt.

'Here goes.' Gil paid the fare then walked into the house, knowing better than to carry his own suitcase here. The butler was holding open the door, a maid was waiting to take his outdoor clothes, while the bootboy slipped up the basement steps to help Horry with the luggage.

From the drawing room came the tinkle of teacups. 'Is my mother entertaining friends?' Gil asked the butler. 'Perhaps I'd better go and sit in the library.'

'I think your mother would prefer you to join them, sir,' Bartlett said.

'Oh.' He braced himself mentally. 'How many am I facing this time?'

243

'Two young ladies and their mothers.'

'Here goes, then.' Gil let Bartlett throw open the door and announce, 'Mr Gilbert is here, ma'am.'

'Ah, Gil dear. I'd expected you earlier.'

And it began again: introductions, small talk, one silly giggling girl, one older, quiet one. Neither of them roused anything but boredom in him, and he followed the advice of the old adage of looking at their mothers to see what they'd become. No thank you.

Dinner brought another pair of youngish women to be displayed for his inspection. He knew one slightly, had met the brother of the other. The evening seemed to go on for ever.

'You're not trying,' his mother said over breakfast the next day.

'I came up to London, didn't I?'

'You'd already made up your mind not to like anyone.'

He looked at her very seriously for a moment, then said, 'No. Actually, I hadn't. I'd really like to marry one day. I love having a child to care for and would like others.'

'You'll keep trying, then? Let me introduce you to girls?'

'Yes, of course I will. I promised, didn't I? But if it comes down to it . . . I won't marry if I don't think I can have a happy life with the woman . . . even if it means breaking my promise.'

'You'd break your word to me?'

'Rather than be unhappy for the rest of my life, yes.'

'Then I shall have to try harder to find

someone. You are staying for luncheon, aren't you?'

'If you wish. I think I'll go out for a walk first. I have to exercise this leg and gentle walking seems to help.'

'Is there nothing they can do about the arm?'

'They don't think so, but we will keep trying if there is talk of any new treatment. Unfortunately, none has proved useful so far.'

* * *

As Renie walked round Yew Tree Gardens during her luncheon break, she sighed. Judson had been here for over a week and was like a shadow looming over her. He hadn't done anything yet, but he'd looked, and smiled slyly, and somehow she just knew he was only biding his time.

Even Mrs Tolson had seen the way he looked at her.

Renie was so lost in thought she almost bumped into someone till that person stopped her with inches to spare by putting a gentle hand on her arm. 'Oh, I'm sorry. I was — Oh, it's you, Mr Rycroft!'

He smiled at her. 'It's been nearly a year, but I've remembered you too.'

'I saw the lists in the newspapers after the *Titanic*. I'm sorry about your brother and his family.'

'Thank you. But at least my niece was rescued. I've adopted her.'

'It's good that she has family left still. I used to have a niece . . . ' She stopped. 'Sorry. You can't

245

possibly be interested in that.'

He offered his arm. 'I am. Why don't we walk a little and you can tell me about it?'

She was so desperate to tell someone about Nell that it all poured out.

He was quiet, then said, 'I don't think you can do anything at the moment. Your sister knows you're here. If she gets desperate she'll turn to you for help. She knows she's not alone in the world.'

As they walked on, she smiled at him. 'I'm sorry. Fancy unloading my troubles on a stranger. You're a very good listener.'

'You don't feel like a stranger. I've remembered you all year.'

'Oh.'

'Look, I hope you don't think this is cheeky of me, but you sound so alone in the world. If you ever need help, let me know.' He fished in his pocket and pulled out his card. 'This is my address.'

'Why would you help me?'

'Because a kindly old lady helped me when I was at the worst point of my whole life, after the accident that left me . . . crippled.'

'You're not crippled, just a bit . . . dot and carry one when you walk.'

He couldn't help laughing. 'Dot and carry one. That *is* how I walk. And it sounds much better than 'crippled'. Anyway, as I started out to tell you, the old lady left me a comfortable amount of money on condition that I help people in need. So if you ever feel you can't manage on your own, write to me.'

She looked down at his card. 'I remembered your name correctly: Gilbert Rycroft.'

'Gil to my friends.'

'I come from Wiltshire, too, but Swindon, not the country. Oh!' She caught sight of the clock on the corner shop. 'Oh, dear! I'm late back. Thank you for listening to me. I have to go.'

'Wait! I don't know your name.'

She called over her shoulder, 'Irene Fuller, but my friends call me Renie.'

She ran back to the hotel, but was ten minutes late.

No sooner had she settled into the tiny room they called her office than the pageboy popped his head round the door, which was always left partly open unless she had someone with her.

'Mr Judson wants to see you.'

He must have noticed her coming back late. He seemed always to be watching her.

She knocked and was told to come in, then kept standing while he continued to write. That was a trick he used to make people feel uncomfortable, but it had the opposite effect on her. She folded her arms and began tapping her foot.

He looked up and put down his fancy fountain pen. 'You were late returning to work this lunchtime.'

'Yes.'

'And it was because you were talking to a man.'

'Yes.'

'You admit it.'

'Of course I do. His family lives at the other

247

side of the gardens. He was telling me about his niece. We met when the news about the *Titanic* came out. He lost several other members of his family then.'

'He looked like a gentleman.'

'He is.'

'What's his name?'

'I don't think that's your concern . . . sir.'

'A gentleman wouldn't be talking to a girl like you unless he had ulterior motives.'

She laughed aloud at that. 'Because he *is* a true gentleman, he wouldn't think of treating me like that. *He* doesn't stare at me like . . . some men do.'

'You are impudent, Irene.'

'No, sir. Only truthful.'

'If you value your job, you'll be careful how you behave.'

'I do value my job . . . sir. But I won't tell lies to keep it, or do anything else wrong.' She could see by his expression that he knew what she was telling him.

'See you make up the time.'

'I work far longer than my stated hours, and am happy to do so.'

'You will stay on for twice ten minutes longer after work tonight to make up for being late.'

She didn't dare refuse, though this was unfair. 'Very well . . . sir.' She hated to call him sir. He didn't deserve that sort of respect.

When Mrs Tolson came in to see her about something, Renie confided what had happened. 'I don't like to think of being alone here with *him* after everyone else has gone home tonight.

The night staff don't use this area.'

'I'll make sure I stay in my office for longer tonight, too. I'll be within call.'

'Thank you.'

Renie got on with her accounts, but three times she pulled out the business card and studied it. She memorised the address and told herself not to be stupid. As if she'd ever dare use it!

But still, a kind gesture like that had brightened the day. She knew instinctively that Gilbert Rycroft would never harm her, just as she knew that Judson would if he got the chance.

She should start looking for another job at once. And she should be very careful not to be alone where *he* could catch her.

14

Renie was lost in thought, thinking about her sister Nell, wondering where she was. She jumped in shock as she suddenly realised Judson was standing right next to her. How could she have failed to sense him coming in?

He took a step closer, so that his thigh was touching her body.

She tried to move her chair away from him, but he followed and her office was so small there wasn't enough space to move again.

He smiled, a slow, gloating smile, as if he understood exactly how trapped he'd made her feel.

'Excuse me, but I need to get something out of the cupboard,' she said.

'Don't let me stop you.' But he made no attempt to move back.

She glared at him. 'You're in my way.'

'Oh, I think there's room to brush past.'

'I don't care to do that.'

He didn't answer, just reached out and grasped her breast, giving it a slow twist that hurt so much it made her yelp in pain and shock. For a moment he kept hold of her breast, his fingers digging in, deliberately hurting her further. Then footsteps came towards them along the corridor and he let go.

She was so shocked she couldn't think straight for a moment or two. No man had ever touched her in this way before, and why should he want to hurt her? She was sure that wasn't normal, even though people didn't discuss such things.

As he stepped quickly backwards, he said in a low voice, 'I shan't wait much longer, Irene. If you wish to stay here at the Rathleigh, doing your imaginary job, it'll be on my terms.' Then he turned and walked away without waiting for an answer.

She sat rigid in her chair, wanting to scream, to rush out and accuse him, to let the world know what he'd just done to her. But she'd seen how he'd got away with similar behaviour at the Rochdale Rathleigh, and knew she had no proof. Her word wouldn't be nearly enough against his, because *he* was the manager.

Even though it was raining lightly, she went out to walk round and round the gardens at lunchtime, walking fast, turning up her face to the cleansing rain. Anger was still burning through her and she felt dirtied by his touch.

Most of all, she was afraid of what he would try next.

More than afraid, terrified.

She couldn't stay here much longer.

★ ★ ★

That evening Renie wrote a letter to Gilbert Rycroft, asking him if she could see him next time he was in London. She needed some advice about setting up a little business, a shop perhaps.

The pen seemed to continue writing of its own accord. He had been so easy to speak to.

251

*I don't like to trouble you, but I'd appre-
ciate it if you could advise me soon. I can't
stay on at the hotel much longer, because a
man is making life difficult for me.*

She stared at the paper, amazed she'd dared to
mention this. She'd have to write another letter
now, because it wasn't the sort of thing you
should confide in a stranger. And yet . . . she felt
instinctively that Gilbert would understand.
She'd never met anyone, apart from her sisters,
with whom she felt so much at ease, as if she was
able to say anything to him, anything at all.

Oh, she was being silly, letting her imagination
run wild. She'd only met him twice.

But she did feel comfortable with him. She
wished . . . oh, the old saying was so right: if
wishes were horses, beggars would ride. *Don't be
so silly, Renie!*

After writing the address on the envelope, she
hesitated yet again, going back to re-read those
final words.

What had she to lose?

She folded the letter, put it inside the envelope
and licked the strip of glue round the pointed
edge, sealing it carefully with no wrinkles. She
stuck a stamp on it because it wasn't a letter to
her family.

Then it occurred to her that if the Carlings
encouraged female members of staff to write to
their families, they must care about their
employees. How much did they care? What if she
wrote to them, told them about Judson?

For a moment hope flared, then it faded again.

252

It all came back to the same thing: her word against his.

When she put the envelope on the table with the other women's letters, something made her pick it up again. Those envelopes went through the general office. Judson must know her handwriting by now. She wouldn't put it past him to remove her letter.

It might be foolish, she might be seeing dragons where there were none, but better safe than sorry. She'd nip out in the morning after breakfast and post the letter herself at the corner of the square. It'd only take a couple of minutes.

As she was making her way to bed, Miss Pilkins stopped her. 'Are you all right, Irene? I couldn't help noticing that you weren't yourself tonight. You haven't heard from your sister, have you?'

'No. I wish I had.'

'Oh. Well, I'm sure you'll hear something soon. And don't forget, if I can help in any way . . .'

'Thank you.' The thought of how caring Miss Pilkins and Mrs Tolson were made Renie feel a bit better, but she didn't want to involve them, because they too would be powerless against Judson and they had a lot more to lose than she did if he sacked them.

As she was getting into bed she had a sudden urge to pack her bags and leave that very minute. She even sat up in bed and flung the covers back.

She could find a cheap hotel and . . .

No! With a sigh, she pushed that thought aside, tempting as it was, and lay down again.

253

She couldn't leave yet. Not till she heard from Nell. She'd already lost touch with Mattie, didn't want to lose her other sister as well.

★ ★ ★

After breakfast the next day, Renie slipped out to post her letter at the corner of the square, but when she got back she nearly bumped into Judson, who was standing in the shadows at the end of the little corridor which the staff used to go into and out of the hotel.

'Where have you been?' he demanded.

'Out for a breath of fresh air . . . sir.'

'Not much fresh air to be found on the way to the postbox.'

She shivered. He must have been watching her out of his office window.

'Why didn't you put your letter with the others?'

'It was important, so I wanted to post it myself.'

'Writing to a lover, eh?'

She drew herself up. 'Certainly not.'

He gave her one of his sneering smiles. 'Never had a lover, have you? But you will. That's what women like you were made for and I — '

'Is something wrong, Meestair Judson?'

He jerked round in shock.

Monsieur Leduc was standing behind him.

'I was just speaking to Miss Fuller about something.' He nodded to Renie. 'You can get on with your work now. I'll see you later.'

She hurried away, hoping Monsieur wouldn't think she'd been encouraging the manager to chat to her.

Judson always seemed to be lurking nearby. She couldn't turn round lately without bumping into him.

Well, at least she could be sure of her letter reaching Gilbert Rycroft.

How long could she keep Judson at bay, though? In such a large building there were places he could catch her where few people were within hearing. Surely he wouldn't . . . force himself on her?

Revulsion at this thought made her feel physically sick. She hated him to touch her, and had a huge bruise on her left breast from their encounter in her office. She hoped none of the girls had seen it as she got dressed and undressed. What would they have thought?

* * *

There was a roar of anger from the stable area at Oakdene and Horry came storming into the house.

'That does it! I'm sleeping near the car from now on. They're not getting the chance to set fire to this one.'

'What's the matter?' Gil asked.

'Come and look at the car. See what someone's done to it.'

Horry led the way outside, across the backyard and into the part of the stable block where the car was kept until a proper building could be provided for it. The area was open to the elements on one side, but at least the car was under cover here and intruders would have to go past Horry's quarters to get there. Or climb over the back wall.

The area had been used as an extra hay store in the days when several horses were kept, and had a tack room leading off it at one side and a storage room next to that for everything from drenches to saddle soap.

'Look at that!' Horry stabbed his finger towards the side of the car's bonnet. There were several scratch marks all along it, as if someone had used a screwdriver or similar metal tool.

'Damn! Those are deep gouges. Is it Chapman's work, do you think?'

'Who else would have done something like that?'

'We'll have to get some doors fitted to this area to keep the car safe till we can build you a proper workshop.'

'We shouldn't need to.' Horry's face was red with fury. 'Don't you waste your money on that! I'm going to sleep out here from now on. He's not getting near our car again.'

'Have you checked for footprints?'

'Yes. Whoever it was got over the wall, but he must have dragged a leafy branch along the ground behind them to brush the footprints out. We used to do that as children when we were playing at stalking in the woods. Come and look.'

They stood together staring down at the thin, whisk-like marks in the dusty ground.

'Cunning, isn't he?' Gil sighed.

'So can I sleep out here?'

'Of course you can. But I hate to think of how uncomfortable you'll be.'

'The weather's not all that cold now, sir, and

I've slept in far worse places. I'll put my mattress on the hay, but out of sight, like. And I'll get the lad to sleep nearby as well, though we ought to pay him a bob or two extra for that. It's always good to have two people around when there's villainy going on.'

'Do as you think best, and if you need to buy anything to help you protect the car and stables, not to mention yourself, don't hesitate to ask for it.'

Gil turned to leave, then swung back. 'It occurred to me that the branch marks might lead you somewhere just as footprints would. Why don't you follow them and see where they go?'

But Horry came back half an hour later, scowling. 'The marks only lead into the village, sir, then there are so many footprints and wheel ruts, it's hard to tell which person was going where.'

'He'll make a mistake one day.'

'Well, he can't make it fast enough for me. Fancy doing that to our car, or to any car! He wants taking out and whipping, that one does.'

* * *

The day got steadily worse. A letter arrived from Gil's lawyer by the first post.

Dear Mr Rycroft,

I've received a communication from someone who claims to be a lawyer. He has rooms in London but the address isn't in a respectable area, and what's more, the names of his colleagues mean nothing to me.

Chapman apparently has proof that he's related to Miss Bennerden and is claiming that he's entitled to a share of her estate.

Standish, the lawyer chappie, says Chapman has a letter from her promising to leave him everything.

They say they are willing to settle out of court, otherwise they'll sue you and claim it all. I doubt they'd get anywhere, but it'd cost a great deal of money to defend you. I think they're counting on that to get something out of us.

Could you possibly come and see me today? We need to discuss this.

Howard Mortlake

There was another envelope underneath it, addressed to him in round, childish handwriting. Thinking it to be part of the hoax, Gil opened it reluctantly.

He found it to be a letter from the nice young woman who worked at the Rathleigh, asking for his help. Renie briefly outlined what she was thinking of doing and asked for his advice. He wanted very much to help her, but had to deal with his own situation first, so he stuffed her letter into his pocket and arranged for Horry to drive him into Swindon.

He wasn't kept waiting long at Mr Mortlake's rooms.

'Do come in, my dear fellow. I hope you're well.'

Gil didn't answer that, couldn't be bothered

with meaningless chit-chat. 'Can I see the letter, please?'

Mr Mortlake handed it over. It was brief and to the point.

On behalf of my client, Duncan Chapman, I wish to inform you that he has proof of his relationship to Alice Bennerden, and also a letter from her stating her intention of leaving her property to him.

I would like to arrange a meeting at your earliest convenience to discuss with you and your client a settlement of this claim.

Given that expectations have been raised for Mr Rycroft, my client has kindly agreed to settle for half the estate.

If this generous offer is refused, we shall take the matter to court and claim the whole.

Yours etc.

Peter Standish

Corson, Standish and Levensworth, Lawyers

'Standish doesn't say what proof he can offer of his client's relationship to Miss Bennerden,' Mr Mortlake said. 'Chapman certainly had no proof to offer when he came to see me, only a tale of being related through a second cousin. Miss Bennerden wasn't even sure about the second cousin's existence. As to the claim for a share in the estate, I'm quite certain she didn't intend to leave him anything.'

He frowned, taking back the letter and holding it between his fingertips as if it were filthy. 'It worries me that I don't recognise this fellow's colleagues. You'd think out of three names, I'd have heard of one of them. I'm pretty well connected in legal circles, for all I live in Wiltshire.'

'What sort of proof could they have?'

'I don't know.' He hesitated, then said in a low voice, 'I shall deny saying this, but I think any proof produced by Chapman is likely to be forged. He once wrote a letter and forged Miss Bennerden's name on it.'

'Did he, now!'

'Yes. I wish I'd kept it. Even she, who always believed the best about people, had to admit in the end that he was a bad 'un.'

'She was right. I can't stand the fellow. I still believe he set fire to my outbuildings, or arranged for it to be done.'

Mr Mortlake shook his head sadly. 'I think I'd better send someone up to London to check the firm out before I proceed any further, just to make sure it actually exists. We also have to verify that Standish really is a lawyer and not merely a crony of Chapman's. I hate to waste your money on this taradiddle, but it's best to be certain before we act so — '

'Why don't I go myself? I have another matter to attend to in London, so I can kill two birds with one stone.'

Mr Mortlake frowned at him. 'Well . . . as long as you don't approach anyone from this firm or do anything rash. Just check out that there is a firm with this name and that they are doing business.'

'Give me the details. I'll leave tomorrow.'

'While you're doing that, I'll write to a friend of mine who has rooms at Lincoln's Inn and ask him to check Standish's legal credentials, not to mention those of his partners.'

'Good.' Gil was glad to be able to do something for himself, instead of relying on others. He was also eager to help Renie. She'd sounded anxious in her letter. Who was making her life at the Rathleigh a misery? His friend Julia had made him realise how vulnerable young women could be in a world ruled by men. He hoped no one ever attacked that bright-faced young woman in the way they had those poor females in the home for women in distress.

When he got back to Oakdene, Gil explained everything to Walter, including Renie's plea for help.

The old man smiled at him. 'There's my lad. I'm proud of you.'

'What do you mean?'

'You're starting to come into your own, not just thinking about yourself. We'll have you a Member of Parliament one day, or at least on the local council.'

Gil gaped at him. 'Me? There's no way I'd go in for that sort of thing. What do I know about running this country? And just think how *Punch* would have a field day about this stupid thing.' He flapped his left arm at Walter.

'And think how many people you could help.'

'I need to help myself first and get rid of Chapman. He's a blight on this village as well as a nuisance to me. Did you know the two Dyson brothers have fallen out because of him?'

'You'll settle his hash eventually, then things will settle down.'

Gil wished he was half as confident as his friend and mentor. Member of Parliament, indeed! What an idea! As if he was capable of something like that! 'I'd better go and pack. Do you feel up to a trip to London?'

'No, lad. I tire too easily these days.'

'Perhaps we should fetch in the doctor again?'

'No doctor can cure old age.' He patted Gil's hand gently. 'I've had a good life and I'm not in any pain. If I'm lucky, one night I'll just slip away, but not quite yet, I hope.'

Gil swallowed hard. Old people did die, but oh, he needed Walter still.

'It's Horry who should go with you this time. He can drive you to London in the car. Though you'd better get him some decent clothes while you're up there. He could borrow one of your suits till then. Were you thinking of staying with your parents?'

'I suppose so.'

Walter chuckled. 'Why don't you stay at that hotel, instead? You'll have far more freedom and you'll be able to have a look round it, to see if you can get any idea of who's causing trouble for that nice lass.'

'As long as my parents don't find out I'm so close.'

'Does it matter if they do? You're not answerable to them any longer.'

The words made Gil pause, seemed to mark an important change in his life. 'No. I suppose not. I'd better tell Horry, then.'

He stopped in the corridor, feeling different, as if . . . Yes, as if he'd finally cut the childish ties to his family, the ties that stopped him acting for himself. Some would call it growing up. He smiled, thinking *and about time too*. What a young fool he'd been.

Whistling, he went to find Horry and explain why they were going to London.

'Um, Walter thinks you should borrow one of my suits. Do you mind? I don't want you getting treated like a servant in this London hotel.'

Horry looked at him in surprise. 'But I am a servant!'

'You've also become a friend, I hope. As Walter has. He always has a room next to mine, and I'd like you to do the same.'

Horry flushed and shook Gil's hand, trying and failing to speak. But there were no words needed for the friendship that was growing between them.

'Let's go and see what I've got. There are some suits that are a bit too big for me now. They might be just the thing for you. Oh, and a hat. We need Walter to tell us what sort of hat you should wear. Let's find him.'

Walter sat on the bed while the two young men went through Gil's clothes. They looked surprisingly alike once they were both dressed in gentleman's clothing. But these days, you'd never mistake which one was the master.

As they were leaving the dining room that evening, Horry tugged Gil's sleeve. 'Are you sure about this?'

'Absolutely certain.'

'You'll not regret it, I promise you.'

Gil laughed. 'One day you'll be famous for designing cars, far richer than me, then it'll be your turn to be kind to me.'

Horry stood stock-still. 'How did you know? That I want to design cars — well, the engines, anyway?'

'I can't help noticing that you've been tinkering with an old engine in your spare time, and making sketches of pieces of machinery. If you need any parts, I'm happy to pay for them. Miss Bennerden left me the house and money on condition I help others, you know. And I find it very satisfying to do that.'

Walter watched them, smiling approvingly.

Gil shot him a quick glance. 'What do you think?'

'I think you two ought to be businesslike about it,' Walter said. 'Go and see old Mortlake when you've sorted out the other stuff and get him to draw up a business agreement between you, then do the thing properly.'

'Good idea!' Gil said. 'We'll do that.'

Horry swallowed hard. 'I'll not cheat you, Mr Rycroft.'

'I know that. And you should call me Gil from now on, don't you think?'

* * *

Renie woke with a start and lay awake worrying. If it hadn't been for Mrs Tolson, Judson would have cornered her near the linen cupboards this afternoon. Why couldn't he leave her alone?

Hadn't she made it plain she wanted nothing to do with him?

She remembered the lust in his eyes, and the way he seemed to puff up with pleasure when he upset her — even more so when he hurt her.

He was enjoying the chase, that's why! He liked hurting people.

She remembered a neighbour's cat, which always toyed with a mouse for a long time before killing it. She'd wanted to intervene, but the neighbour had told her to leave things be. The cat was only doing its duty and deserved its fun.

If only she had some way of contacting Nell, she'd leave. Perhaps Gilbert Rycroft would contact her soon. She didn't know why, but she felt quite sure he'd help her.

Feeling better for taking that decision, she snuggled down in bed. Thank goodness she slept in a dormitory with the other women. She felt safe here, safer than anywhere else in the hotel.

Other people must be aware of what Judson was doing, though perhaps they didn't know all the details. Didn't they care? Or were they too worried about their own jobs?

Perhaps they were as afraid of him as she was? Probably.

How could one man make so many people nervous?

15

Gil set off the following morning, with a self-conscious Horry, dressed in one of his new suits. He felt a sense of freedom as they drove along the quiet roads. They didn't say much, but Horry looked happy at the wheel and the car chugged along merrily, as if it too wanted to be out and about.

Once they arrived in London, Gil had to direct Horry. They went to the hotel, booking rooms and leaving the car there, parked in what had been the mews.

Then they had a quick snack in the tea shop at the hotel, before finding a cab driver who was prepared to take them to the rooms of Corson, Standish and Levensworth, then wait for them. That would be easier than Horry trying to find his way round the city.

Horry had wanted to find a motor cab, but Gil insisted on a horse-drawn vehicle. 'This is one time where we don't want to attract onlookers if we have to stop.'

He was quite frank with the cab driver. 'We want to check what these gentlemen are like, whether they're a reputable firm or not.'

The driver hesitated. 'That lot aren't the sort of lawyers toffs like you use, sir.'

'Oh? Why not?'

'I know the street. Lots of businesses along it share premises. Nobody's making a fortune, not if they work there. I take quite a few people to that particular building, though whether it's to your firm or to one of the others I don't know. They're usually people who don't want their faces to be seen clearly: gentlemen with hats pulled down, ladies with heavy veils. I reckon most of them as work in that building deal in divorces, that's what I reckon.'

Gil knew about the divorce laws from Julia, that women had to prove both adultery and another serious fault, like cruelty or incest. He didn't blame people for hiding their faces. It must be very difficult for them.

When they arrived, he suggested the cab driver stop further down the street and put a nosebag on his horse. 'Don't worry. I'll pay you a guinea for your time.'

The man beamed at him. 'You're a gentleman, sir.'

Because Gil's limp attracted attention, Horry got out of the cab and strolled along the street, studying the various premises and their brass plates, some of which would have been the better for a good polishing.

When he came back, Horry stood pretending to talk to their driver but in reality addressed his words to Gil, who had kept out of sight in the cab. 'There are four firms in that house. Your lot are on the first floor. There's another lot there too, so they can't have much space, can they?'

'Why don't you go and get a shoeshine from that old fellow on the corner? Ask him about them. Pretend you're wanting a divorce from a cheating wife.'

Horry glanced down at his ankle boots. 'Better get a bit of muck on these first, then. I gave 'em a good shine this morning.' Surreptitiously he scuffed dirt from the gutter over his boots, then grinned. 'I've never had anyone else shine my shoes for me. I'll feel like a proper toff.' Straightening his curly-brimmed bowler, he adjusted the jacket of his three-piece suit and sauntered off again.

When he came back, he got into the cab. 'Well, the old guy who did my shoes doesn't like Standish at all. Says he's a mean sod. The other two men in his so-called firm have never been seen, if they ever existed, so it's only Standish, really.'

'I suppose it sounds better to have several names in a legal firm. Hmm. I don't think we'll find out any more without going in to see him.'

'I could come back later, dressed in my own clothes,' Horry volunteered. 'I'll go into a pub — look, there's one on the corner — and ask about divorce lawyers. People will talk if I buy them a drink or two — especially if Standish isn't liked round here.'

'Good idea. You do that.'

★ ★ ★

When they went back to the hotel, Gil glimpsed Renie hurrying across the foyer. She saw him and her face lit up for a moment, but the glow faded almost immediately. With a slight shake of her head, she hurried through a door.

Which presumably meant he was not to

contact her in public.

Then Gil noticed a burly man dressed in a good suit following her. The fellow's eyes were on Renie and you couldn't mistake that look of lust. This had to be the one who was making her life miserable.

He stopped a page. 'Who's the man over there, the one just going through the door? He looks familiar. I'm sure I've met him somewhere.'

'That's Mr Judson, the manager.' The boy's voice was toneless, and from the look in his eyes, he didn't like Judson.

'I must have been mistaken, then. The fellow I know is called Hepworth. Thanks.' He gave the lad sixpence, which sent him on his way, whistling cheerfully.

'I didn't like the looks of that manager,' Horry said quietly. 'I've met his sort before. Had to thump one fellow for pestering my cousin.'

Which left Gil with two things to worry about: his own situation and how to help Renie. Even from across the foyer, he could tell she'd lost weight and you couldn't miss the dark circles under her eyes.

His heart went out to her. If she needed help, he'd do whatever was needed.

* * *

Renie stood in the linen cupboard, with the door open a crack, and watched Judson hurry past. When he'd gone, she slipped out and hurried off to see Miss Pilkins.

269

'Do you have any jobs where I can work with someone?' She was beyond pretending now.

'Please close the door.' Miss Pilkins waited till she'd done this, then asked, 'Is it Mr Judson?'

'Yes.'

'It's becoming very obvious that he's pursuing you. I've never seen anything as blatant. It's disgraceful.'

'I've done nothing to encourage him, I promise you.'

'You don't need to tell me that. I'll speak to Mrs Tolson and we'll see what we can arrange. If you like, you can go over my accounts with me this afternoon and — '

There was a knock on the door and it opened almost immediately, before Miss Pilkins had time to say 'Come in.'

Judson stood in the doorway. 'Irene, I'm sure you have work to do. I need to speak to Miss Pilkins.'

Renie stood up and went towards the door, noticing that the assistant housekeeper was looking apprehensive.

Judson was blocking her way, so Renie stood waiting until he stepped aside. She wasn't going to touch him if she could help it. The door shut behind her with a bang.

She waited round the corner until she saw him leave the office, then went back to see Miss Pilkins.

The other woman was in tears.

'What's wrong?'

'I'm to stop taking you away from your work. What he really means is to stop protecting you.

270

And the trouble is, I need this job. My mother depends on my wages. She has no other money. I'm sorry, Irene, so very sorry. I daren't help you, though I *will* mention it to Mrs Tolson next time I see her.'

'I'm sorry to have dragged you into this.' Renie walked away, feeling outraged, went to her office and wrote out her resignation there and then. She took it to the manager's office and gave it to his secretary. 'Please see that Mr Judson gets this as soon as possible.'

Then she went back to her office and began to get the papers in order for someone else to take over.

She half expected Judson to turn up once he'd had time to read her letter of resignation, but the minutes ticked slowly past and there was no sign of him, or of anyone else. Which was unusual.

An hour later the pageboy delivered an envelope. When she opened it, pieces of paper fell out — her letter of resignation.

Well, she would write another one and hand it to him in the presence of someone else so that he couldn't pretend he hadn't received it.

Inevitably her thoughts turned to Gilbert Rycroft. Had he come to the hotel to help her? She hoped so. If Judson caused any more trouble, she was going to beg Gilbert to help her get away at once. She could slip out easily enough, but she didn't see why she should lose her possessions if Judson tried to stop her. He could claim anything — that she'd stolen something, even.

She didn't care now whether she got the wages

that were owing to her or not. All she wanted to do was leave and never see Judson again.

After a while, she couldn't bear to sit there any longer and went out into the foyer. There was no one at the desk, so she nipped across and checked the sign-in register to find out Gilbert's room number. First floor, number eight.

She couldn't go and see him without people noticing, not yet anyway. But later she'd go and ask him to help her get away. She wanted to leave tonight.

She felt certain Gilbert Rycroft wouldn't turn away from her.

And she had her savings. Thank goodness she'd been careful!

★　★　★

Gilbert took Horry down for afternoon tea in the café just off the foyer. He knew Horry had an excellent appetite, and he was feeling quite peckish again himself.

As they sat there, people passed by. The pageboy went to and fro at a trot, glancing over his shoulder occasionally, as if he felt someone was watching him.

When they'd finished their tea, Gilbert said he'd go back to his room and have a rest for a while. 'My leg's aching.'

'I'll take a turn round those gardens outside, if you don't mind,' Horry said. 'I could do with some fresh air.'

'What time are you leaving this evening? Do you want to have something to eat first?'

'I'll go about six, I think, but I'll find somewhere to eat near the pub. There's always somewhere in an area like that and maybe they'll know something about Standish too.'

'I'll book a table in the restaurant here, then. I don't feel like going out.' Nor did he want to see his parents.

He shared the lift with the pageboy. 'Running the lift now, are you?'

'Just while Bob's at tea, sir.'

The lift shuddered and came to a stop between floors.

'Has it broken down?'

'Well, it does this sometimes. If we wait a couple of minutes and try again, it should work. Sorry for the inconvenience, sir.'

'I don't mind. I wanted to ask you something privately, anyway. Do you know a young woman called Irene Fuller?'

The pageboy looked at him in surprise. 'She works here, but I don't know her well.' His tone didn't encourage further confidences.

'My cousin knows her family and asked me to find out how she is. She didn't sound happy in her last letter, apparently, and when Julia found I was coming to stay here, she asked me to check on Irene. I saw Irene in the foyer when I arrived, but she was hurrying off somewhere. Could you take a message to her, do you think?' He pulled out half a crown and flipped the silver coin in the air a couple of times.

The lad hesitated. 'You're not . . . trying to hurt her, are you?'

'Certainly not. I'm trying to help her. We know

273

something's wrong.' He took a risk. '*I* think it's to do with the manager.'

Another silence, then the lad said, 'She's a decent girl, sir. It's not right what he's doing. I'll give her your message.'

The lift chose that moment to jerk and start rising again.

'I won't write anything down. It might get into the wrong hands and then you'd be in trouble. She knows my name, because we've met before. Tell her I'm in room eight and would like a quick word when convenient.'

'That's all?'

'Yes.'

Gil handed over the half-crown, which vanished into the lad's pocket before the lift doors were even half open.

Renie didn't come to see him, though, and when Gil went down for his evening meal, there was no sign of the lad to ask if she'd received the message.

Nor was there any sign of the manager.

★　★　★

Just before her day ended, Renie received a note from Miss Pilkins asking her to collect a lady's spare nightdress, which had mistakenly been left in a suitcase by her maid.

She'd had to fulfil such errands before and she recognised Miss Pilkins' handwriting, though it wasn't as neat as usual and must have been written in a hurry. She wished this hadn't happened just as the daytime workers would be going off duty. Still, it wouldn't take her more than a few minutes and she could trust Miss Pilkins.

She was careful to check that Judson was nowhere around before she left the foyer and she took the fire escape stairs down to the basement, an echoing series of plain concrete stairs. This was not only the quickest way, but also would let her hear and see if anyone else was on the stairs following her.

She'd go back a different way. The cleaning staff had shown her at least two other little-used exits from the basements as well, one of which they used to keep dirty linen out of sight of guests. They knew the building better than anyone.

She lit an oil lamp because there was no gas lighting down here, then went into the room where the most valuable luggage was stored. She saw the suitcase that had been described to her, feeling relieved that this errand could be quickly accomplished, because she felt uneasy on her own down here.

As she bent to open the case, the door of the room slammed shut behind her and the key turned in the lock.

★ ★ ★

Horry had an excellent meal at a chophouse patronised by clerks and decent working men, the sort of hearty food he liked best, if truth be told. Pork chop, heaped-up mashed potatoes and carrots, all covered by a savoury onion gravy, followed by suet currant pudding and custard.

He chose to sit at a long communal table and easily got into conversation with his neighbours, mentioning that his master was looking for a lawyer to help him get a divorce.

'Wish I could get rid of my old lady!' one man joked.

'Wish I had the money to do it. Though I'd not need to then, because if I had money, she'd stop nagging me and life would be a lot easier.'

'Not married yourself?' an older man asked Horry.

'Nah. Who'd have someone with a scarred face like this?' He pointed to his cheek.

'I don't think they look at you much once they've got their hooks into you,' said a gloomy-looking fellow. 'It's whether you're a good breadwinner or not that matters to them. If your master is looking for a divorce lawyer, he could try that Standish fellow on Person Street. I've heard he's a tricky devil and that's what you need.'

'Does he do divorces regularly?'

The old man laughed. 'He does anything that'll make him money, that one.'

'I thought all lawyers were rich.'

'Not him. Nearly lost his licence, he did, and got thrown out of his last place by the other lawyers because of it. Had to set up on his own then.'

'How do you know all this?'

'Got a nephew who was in the thick of it. Good as a play, it was, to hear what happened each day.'

'Give me the name of his old firm and I'll check it out.'

'Why doesn't your master do his own hunting for a lawyer?'

'He's lame. Can't walk about much. Good master, though. Looks after us servants.'

'You can't ask more than that,' the old man said.

The talk moved to other topics and Horry let it, satisfied he'd found out something useful.

Horry accompanied some of his new friends from the chophouse to a pub and enjoyed a pleasant evening, relaxing and chatting, drinking far less than his companions without letting them see that. He didn't pick up any more information but they had a few laughs.

★ ★ ★

After he'd finished a leisurely meal, Gil returned to his hotel room. The lift behaved itself, under the care of a fellow with grizzled hair and a lined face, who was perfectly civil but not interested in chatting.

While Gil had been in the restaurant, a maid had turned down his bed and lit a small fire in the grate, putting a fireguard round it. The two gas wall lights on either side of the mantelpiece were lit but turned right down, so he turned them up again, took out his book and began to read.

But he couldn't concentrate because he continued to feel uneasy. Surely Renie should have contacted him by now? She'd definitely seen him in the foyer. If she didn't at least push a note under his door tonight, he'd make enquiries about her openly in the morning, preferably from someone other than that manager. And he wasn't leaving the hotel until he'd spoken to her.

He wondered how Horry was getting on, hoped he'd found something out.

★ ★ ★

When she realised she was locked in the storeroom, Renie was so shocked she couldn't think what to do. She stood motionless, holding the oil lamp she'd brought with her, but it was a big room and the corners were still shadowy.

It must be Judson who'd done this. She didn't have the slightest doubt of that, because no one else would do this to her.

But the note asking Renie to come down here had come from Miss Pilkins. How had he forced her to write it? Whatever threats he'd used, Renie thought the worse of her for giving in to him, because Miss Pilkins must have guessed what he intended to do.

No wonder he got away with so much. He found people's weak points and used them.

And now he'd trapped her. Renie had no doubt about what he intended to do to her. She moaned and a few sobs escaped her, then she stiffened her spine. She couldn't waste time crying, had to think what to do. Surely there must be some way of escaping? She went to the door, but it was a solid one and there was no key this side, no possible way of opening it with only her bare hands.

He'd be back. She had to be ready, had to find something to use as a weapon. He wasn't going to overcome her easily, she was determined about that.

She checked the oil reservoir in her lamp. It was less than half full. She'd better explore this room before the oil ran out . . . try to find some way of protecting herself before he came back.

Setting to work, she went round the room, searching, finding out what it contained. That turned out to be mainly piles of luggage — beautiful, expensive luggage. Not much use for defending yourself with.

Methodically, listening carefully for sounds outside as she worked, she opened the cases and hatboxes, the trunks and the Gladstone bags. Most were empty. One or two contained crumpled or dirty clothing.

There was nothing she could use as a weapon.

Once she thought she heard a sound outside so went to the door and yelled for help at the top of her voice. But no one answered her call, so she must have been mistaken.

In one suitcase she found some shoes with Louis heels. Better than nothing to hit someone with, she supposed. She thrust one shoe into her side pocket.

But it was a forlorn hope and she knew it. Judson was a big, strong man. Unless she took him by surprise, and had a weapon, he'd easily overpower her.

In the last corner, behind a cardboard box, she

found a pile of old rugs and cloths. She nearly moved on, then decided to check underneath them and found a battered old lamp. One of its glass panels was broken and it should have been put in for repair. Could she use this? She had to fiddle with the spiky pieces of broken glass and cut her finger, but managed to wiggle a shard out. It was nearly as sharp as a dagger. She put that into her other side pocket.

She should have thought of this use for the lamp she was carrying, only if she had used that one, she'd be in the dark.

Could she really stick a piece of glass into someone's flesh? She pulled the shard out again and pressed it lightly against her thumb. The edge was so sharp a drop of blood welled beneath it. She didn't like the idea of using it, but if it was a choice of slicing him open or being ravished, she was definitely going to fight him every inch of the way.

With a sigh she went across to sit on a box near the door and put out the lamp, because the oil reservoir was quite low now. She had some matches to light it again. You always took matches along with a lamp, in case it blew out.

It was worse sitting in the darkness. She didn't feel alone; her fears were crawling round her all the time and she felt literally sick with fear.

★　★　★

After what seemed a very long time, Renie heard footsteps outside and saw a thin line of light coming from the other side of the door.

Someone put a key in the lock and turned it.

Heart pounding, she stood up and tiptoed across to flatten herself against the wall near the door. She had a stout hatbox in her hand.

As the door opened she swung it at Judson's head, taking him by surprise and making him cry out.

But as she swung it again, he grabbed her wrist with one hand and tore it away from her with the other, flinging it aside.

She tried to pull away but he kept hold of her arm as he hung the lantern on a hook and kicked the door shut with one foot. 'You'll be sorry for that, you stupid bitch!'

She didn't answer, would have moved further away but his grip was too strong.

When he swung her round to face him, she tried to surprise him by kicking him in a very tender place.

He laughed as he avoided her kick and sent her flying across the room with one sideways sweep of his fist. She landed awkwardly on a trunk and hurt her side.

His laugh was low and confident. 'I like it when they fight.'

She felt so sick with terror, she wondered if she was going to vomit. Hauling herself to her feet, she faced him from a slightly crouching position, one hand fumbling for the shoe in her pocket.

When he grabbed her, she hit him with the shoe's wooden heel as hard as she could.

He roared with pain as it connected with his temple then thumped her again, sending the shoe flying one way, her the other. 'That's it! I might have made it easy for you, but now you deserve all you get.'

This time she landed on her back, and before she could get up, he threw himself upon her, tearing at her clothes.

She heard her blouse rip, then his hand started fumbling up her skirts. Desperation lent her strength and she managed to get the shard of glass out of her pocket. She lashed out blindly at his head, feeling it connect with something soft.

This time his yell was of pure pain and for a moment the weight jerked away from her.

It was enough for her to roll sideways and lunge for the door. Every second she expected him to grab her but he was making whining, moaning noises and clutching his face. Blood was dripping through his fingers, dark in the flickering lamplight.

She flung the door open and ran off along the dark corridor, knowing the way in her mind because she'd been here many times before.

There were footsteps behind her, but he wasn't yelling or making threats now, just running in silence, which was even more frightening. His feet thumped down one after the other, heavy, getting closer.

She didn't make the mistake of trying to look behind her. She put all her efforts into running faster. She had to get away, right away, because he'd kill her if he caught her, she knew he would.

★ ★ ★

The watcher hiding in a nearby alcove put a hand to her breast and tried to still her pounding heart, praying poor Irene would get away from that brute.

Doors banged from round the corner, but she didn't follow them. She wasn't moving out of this alcove until she was certain *he* wasn't coming back.

She was trying to do what she could to help poor Irene, but she didn't want to do anything openly after the threats he'd made, so would have to be very careful. Only as a final resort would she act openly.

It might already be too late to help, in which case she would never forgive herself.

Oh, please, let her escape!

16

Gil grew more and more anxious, and wasn't at all sleepy, so didn't even try to go to bed. He heard the sounds of movement outside his room from time to time, and walked up and down the corridor a few times to stretch his legs. Sounds grew fewer as people settled down for the night. He took out his pocket watch. Half past midnight now.

By one o'clock it was completely silent outside and he hadn't heard anyone passing by for half an hour. He still felt restless, so he went outside. It'd do his bad leg good to walk up and down the corridor again.

He walked to the far end and back, then went to the head of the main stairs and stared down at the shadowy foyer. Lights there were burning low and a sleepy night porter was dozing in his armchair near the entrance. Nothing to see.

Renie wasn't coming to see him tonight. It was far too late for that. He should go to bed.

As Gil reached his door, he heard something and stood still, listening hard. The sound came from the fire escape at the end of the corridor. Even as he turned to look, the door opened and a figure hurtled out. Renie!

She saw him in the dimly lit corridor, stopped with an expression of terror, then realised who he was and rushed towards him. 'Please hide me. Quick!'

Already he could hear other footsteps. Someone was labouring up the last few stairs of the fire escape. Quickly he gestured to his room and followed Renie inside.

'The lights!' she said.

He locked the door then moved towards the gas wall lights and turned them down to a dim glow. She was shaking so hard, he wanted to take her in his arms and comfort her. Her clothes had been torn and her face bruised.

Someone had attacked her. Not difficult to guess who. He'd like to beat the brute to a pulp, only he could no longer do that, couldn't even protect her physically with his stupid arm.

The room was almost dark and he stood perfectly still. She must have been standing just as quietly.

He stiffened as he heard footsteps outside. Once there was a soft moan, and as whoever it was passed the room, they could hear his rasping breaths. Judson, presumably.

As his eyes grew more accustomed to the darkness, Gil saw Renie's silhouette outlined against the faint glow from the street lamps and realised she was still shaking. He couldn't leave her like that, just couldn't.

Giving in to instinct, he moved across the room and stopped beside her, whispering, 'I won't hurt you.'

She turned towards him, shoulders hunched, arms crossed over her chest holding the torn blouse in place.

He paused for a moment to give her time to back away if she didn't want him to touch her.

'My dear girl, what has that brute done to you?'

Only then did he take her in his arms, holding her loosely, making sure she knew she could move away if she wanted to.

But she didn't pull away; she moved closer, shivering and trying to control her sobs.

He cradled her against him with his good arm, and the bad arm chose that moment to jerk and flap about.

He felt humiliated by that. Fine hero he made. He moved his lips close to her ear and whispered, 'Sorry. I can't help my arm.'

Her voice was only just audible. 'The arm's part of you. It doesn't matter. You're normal and sane and kind. That's what really matters.' With a long sigh, she rested her head against his chest and they stood there for a few minutes, body against body, sharing comfort and warmth.

Gradually he felt her relax a little.

A few moments later, she took a deep breath and tried to move away, so he stepped back at once.

'Don't turn the lights up yet,' she begged in the barest thread of a voice. 'He might come back and see them.'

'We'll do whatever you want. Shall we sit down? There are two chairs.'

But she said in a rush, 'I'd rather you held me, if you don't mind. It makes me feel safe.'

'I'd love to. You could sit on my knee. You're not a big woman.'

Again, he had the satisfaction of comforting her.

After a while, he said, 'Do you want to tell me what happened?'

She did that in a halting whisper, giving the barest outline.

When she'd finished her tale, Gil couldn't hold back his anger. He'd seen the bruises and the torn clothing. 'A man like that ought to be whipped and locked away for the rest of his life.'

'Shh! Keep your voice down. He'll probably go on being the manager of this hotel or one like it, and hurting other women. There's nothing we can do.'

'There must be something.'

They fell silent again. Her head was warm against him, her hair tickling his nostrils. It smelt of soap.

'I'll leave as soon as it's light,' she said after a while. 'I can't impose on you.'

'Impose!' He let out a mirthless snort of laughter. 'It's my pleasure to help you, Renie . . . and it makes me feel better. Since my accident, I've felt so . . . useless.'

'Just because of your arm?'

He could hear the surprise in her voice and that pleased him. 'It makes me look like a badly made puppet.'

'You're a good-looking man still, with all your wits and in good health. What does that arm matter?'

He relaxed. 'You're good for me.'

'I am?'

'Yes. You make me feel . . . whole again.' He hesitated, then added, 'I've never forgotten you, you know. Not since the first time we met in Yew Tree Gardens. Tell me about your family. Are you going to them now?'

287

'I've still not heard from Nell or Mattie. And Nell won't be able to find me once I leave the Rathleigh.'

He could feel the dampness of her tears.

'I've remembered your sister's loss. It's hard to lose people you love.'

'You've lost them too. I only stayed here because if Nell comes to the hotel, *he* won't tell her where I am. He'll probably forbid people to even mention my name. Only I have to leave now . . . and I may never find her again.'

It was then the idea struck him, but he couldn't just rush into it, so he held on to the thought and merely said, 'We'll think of something. But in the meantime, you'll need somewhere to stay.'

'I've got money, so I can get some lodgings. I've saved up hard because I never wanted to be dependent on someone like my brother-in-law again. I'll be all right till I find another job, though it'll be harder without references. Or I can start a little business.'

He didn't want to lose her and the cosy darkness was ideal for confidences, so he took a deep breath and said, 'Or I could suggest something.'

'Oh? Do you know someone who needs a maid? I don't suppose I'll find another job like the one I was doing here.'

'Not a maid, no.' He told her about the bargain he'd made with his mother to marry within eighteen months. Before he continued, he turned up the lights a little, wanting to see her face as he asked her. 'I wonder if you'd consider marrying me instead?'

She gasped and said nothing.

'I feel very comfortable with you and I'm sure you'll be good with Beth.' He saw her expression soften and for the first time felt real hope.

'I feel comfortable with you, too, but Gil . . . I'm not of your class!'

'What does that matter if we get along well?'

She was frowning again. 'But your mother . . . doesn't she care who you marry? It sounds as if anyone would do.'

'I don't think she cares greatly, as long as it's someone respectable. She's almost given up hope of me, you see. People like my parents feel a man should marry and have children. It's what one does. Only I couldn't marry just anyone, not now. I'd like to marry you, though. You make me feel . . . a whole man still.'

'But — '

He took her hand. 'Don't say anything or I'll lose my courage.'

Her face softened a little as she looked at him. 'Does it take courage to ask me?'

'To ask anyone, given my problems.' He explained about his reaction to her. 'I don't want to marry a young woman of the sort my mother's been introducing me to. I'm no longer the empty-headed young idiot I used to be. And anyway, none of them have made me feel . . . as if I could do all that marriage entails. In bed, I mean.'

'Oh. I see. You would need to like the person you marry, wouldn't you?'

'Definitely. And I want someone with . . . a bit

of gumption. Someone like you.'

She frowned. 'But you hardly know me.'

'Sometimes you feel at ease with another person from the very first moment. We've been like that, haven't we? Able to talk to each other easily, even that first time in Yew Tree Gardens?'

She didn't speak but gave a quick nod.

'You can't tell yourself when to feel attracted. It just happens. Though I never thought it could happen so quickly.'

She stared down at her lap.

'Perhaps it isn't like that for you? Perhaps I'm seeing things that aren't there? If so, I won't trouble you again and I'll still help you to escape.'

She looked up. 'You're not imagining it. I do feel attracted to you . . . though I never believed it could come to anything, because we're from such different backgrounds. Yet tonight, I felt so safe with you, so cosy. So right.'

'Then, is there a chance you might say yes?'

The frown came back. 'I don't know. Could we spend some time together first, just a few days? I know people wouldn't approve of us doing that, but our whole lives and happiness depend on us getting on with one another, so it's important not to rush in blindly.'

His heart lifted. 'So you're not saying no.'

'I'm too upset to think straight, Mr Rycroft. I'm saying . . . perhaps.'

Relief made him feel dizzy for a few seconds, as if the room was whirling round him. 'Call me Gil. Please.'

'Gil.'

'Why don't you come and visit me at Oakdene? I promise you'll have your own bedroom. I won't . . . pester you for favours. Whether you accept my proposal or not, it'd give you a breathing space. And you can see whether you get on with Beth.'

'Yes, that's important too. I like children.' Silence ticked along for a few slow minutes, then Renie said, 'All right.'

Could a woman be as straightforward as that? he wondered. None of the women of his class were. In fact, he mostly didn't have a clue what they were thinking, and he'd watched his mother manipulate his father for years. He didn't want anyone manipulating him that way, as if he were a naughty child.

'Gil?'

'What? Sorry, my attention wandered for a moment.'

'There's just one thing. I don't want to see Judson again. I don't want anyone investigating what he tried to do, because he'll only blame me and say I egged him on. That's what always happens. And they might arrest me for wounding him. I don't even know how badly I cut his face.' She shuddered at the memory of slicing at him with the glass.

'I hope you've marked him for life.'

'I didn't want to do it.' She shivered and looked towards the window. 'It's nearly morning, soon be light. Could we get away from the hotel before people start work, do you think?'

'We can try. But you know the place better than I do. Can you think how to get out of the hotel without anyone seeing us? We can get away in the car.' He explained about Horry.

She gave him a beaming smile out of her poor, battered face and he just had to hug her.

'Why did you do that?'

'Because you smiled and you're so brave.'

'Oh. I'm not really.' She blushed.

'No other woman that I know could have fought him off. Sorry . . . you were saying?'

'If you have a car, that makes it much easier to get away. They keep the guests' cars in the old mews. If your Horry could bring the car to the back of the hotel, I could slip out up a chute from the basement, and hide in the car under a blanket, if you have one.'

'I'm sure we could do that. I'd better go and wake him.'

There was a knock on the door and he stiffened, then gestured to her to hide. She went to crouch on the other side of the bed.

When he opened the bedroom door, he found a woman there.

'Get her away from here,' she said, and ran off down the corridor.

He took a step forward and nearly fell over a suitcase. 'What the — ?'

He carried the case into the room. 'I think these are your things. A woman just left them. I'll go and tell Horry. He's only next door.'

After explaining, he brought Horry in to meet Renie.

'We'd better not leave too early. We don't want to look as if we're doing anything out of the ordinary. Can you bear to stay hidden in the car for a couple of hours, Renie? I don't think you'll be disturbed there.'

'I can pretend to work on the car, sir,' Horry said. 'I'll keep an eye on her, I promise you. Our car's at the end, so it'll be quite easy to hide in it.'

'Thank you.'

'Let me take her out, sir,' Horry said. 'You'll slow us down.'

'Damn this leg! Oh, sorry for my language, Renie.'

'It must be frustrating.' She turned to look at Horry. 'What if we meet Judson?'

'If he tries to attack you again,' Horry said quietly, 'I'll make sure he regrets it.' He led the way, taking the corridors she pointed out in whispers, and they made their way down to the basement.

They met no one and stopped to get a lamp from a cupboard and light it, as she indicated the way to the lowest level.

There, they stopped again as they heard faint footsteps.

Horry came to stand beside her. 'I'm as strong as he is.'

She shook her head, praying hard for it not to be Judson. It turned out to be one of the men who cleaned out the stables. He walked across where the two corridors met without even looking sideways.

'That's not him,' she whispered. She couldn't move for a moment or two from sheer relief, then Horry nudged her and she nodded, leading the way again.

As they climbed the narrow brick stairs to the rear yard, she tensed up again. What if . . . ? But there was no one around, so she let Horry walk across first to where the cars were kept. When he beckoned to say it was safe, she ran over to join him as fast as she could.

'This one.' He opened the car door, covered her with a rug, then opened the bonnet and stood with his back to the wall, a spanner in his hand.

She managed to watch through a gap in the blanket covering her. He was thumping the spanner against his hand, as if eager to use it as a weapon. He was a big, strong man too. She was safe now, surely?

As sleep tugged at her eyelids, she let them close, just for a minute . . .

* * *

Gil packed his bag and went down for an early breakfast. He ate quickly and went to the desk, where a clerk was just starting the day. 'As I said yesterday, I wish to leave early. Have you got my bill ready?'

The man fumbled through the contents of a drawer with narrow compartments but found nothing. 'Did you arrange for an early departure, sir?'

'Of course I did. Isn't it ready?'

'I'm sorry. Your bill must have gone astray. It won't take me a minute to write out a new one, sir.'

When that was done, Gil asked them to call

his chauffeur and send someone to bring down his luggage, before moving to wait outside the front door.

Horry brought the car round and Gil was escorted out to it by the doorman, who opened the front door of the car with a flourish, accepted his tip with a touch of his hat, and helped load the luggage. There was no sign of the manager.

Not until the car had pulled away did Gil glance into the back, expecting to see Renie looking at him.

'She's asleep, sir, still lying down under the blanket,' Horry whispered. 'She was exhausted, poor thing.'

'I'm rather tired, myself. I didn't get much sleep.'

'If you can doze off sitting upright, you go ahead and do it. I know my way back.'

As he closed his eyes and wriggled in a vain attempt to get more comfortable, Gil wondered if Judson would guess he'd been involved in helping Renie escape. He hoped not. But too bad if he did. Gil intended to make sure no one hurt her again.

★ ★ ★

The bitch had gone to ground. Someone must be sheltering her, only if they were, it wasn't immediately obvious which room she'd gone to.

Judson gave up the hunt because his face was hurting and blood was still trickling down his cheek. He pressed his handkerchief over the cut and groaned as he entered his suite.

He went into the bathroom and gasped as he saw what she'd done. Not only deep but long, the cut ran from his forehead down his cheek. That eye was closed and puffy, and he could see nothing out of it.

Rage filled him, but he didn't let it loose, because it was obvious he had to get help for his injuries.

How to explain this? He looked round the room, picked up his shaving mirror and smashed it on the ground. Then he took his handkerchief away from his face and smeared blood on the ground nearby. More blood dripped down as he worked.

He still couldn't see anything out of that eye. It must be because it was so swollen.

He went to get a clean handkerchief then stumbled out to the lift and rode down to the foyer.

The watchman stood up as he stumbled forward, feeling dizzy now.

'I've had an accident, cut my face. There's a doctor in number fifteen. Wake him up and ask if he'll see me. I'll be in my office.'

The doctor arrived, wearing a dressing gown. He sucked in a breath of shock as he examined the eye. 'You need specialist help for this. You may have injured your eyeball.'

'I'm not going to hospital.'

'But I'm not qualified to treat eyes!'

'Damn you, clean up the cut and I'll cover it with a patch. I'll be all right.'

The doctor drew himself up. 'I'm sorry, but I can't reconcile it with my conscience to do that.

You need specialist help if you're to save the sight in that eye.'

Judson stilled. '*Save the sight?* Is it that bad?'

'I'm afraid so.'

'If that bitch has blinded me, I'll make sure she pays for it.'

The doctor stared at him in shock. 'A woman did this to you? But you said you'd fallen.' Then his eyes narrowed. 'Why would anyone do that?'

'Never you mind.'

The doctor stepped away from him. 'I can't help you. You really do need to go to a hospital.'

Judson watched him go, then yanked the bell pull. He'd better keep his mouth shut about her doing this.

'Get me a cab. I need to go to hospital.' The room seemed to be wavering round him. 'Don't . . . disturb guests.'

He didn't regain consciousness fully till he was lying on a hospital bed.

They told him they'd have to operate, remove the injured eye, which was too badly slashed to save.

His last thought as the anaesthetic took effect was: once he recovered, he'd make sure she paid for it, by hell he would.

17

Gil woke before Renie did, not sure where he was for a minute. Oh yes, in the car. Going home. Good.

'She hasn't stirred,' Horry said quietly.

Not until they were almost at Oakdene did sounds from the back seat indicate that Renie was waking up.

'Is it safe to sit up?' she asked in a whisper. 'Are we out of sight of the hotel?'

Gil laughed. 'We're nearly at Oakdene. You've been asleep for hours. It's quite safe to sit up.'

He turned to see her staring round, hair tousled, face bruised. Something twisted in his heart at the sight of the bruise, the thought of Judson hurting her. And at that moment he admitted to himself that he loved her.

It surprised him — and yet, didn't really surprise him. She was very easy to love.

She returned his smile shyly. 'Sorry for falling asleep.'

'Why be sorry? It was the best thing you could do.'

'I haven't been sleeping well lately.'

'I'm not surprised. But you'll be quite safe at Oakdene, I promise you.'

When they arrived, she kept the blanket round her shoulders as she got out of the car, to hide her torn blouse.

But it was her face he was looking at. He

touched it gently with one fingertip. 'Oh, my dear girl, that bruise and swelling must hurt.'

'It's not too bad, but it must look awful.' She gave him a wobbly smile. 'Judson didn't get what he wanted. I fought him off and then you saved me. I wonder who packed my case?'

'An older woman, thin, that's all I could see.'

'It must have been Miss Pilkins. But I don't understand, because it was she who wrote the note that sent me down to the cellars.'

'*She did what?*'

Renie explained.

'I can't believe any woman would do that to another.'

'He must have threatened to dismiss her. She's the sole support of her invalid mother.'

'Even so. Anyway, let's forget about her for the moment. Come inside and meet everyone.'

He led the way into the kitchen and introduced her to the servants, saying quite openly, 'Miss Fuller was attacked last night in London, but she managed to fight off her attacker and escape. I'm sure you'll all want to help her.'

There were gasps, then Lizzie came and put an arm round Renie, drawing her towards the warmth of the stove. 'You poor thing! Would you like a bath first? If you've been sleeping in those clothes, you must feel all itsy-twitsy.'

Gil smiled. He loved Lizzie's made-up words.

Renie held out one hand to the warmth. 'I'd love a bath, if it's not too much trouble.'

'She can use the blue bedroom,' Gil said, making it clear she was a guest, not another servant.

Lizzie nodded. 'Do you have some clean clothes, Miss Fuller, or would you like to borrow some of mine? Though they'll drown you, because I'm much taller.'

'I have some clothes.'

Horry came in just then with her suitcase and Lizzie swept her upstairs.

It wasn't proper for a man to intervene, so Gil could only watch them go.

Madge Hilton set the stove to burn more quickly and heat the water, then looked across at him. 'You keep saving people, don't you?'

He smiled back. 'I've saved this one for myself, I hope.'

She raised her eyebrows. 'She must be special.'

'Very special. I've met her a time or two in London.' Thus, casually, he'd also ensured Renie a permanent place in the household, if she chose to accept it, and the respect of the other people who lived and worked there.

Now, all he had left to do was make sure Renie accepted his proposal. He thought she might, hoped she would. Not for the convenience of the arrangement, but because she liked him too. He was fairly sure of that.

He realised he was smiling foolishly and Madge was still watching him indulgently.

The words were out before he could stop them. 'I love her.'

Madge came and plonked an unexpected kiss on his cheek. 'About time you found someone.'

★   ★   ★

Renie let Lizzie and a younger maid bring up ewers of water, then they left her to take a bath in front of the fire like a lady, with a screen to hide her from view. She was still tired, but oh, it was wonderful to feel safe and lie in a tub of warm water.

She dipped the facecloth in the water and held it to her bruised face, murmuring at the comfort of that. The other women hadn't commented on the bruises. She hoped Gil would tell them what had happened. She didn't want to have to explain it to strangers, even kind ones.

Suddenly she realised she was ravenous, so didn't linger any longer in the water. When she'd dried herself on the big, soft towel, she wrapped it round her and checked the contents of the case someone had packed for her, looking for the most important thing of all, her savings bank book. Her heart pounded with panic when she didn't find it at first.

Calm down and check properly! she told herself, and started again.

They must have packed it in a hurry because things had been crammed in anyhow, all her decent clothes and the contents of her bedside drawers, though none of the things from her trunk in the attic. She could manage quite well on these and could buy others if only she had her bank book.

And then there it was, tangled in her nightdress. 'Oh, thank goodness!'

She finished getting dressed and lingered for a moment or two, staring at her bruised face in the mirror. She felt a bit shy of going downstairs. The house was so beautiful. How could a gentleman who was the owner of all this want to marry her? Only . . . the gentleman was Gil and he was like no one else she'd met before, not because of his arm but because of his kindness.

Perhaps he'd changed his mind about marrying her. He probably had, so she wouldn't say anything more about it until he spoke again.

But she could hope, couldn't she?

There was a knock on her door, and when she called to come in, Lizzie appeared again.

'Is there anything else you need, Miss Fuller?'

'No, thank you. My clothes are a bit crumpled but at least I feel clean and decent again.'

'Whoever attacked you must have thumped you hard. I hope you hit him back.'

Renie hesitated then decided on the truth. 'He was much bigger than me. All I had was a piece of broken glass, so I sliced his face for him.' She shuddered at that memory.

'Good for you, miss. Serves him right. Now, can I call Beth in? She's Mr Rycroft's niece and she's six, nearly seven. She's dying to meet you. We don't get many visitors here.'

'I'd love to meet her, too. Gil's told me about her.'

Beth mustn't have been far away because she was with them in a minute, standing shyly by Lizzie's side, staring at the visitor. 'Did you fall over?'

'A nasty man hit her,' Lizzie said before Renie could reply. 'So don't you ever talk to strangers, as I keep telling you, young lady.' She smiled at Renie. 'She'd talk to the moon if it said hello, this one would.'

'I'm sorry you're hurt, Miss Fuller,' Beth said. 'I hope your face gets better soon.'

Her concern warmed Renie. 'I'm sure it will.'

'Let's go down now and have something to eat,' Lizzie said briskly. 'We have high tea here, miss, not dinner.'

Renie looked at the tub of dirty water. 'I need to clear this up first.'

'Bless you, we'll do that. It's our job, after all. You let Beth take you down to the dining room and I'll make a start here. Oh! Shall I throw the blouse away? I don't think it's worth mending.'

'I never want to see it again.'

Beth slipped her hand in Renie's and tugged, so they went downstairs together.

The child said nothing, but she didn't let go. It was comforting, that little warm hand was. Like Lizzie's kindness.

In the sitting room, Gil was waiting for them, standing in front of a cheerful fire, even though the day wasn't cold.

Horry was reading a newspaper, but he put this down when he saw Renie. A much older man, who was sitting in an armchair staring into the flames, turned to give her a smile and she remembered meeting him in London a while ago. There was also an older lady, who was the governess.

They all went into the breakfast room and a maid brought in the food. Gil took the trouble of introducing the cheerful young girl as Dolly. Most people wouldn't have bothered to do that.

Everyone filled their plate and there was mainly silence as they ate.

'That's a wonderful apple pie,' Renie said, when she'd finished the dessert.

'The apples were grown in our own garden,' Walter told her. 'An old-fashioned type of tree, the fruit's a bit tart, but perfect for cooking.'

Renie didn't talk as much as the others, but she listened carefully to everything they said.

She especially enjoyed listening to the bright-eyed child, who was chatting to Gil about her day. No one told Beth to be quiet, as some families did when they brought their children to the hotel. How different that was from Renie's father, who had been such a bully she and her sisters had hardly dared open their mouths at table.

Gil didn't talk as much as the others, but every time Renie caught his eye, she saw his face soften into a smile. She couldn't help smiling back, even though it hurt her face. After one horrified glance sideways, she avoided looking in the big mirror over the fireplace.

After the meal was finished, the governess took the child away, waiting for Beth to give everyone a kiss, Renie included.

They began to chat about what Gil had found out in London. She hadn't thought a man with money would have problems that were hard to solve, but he did. Life was never perfect, was it?

It was only when someone touched her arm gently that Renie realised she'd nodded off.

'I'm sorry. How rude of me!'

'Nonsense,' said Walter. 'You're exhausted, lass. Anyone would be after what you've gone through. And Gil's been trying to hide his yawns as well. Why don't we all have an early night?'

'Good idea.' Gil stood up. 'I'll walk you up to your bedroom, Renie.'

Renie ran her fingers lightly up the banister rail as they walked up the stairs. 'I really like your house.'

'So do I. It was left to me by a very kind lady and it brought me out of an unhappy time after my accident.'

'I think your niece is lovely, too. She's a proper little chatterbox, isn't she?'

'Nowadays she is. When she came here at first, after losing her family, she was very quiet.'

At her bedroom door, he stepped back. 'Here we are. I hope you sleep well, Renie. There's a key on your side of the door, in case you feel nervous in a strange house.' He hesitated, then stepped forward to kiss her cheek. 'I haven't changed my mind about us getting married, in case you're worrying.'

'Are you sure?'

'Very. Especially now I've seen you with Beth and the others. You'll fit in well here.'

'That's easy to do. They're all so kind.' She raised one hand to touch his cheek, then felt shy of even this tiny intimacy and let it fall again. 'Good night.'

When she'd closed the door, she did lock it, but didn't move away. Leaning against it, she stared round the beautiful room. She felt as if she'd come to live in paradise.

And he hadn't changed his mind.

Could life really be so wonderful?

In London, the hotel staff were astonished to hear that Mr Judson had had a bad accident and had to be rushed to hospital. No one believed he'd fallen and cut himself on the shaving mirror because the maid who'd cleared it up said there were no long shards.

So how had he got hurt?

However it had happened, no one felt sorry for him. He was a nasty fellow, that one, not only the way he treated women members of staff, but the way he treated everyone. And no one had seen Irene this morning, had they?

It wasn't hard to put two and two together.

Good for her if she'd hurt him.

Miss Pilkins had been trying desperately to continue working as usual. She hadn't told anyone that Renie had left permanently and wasn't sure how to do that. But when the news about Judson broke, she could stand her own guilt no longer.

She knocked on Mrs Tolson's office door, didn't wait for an answer and nearly fell into the room. 'It's all my fault. I've done something dreadful.' She burst into tears, unable to hold her feelings back any longer.

'I was hoping you'd come and see me. Sit down and tell me about it.'

'I betrayed Irene, let that brute trap her and — ' She couldn't speak for sobbing, rocking to and fro, sure that any decent woman would hate her, sure that she'd lose her job.

It was a while before she could calm down

enough to explain the events of the night and Judson's threats not only to her job, but to her invalid mother's safety. She sat mopping her eyes, waiting to be dismissed.

'Irene must have stabbed him,' Mrs Tolson said, thinking it through. 'I thought he couldn't have caused so much damage with a shaving mirror. I hope she wasn't badly hurt.'

'She was well enough to run away. How bad is his injury?'

'The doctor staying at the hotel was worried he might lose the sight in one eye, insisted on him going to hospital.'

'Judson deserved all he got. He's a horrible man.' Another sob escaped Miss Pilkins and she mopped her eyes again. 'But he'll sack me when he comes back, I know he will.'

'Calm down, my dear. You're not going to lose your job, though I hope you'll learn from this and never, ever let anyone bully you into doing wrong again. Where do you suppose Irene went?'

'To that nice Mr Rycroft in number eight. I crept along the corridor after Judson had gone to his room and that was the only room where people were talking. If I didn't have such good hearing, I'd not have heard them myself. So I packed her things in a suitcase and took it to his room. I didn't see her. I just gave it him and ran.'

'So she's got her things? Good. Now, let me think what to do next.'

After a few moments, during which Miss Pilkins alternately sniffled and looked at her hopefully, she said, 'I think I'd better go down to Brighton and consult Mr and Mrs Carling about

Judson. They'll understand what to do in this situation better than their son will, because they went through some hard times before they made their fortune. They'll want us to keep this whole affair quiet, for the sake of the hotel's reputation, so I'm afraid he'll get away with it.'

Her companion shuddered. 'But Judson's bound to say something. He may even report her to the police for attacking him.'

'Just let him dare! Hmm. I suppose I'd better speak to him before I leave for Brighton. He definitely ought to be locked away for what he did, but how can anyone prove it? Perhaps we can use the threat of revealing all to stop him laying charges against Irene, though, make him think someone saw everything.' She looked severely at the other woman. 'I'm assuming you would be prepared to bear witness to his attack on her, if necessary? Did you see much?'

Miss Pilkins nodded. 'Not the actual attack, but I heard what he said. I hid nearby and saw him go into the storeroom. Then I heard Irene screaming for help. It was terrible. He taunted her. He's a wicked creature. Then he yelled in pain and she ran out with her clothing all torn.'

She gulped and mopped her eyes again. 'I was terrified he might kill her. I waited till they were out of sight and crept after them. I hid in that alcove on the fire stairs landing and saw him come in and out of the stairs. I think he must have searched every floor. But I didn't see Renie again.'

She bent her head and said in a muffled voice, 'I'm so ashamed of myself.'

'No time for that now. Pull yourself together. You'll have to take over from me at the hotel while I go down to Brighton to see the Carlings. And don't say a word about what really happened, not a single word to anyone.' Mrs Tolson got up, then stopped to ask, 'Oh, what about Irene's other possessions?'

'They're in her trunk in the attic, I suppose. I emptied all the things from her drawers into an old suitcase a guest had left behind.'

'The others will be quite safe in the attic. We'll leave them there till she sends for them.'

'How do we explain her absence?'

'Did the others know about her sister?'

'Yes.'

'Then it's easy to explain. She's gone to her sister. I'll tell Judson *I* helped her get away. I doubt he'll ever dare to come back here.'

She looked at her fob watch. 'I must hurry up and pack now. I doubt I'll be able to get back from Brighton until midday tomorrow. I'm trusting you to keep everything quiet in the meantime.'

'I'll do my very best . . . unless *he* comes back.'

★ ★ ★

At the nearby hospital, to which Judson had been taken, Mrs Tolson was shown to a ward with several beds down each side. He was lying in one of them with a big bandage round his head, covering one eye. She asked the nurse in charge if he could be put in a wheelchair and taken somewhere private, since she had some bad news to tell him and he might make a fuss. To her relief, that was agreed. From the looks they gave him, he wasn't a favourite patient.

She waited in a side room until he was wheeled in and made sure she was nearer the door than him, in case he attacked her. Though he didn't look at all well.

He squinted up at her. 'What do *you* want, Tolson?'

'To speak about what happened and arrange what to say.'

'As soon as they let me out of here, I'm going straight to the nearest police station to lay a complaint about Irene attacking me. There's no *arranging* needed. I only have to tell the truth. The bitch has blinded me in my left eye.'

Eunice abandoned any attempt to reason with him. He looked so wild, she was glad there were people within call. 'If you do that, I'll lay a few complaints against *you* on behalf of young women who work at the hotel. Whether the police can prove anything or not, I think my reputation is such that I'll be able to make sure you never get a job in a decent London hotel again.'

He gaped at her for a moment, anger colouring the pallor of his face suddenly, then he banged his clenched fist on the arm of his wheelchair. 'I'm *not* letting her get away with blinding me. I'm definitely going to the police and if *they* don't arrest her and charge her with attempted murder, I'll track her down and see how she likes it with only one eye.'

The chief nurse poked her head round the door. 'Keep your voice down, if you please, Mr Judson.' From the look on her face, she'd overheard what he said.

He scowled and waited till she'd gone to continue more quietly, though no less viciously. 'I meant what I said.' He plucked at the bandage as if it hurt, then studied her sourly. 'She came to you for help, didn't she?'

'Yes. I helped her leave the country. It seemed best then and you've confirmed that for me with what you've just said.'

'*What?* You interfering old biddy. I'll remember that and make sure *you* regret crossing me. And I'll still find out where she went. See if I don't. I'm not . . . not giving up. Not after this.' He fingered the bandage.

Clearly nothing she said or did would persuade him to change his mind. He was flushed, starting to ramble. She'd done her best, so stood up. 'I'm going down to see the Carlings. I think you can be sure you'll lose your job. If they'd still been in charge, you'd not have lasted this long at a Rathleigh hotel.'

She left to a hail of curses, thanked the nurse in charge, then went to Victoria Station and took the train to Brighton. She'd known the Carlings for many years and thought they'd listen to her about Judson, but she also had to protect Irene, so couldn't tell the complete truth to anyone.

She didn't know for certain where the poor young woman was now, though she hoped Mr Rycroft would keep an eye on her.

She was going to do her best to convince

everyone that Irene had left the country, even the young woman's own family, if they ever turned up.

Judson was a very dangerous man when crossed. If he went round making enquiries, she had to make sure he got the same answer everywhere.

★ ★ ★

Renie woke with a start, wondering for a moment or two where she was. Then she remembered and snuggled down again in the big, soft bed. She was safe. With Gil. And he'd said he meant it about marrying her.

Surely Judson wouldn't be able to get to her here?

She lay there until she heard people stirring, then got up, washed quickly in cold water and went downstairs, following the sound of voices into the dining room. She hesitated in the doorway, still feeling a little shy.

When Gil noticed her, he got up with a beaming smile to kiss her cheek and lead her to the seat next to his. 'Did you sleep well?'

'Better than I have for ages. Ooh, something smells wonderful.'

She let him serve her with a plate of fried eggs, bacon and kidneys. 'Isn't Beth up yet?'

'She has her breakfast in the schoolroom, then does lessons all morning.'

'Oh. I was looking forward to seeing her again.'

He grinned. 'We can always interrupt them. I

do that sometimes on fine days, because I think children should get plenty of fresh air.'

'Could we interrupt them today? I'd like to make sure I get on with her.'

'Good idea.'

His eyes were so warm on her face she felt herself blushing. Walter winked at her from across the table.

There was one person still missing. 'Isn't Horry coming to breakfast?'

'He's been and gone. He's an early bird, our Horry. He wanted to check the car and then work on an idea he has for an improved motor car engine.'

'How clever he must be!'

After breakfast Gil took Renie up to the schoolroom, where Beth was reading a poem aloud. She didn't notice them and they stood in the doorway to listen:

He thought he saw a Rattlesnake
That questioned him in Greek:
He looked again, and found it was
The Middle of Next Week.

Beth stopped reading. 'That's silly.'

'It's meant to be,' her governess said. 'It's meant to make you laugh. We'll start reading *Alice in Wonderland* next.'

'I love that story,' Renie said without thinking.

Beth turned round and clapped her hands. 'Good morning, Miss Fuller. Are we going for a walk, Uncle Gil?'

'Whatever makes you think that?'

She got up, so sure of her welcome in his arms that Renie's eyes grew moist. This was how children should be treated.

Beth turned to her. 'Did you really like the story, Miss Fuller?'

'Yes, I did. I never did anything that was fun when I was at school, and I went to work in the laundry as soon as they let me leave school. My father wanted the money and he didn't believe in educating women. Thank goodness for libraries! My sisters and I were always borrowing books. You're lucky to be able to read stories that are fun.' She smiled at the governess as she spoke.

'Well, we have plenty of books here, so if you want to read some more nonsense verse, I can find you several books of it. Miss Bennerden must have had a wry sense of humour.' Gil turned to the governess. 'Would you mind if we interrupted for just an hour, Miss Bramber? I promise to bring Beth back then.'

'Would it matter if I did?' She waved one hand dismissively, an indulgent smile on her face.

He held out his good hand to his niece. 'Come along, young lady. We'll show Miss Fuller the gardens.'

They walked out through the French windows in the sitting room.

Renie stopped almost immediately. 'Oh! Look at all the flowers! Already! And everything's so green.'

She followed Gil past flowers, shrubs, through a vegetable garden, with neat rows of young plants, to a swing hanging from a big old tree. There were wooden seats here and there,

314

tempting you to sit.

'I shan't recognise all the flowers and plants because I've never spent much time in gardens.'

'Beth and I will teach you. You could bring a book out here this afternoon and sit reading in the summer house. It catches the sun nicely. I'm afraid I have to see someone, so can't join you.'

After luncheon, Renie did just that, sitting in a delightful little summer house, feeling guilty at not working. She didn't intend to go into the village until her face got better, though. She didn't want people to see her looking like this.

She found herself dozing and gave in to temptation, leaning her head back. Just as she was nodding off to sleep, she thought she heard footsteps and jerked awake again. But when she glanced round outside, she could see no one.

That was strange. She was sure she'd heard something in the bushes.

Then Gil called her name. He came across to join her from another direction so it couldn't have been him she'd heard moving about.

She forgot about the footsteps in the pleasure of chatting to him. They never seemed to run out of things to say.

She was already sure that if he didn't change his mind, she'd accept his proposal.

He didn't love her, just wanted to find a wife. But he liked her, felt comfortable with her and maybe he'd grow fonder of her as time passed. She'd grown to love him, though. How could she not, when he was so wonderful? She'd been foolish enough to dream about him since the very first time they met.

As for Beth, she was a delightful child. It would be a pleasure to help raise her, and other children too, perhaps.

Could life really be this good?

If only Renie could find her sisters again, it'd be more perfect than her wildest dreams.

18

Eunice arrived in Brighton, deeply worried about what she had to do. The older Carlings lived in a suite at the Brighton Rathleigh and she was shown straight up to it.

To her dismay she found Dennis Carling visiting his parents.

He stood up and gave her a dirty look, not even having the common politeness to suggest that she sit down.

'Perhaps it's as well you came, Mrs Tolson. We need to do something about the vicious attack on Mr Judson.'

She was startled by this and had to catch her breath before she could respond. 'It's the other way round: it was he who attacked a young woman.'

'He told me about her claim. They always say that. It's only her word against his. I'm afraid she's taking you for a fool.'

Maurice Carling cleared his throat. 'Just a minute, Dennis. You've only heard one side of the story, and that was on the telephone, not face to face. And what a way to greet a visitor, who's also an old friend. My dear Eunice, do please sit down. May we order some tea for you?'

'I'd rather settle this matter first, if you don't mind, Maurice.' She looked at him and his wife. 'Have you ever known me lie to you?'

It was Lois Carling who answered that without

317

hesitation. 'Never. Nor are you a fool.' She frowned at her son when he started to speak and he snapped his mouth shut.

'There was a witness to what happened,' Eunice said. 'Judson didn't know about that when he concocted his tale. Unfortunately, the witness was too frightened of him to intervene.' She explained what had really happened.

Dennis sat frowning. 'It's still the young woman's word against that of a man I know and respect. And I gather she was rather lax in morals.'

'She was not! She was a quiet and hard-working young woman.'

'She had you fooled there. She was leading Mr Judson on all the time.'

'He's lying. I've known him for several years, have worked with him before, and he's annoyed other young women during that time. I've had to speak to him about it more than once. Some of them even left our employment because they were frightened of him.'

'That's a very serious allegation, Mrs Tolson. Are you quite sure of this?'

'I'd stake my life on it being true.'

He was speechless for a moment.

'Is the young woman all right?' Lois asked. 'Do we need to help her?'

'She's all right, though her face is somewhat battered from where Judson beat her.' Eunice found the next lie came more easily than she'd expected. 'She's terrified of him, though, so I helped her escape to France, where she has a friend.'

'France?' Lois looked at her in shock.

'I was afraid Judson would go after her. After all, his job is at stake . . . surely?'

'He can hardly go after anyone at the moment,' Dennis said. 'His injured eye needs attention. That's why he telephoned me from the hospital to ask my help. And, I might add, what sort of woman slashes a man's face with a piece of broken glass? That's not a sign of respectability.'

'On the contrary. Irene had no other weapon and was in danger of being raped. I'd have done the same myself.' She saw Lois suck in her breath at this blunt speaking, so pressed the point. 'I firmly believe he'll go after her again once he recovers.'

'Of course he won't!' Dennis glared at her.

'He said he would when I went to see him in hospital. He was . . . very unreasonable.'

'Well, I'll believe you over him any time,' Lois said. 'You have no reason to lie to us and we've known you for more than thirty years. That poor girl! I can't bear to think of this happening to her in our hotel.'

'Judson must be dismissed,' Maurice said. 'We can't have such people working for us. What if he attacks a customer?'

'He's a good manager,' Dennis insisted. 'I'll talk to him about it, make sure he changes his ways.'

'I've already talked to him more than once and so did Mr Greaves. When Judson was younger and working at the various hotels in a lesser capacity, he spent some time at the London

Rathleigh. Mr Greaves spoke to you then, I believe, Mr Carling, worrying about him, without telling you his name. And you said to give him a second chance.'

'I'd forgotten that,' Maurice said. 'Was it him? Are you sure?'

'Yes. It was at my instigation.'

She looked at Dennis as she added, 'Each time we spoke to him, he promised not to behave like that again, but he didn't change much, simply became more cunning.'

'But he's such a good manager,' Dennis protested. 'Makes the hotel very profitable.'

She glared at him. 'Don't you care about the women he's upset, or the women he'll continue to upset?' When he didn't answer, she said firmly, 'I regret to tell you that if Judson continues to work at any of the Rathleigh hotels, I shall tender my resignation.'

'She's right, and I've spoken to you before about this,' Maurice told his son. 'Money isn't everything. The man must go. And if I ever hear of anyone else in our employ molesting the young women who work for us, I shall myself take action against them.'

'Think if it were your sister, Dennis dear,' Lois said.

He turned to Eunice. 'You're sure of your facts about this incident?'

'Absolutely certain.'

'Then Judson was lying to me.'

'We can't leave Miss Fuller on her own overseas, surely?' Lois asked. 'She must be brought back and reinstated.'

'I think it'd be best to leave her where she is. She's with friends who'll protect her. Even if he's dismissed, I fear Judson will still seek revenge if he can find her.'

Eunice stayed the night at the hotel, dining with the older Carlings. In the morning she went back to London. Dennis accompanied her. He was to go and see Judson at the hospital and dismiss him, then take over at the hotel till a new manager could be appointed.

Eunice watched him bustle around. She could have done the manager's job, knew more about it than Dennis, but even Mr and Mrs Carling would never consider a woman for that post. Life wasn't fair.

* * *

Two days after their arrival at Oakdene, Mr Mortlake sent a messenger with a letter from Chapman's lawyer, again demanding a share of the inheritance. Mr Mortlake's note said: *I was so sure of what you would want me to do, I've written back to say we do not accept their view of the situation and you won't be paying out any of your inheritance to Chapman.*

Gil told the others what had happened, then frowned. 'Why do I feel we've not heard the last of this?'

'Because Chapman's a villain,' Horry said.

The next day Gil was accosted by Chapman in the village. The fellow must have been waiting in the garden to speak to him when he went out for his usual early morning stroll.

'What do you want here?' he demanded.

Chapman glared at him. 'I want my inheritance.'

'You're not legally entitled to anything.'

'I'm morally entitled. I was her only close relative.'

'So closely related that no one can trace the connection.' Gil turned to leave.

Chapman moved to bar his path. 'You may find you change your mind. You wouldn't want those you love getting hurt, would you? Think about it.'

He smiled, then walked off without a backward glance, leaving Gil still gaping in shock.

He hurried to tell the others what had happened, adding, 'Don't go outside in the garden on your own, Renie, or let Beth go, either.'

★ ★ ★

A few days passed and nothing happened, but Renie took care not to leave the garden when she played with Beth because she couldn't bear it if anything happened to such a delightful little girl. Just before teatime on a day of showers and cloudy skies, the sun came out.

'Can we play catch?' Beth begged.

Renie looked outside. 'Just for a while.'

When she grew breathless, she insisted they needed a sit down. 'I'm not young like you.'

'I'll go and pick us an apple each,' Beth said. 'It's still a long time before dinner and they're delicious straight from the tree.' She didn't wait for an answer but hurried off down one of the narrow paths through the garden.

322

Renie had just sat down on the bench when she heard the child cry out. But the cry was cut off abruptly.

Had Beth fallen?

'Beth? Are you all right?'

There was no answer, but there was a scuffling sound beyond the bushes.

Worried, Renie rushed down the path Beth had taken. 'Beth? Beth, answer me!'

As she turned into an open space near the kitchen garden, she saw Beth struggling in the arms of a man who had a sack over his head with eyeholes cut in it. 'Stop that! Let her go, you brute!'

He picked up the child, still keeping one hand over her mouth.

'Help! Someone help me! He — '

Someone grabbed Renie from behind and a heavy hand was clasped over her mouth. She tried to kick the person, but it wasn't possible to kick hard enough in a backwards direction and the man was so big, he was easily able to control her.

She couldn't believe this was happening a second time. Had Judson tracked her down? Or was this to do with Chapman?

Her attacker threw her to the ground and pressed her face down so hard she got a mouthful of earth. She struggled in vain, half smothered, as he tied her hands behind her back, then he stuffed a piece of cloth in her mouth, still keeping her face down. All she could see of him was his boots, heavy working boots, one tied with a piece of twine.

She waited, terrified of what he was going to

do next, but nothing happened. When she rolled over, there was no sign of her attacker . . . or of Beth.

It was difficult to get to her feet with her hands tied behind her back and it took her a while. The cloth was tied so tightly she couldn't remove it to call for help, even when she rubbed her face against a tree.

Staggering, shocked, terrified for little Beth, she stumbled along the path towards the house, moaning in relief when she heard someone cry her name.

Within seconds, Gil was there. He managed to untie the gag, but the twine that tied her hands was knotted so tight it was digging into her flesh.

'Never mind me. They've taken Beth.'

'*What?*'

'She went to pick some apples and I heard her cry out. When I ran to see what was wrong, I saw a man carrying her away. Another man pushed me to the ground and tied me up. I didn't even see his face.'

Gil lost every vestige of colour. 'Let's get that rope cut off your hands.'

'You get Horry and go after her. Someone else can help me.'

He insisted on going with her to the kitchen. 'Help Miss Fuller. She'll tell you what happened.' Yelling for Horry, he hurried off back towards the path.

Lizzie, who was having a cup of tea with Madge, got a sharp knife and cut the twine. It took a while. 'The brutes! They didn't need to tie it so tightly. It's dug right in and cut you. You'll have bruises on your wrists.'

'I don't matter.' Renie explained that someone had kidnapped Beth.

There was dead silence in the kitchen, then Lizzie stood up. 'I'm going to look, too.'

'You can't do much against a strong man,' Renie said. 'You might make it worse.'

Lizzie stopped for a moment, frowning in thought, then said, 'I can get my brothers out looking, though. If my little love is still in the village, they'll find her, if anyone can. They're into everything, the little monkeys.'

She was gone before anyone could stop her.

★   ★   ★

Gil followed Horry into the village, unable to keep up. When he got to the green, he found Horry questioning an old man.

'No one came this way,' the fellow was insisting. 'I'd ha' seen 'em, for sure.'

'But they must have come through here.'

'There are all sorts of ways through the village, zur. In and out of gardens, through the back of the churchyard. All sorts.'

Gil laid a hand on his friend's arm. 'We'll go straight to see Chapman. We'll beat it out of him if we have to.'

'He's in the pub,' the old man called. 'Went in there an hour or more ago. Hasn't come out that I've seen.'

'That means he's got someone else to do the dirty work,' Gil said.

'What's the matter?' the old man asked.

'Someone's kidnapped my niece.'

The man jerked upright. 'That little lass as 'as lost her parents?'

'Yes. My fiancée saw someone kidnap her, but they tied Renie up so she couldn't follow them.'

'Dear-oh-Lord, whatever will happen next?' He raised his voice. 'Jem? Jem, get out here this minute.'

A man looked out of the smithy, a burly fellow with a big hammer in his hand. 'What's up, Granddad?'

Gil left the old man to explain and led the way into the pub. Chapman was sitting there with a couple of men from the village.

Gil marched up to the table. 'What have you done with her?'

Chapman gave a knowing smile. 'I don't know what you mean.'

'My niece. What have you done with her?'

The landlord came across to join them. 'We don't want no trouble, Mr Rycroft.'

'This fellow's kidnapped my niece. If she's hurt in any way, I'll make sure he pays for it.'

Chapman laughed. 'You couldn't fight a scarecrow, let alone someone who can fight back. And if you continue to threaten me, I'll complain to the police.'

The landlord frowned. 'When did this happen, Mr Rycroft?'

'About a quarter of an hour ago.'

'Well, then, there's one thing certain: Mr Chapman couldn't have done it. He's been sitting here for an hour or more. I'd ha' known if he even went out to the privy.'

'Then he's arranged for someone else to do it.'

'I can see you need convincing.' Chapman stood up. 'Let's go to my house. You can search it from top to bottom and you'll find no one there.'

Which meant, Gil guessed, that Beth wasn't being held there. But he still had to search, in case it was a bluff. 'Very well.'

Chapman turned to the landlord. 'I'd be grateful if you'd come with me, Ozzie. I don't intend to put up with being manhandled, and I want this matter settled once and for all.'

In grim silence, the group of men walked out of the pub and across the green, then down a short lane to Chapman's house. To his chagrin, Gil again couldn't keep up.

'Oh dear, walking too fast, am I?' Chapman threw his head back and laughed. 'As if a cripple like you could look after anyone.'

'Mind your mouth or I'll mind it for you,' Horry growled. 'And Mr Rycroft has a lot of friends who feel the same.'

'If they're all like you, heaven help him.'

They were at the house by then. Chapman flung open the door and stood with arms folded. 'Go on! Search. I'll wait for you here.'

By that time, others had joined them, including some women, one telling another what had happened.

'We'll all go inside,' Jem said.

It took half an hour to search the house, which they did from the attics to the cellars. When they'd finished, Horry and Jem went to find Gil, who was pacing up and down the hall.

'She isn't here.'

'Then he's got her hidden somewhere else.'

'Are you sure it's him, sir?' Jem asked.

'As sure as I'm breathing,' Gil said. 'No one else would have kidnapped that child.'

'But why would he do it?'

'He's claiming a share of my inheritance. He threatened me the other day, though he made sure there were no witnesses. Said I'd regret it.'

Jem frowned and looked thoughtfully at Chapman. 'Wouldn't hurt to search the whole village. I don't like to think of a child being took.'

'You go and wait on the village green, sir,' Horry urged. 'We'll all report to you and then you can keep track of what's going on.'

* * *

Bitter that he couldn't do more to help, Gil went to sit on a wooden bench given to the village by Miss Bennerden. He sat rubbing his aching leg as people gathered at doors and garden gates. Some scowled at him, clearly on Chapman's side, others gave him sympathetic looks.

A woman came hurrying down the path leading from Oakdene. Renie. He felt better just to see her.

She came to sit on the bench beside him and he picked up her arm, looking at the weal on her wrist.

A woman who'd come to join him stopped to look. 'Whatever happened to you, miss?'

'Someone tied me up when they kidnapped Beth.'

'I'll fetch you some goose grease, and my daughter's got the kettle on. I'll bring you a cup of tea. It's a comfort, a cup of tea is.'

Mrs Wyndham made her way across to join them, with one or two of her friends. Most of the men were still out searching.

One by one they came to report their inability to find any sign of the little girl.

They gathered in groups, murmuring, jerking round when any new person came into view.

'Do you want to come and sit in my front room, sir?' Mrs Wyndham asked. 'You and the young lady.'

Gil realised most of them didn't know Renie, so introduced her, adding, 'We're engaged to be married.'

'That's a blessing for you.'

'Heaven help her with a husband like that,' someone called.

Jem marched across to the smaller group of men and shoved one so hard, he stumbled backwards.

'Here, what do you think you're doing, Jem Rossley?' The man shoved him back.

'Making you mind your manners, Shep Horton.'

It looked as if a fight was about to erupt, with other men taking sides.

★   ★   ★

Renie had been staring at them idly, more concerned about Gil's feelings than the crowd around them. Suddenly she noticed Shep's boots

329

and bounced to her feet. Most of the men were wearing very similar footwear, but one of his was tied with twine, the same sort of twine that had been used on her wrists.

'It was him!' she yelled, pointing. 'He was the one who tied me up. He's one of them.'

The men around him stepped back quickly, but Horry grabbed him as he turned to run.

'Where is she?' He shook Shep hard.

'I don't know what you're talking about.'

Horry drew his fist back and punched Shep, knocking him to the ground.

Jem joined in, hauling him to his feet by the front of his jacket and shaking him like a rat. 'Let me deal with him. I've been itching to give him a thrashing ever since he kicked my dog and broke her back.'

As his fist connected with Shep's cheek, the crowd gasped, but no one stepped forward to help till Chapman came striding across the green.

'Stop! What the hell do you think you're doing?'

The group of Gil's supporters at once surrounded him protectively, but Chapman wasn't interested in him.

'Lay one finger on me and I'll have you up before the magistrate. Let me through.'

Reluctantly they fell back, but even as they did so, Horry laid into Shep again.

He lay on the ground, winded and groaning in pain.

'Get up, man!' Chapman said.

'Stay away from me, you. This is all your fault. I said we shouldn't take the little girl.'

Breaths were sucked in all around them and

suddenly women were joining the circle.

'I don't know what you're talking about.' Chapman started to walk away, shoving people aside and yelling, 'You've searched my house. She isn't there. This is nothing to do with me.'

Mrs Wyndham yelled, 'Stop him! I've remembered something.'

The men immediately regrouped around him.

'I'd like it if I have to force you to stay here, Chapman,' Horry said with quiet menace.

'He borrowed the church key. I saw him take it yesterday.' She pointed her finger at Shep, who cringed. 'And I saw him coming out of the churchyard this afternoon.'

Chapman laughed, but it sounded forced. 'Go and search the church, then. You'll not find the girl there.'

But a lad pushed through the crowd as he spoke, followed by Lizzie. 'I know a hiding place in the crypt. I bet she's in there.'

Renie watched Chapman lose his smile, watched anxiety replace it and knew they'd found the answer. 'Can you take us to the hiding place, lad? Jack, isn't it?'

The boy nodded. 'Only don't get mad at me. We only play there sometimes on rainy days an' we don't do no harm.'

'No one will get mad at you, I promise.'

★ ★ ★

Gil stood up. 'I'll go with young Jack. I don't want anyone frightening my girl.'

Renie went to walk by his side and Mrs

331

Wyndham followed her.

The crowd held back, silent for the most part, though some were muttering to one another. Others made sure Chapman didn't get away, ignoring his threats. Jem and Horry kept an eye on Shep, prodding him to go with them. One of his eyes was puffy and closed, there was a graze on his jaw and he was limping.

The front church door was locked.

'Try the side one,' a woman called.

The side door was locked as well.

'Where's the key?' Gil asked Chapman.

'How should I know? This is nothing to do with me.'

Mrs Wyndham pushed forward. 'Try the back of the offering box in the church porch. I doubt there'll be anything else inside. That's where the curate hides his key because it's a heavy old thing.'

There were one or two mirthless sniffs. No one liked the curate's idea of what they called 'the begging box', so no one from the village put extra money into it. They put their pennies into the collection box on alternate Sundays and that was enough.

One of Lizzie's brothers ran round to the front door and returned carrying the box.

It rattled as Gil took it from him. He undid the hasp at the back and tipped out a large key.

Mrs Wyndham took the key from him. 'There's a trick to this door.' She slid it into the lock, tugged the door towards her and then the key turned. 'There.' She stepped back and gestured to him.

Gil beckoned to Lizzie's brother, who led the

way confidently down the worn stone steps to the crypt. No one pushed ahead of Gil's slow, limping pace. And they made sure Chapman and Shep stayed with them, guarded by Jem and Horry.

In the crypt the lad went to one corner, behind a raised grave. 'You have to push it here.' Something clicked and a stone slid away, to reveal a low doorway.

'About time,' a voice said from inside. 'You said I'd not be here for long, Mr Chapman. I want my money now and you can look after her. She's a cheeky little devil, this one.'

'Shut up, you fool!'

A man stuck his head out of the opening, gasped and yelled in shock as Horry yanked him out through it by the front of his shirt and slammed him against the nearest wall.

Renie didn't wait to see what happened to him, but bent down and eased herself into what proved to be quite a big space. 'Beth love, we've come to rescue you.'

There was the sound of a child sobbing, and Gil pushed forward, ignoring his arm as it knocked against the entrance stone, managing somehow to get inside as well.

Renie was already cradling a sobbing Beth, making hushing noises and rocking her. 'You're safe now, my darling, safe from those men.'

Beth sniffed and tried to cuddle her uncle and Renie at the same time.

A woman next to Beth's captor slapped his face good and hard. 'I'll never speak to you again, you brute. A little lass like that. She must have been terrified.'

'Shh,' Gil called. 'Don't frighten her.'

'She don't frighten easy, that one,' her captor said. 'Who do you think bit my hand?'

'Good for her!' someone called. 'I'd like to set my dog on you. Frightening a child as has already gone through so much.'

Gil and Renie eased themselves and Beth out of the hidden chamber and she stared round, wide-eyed.

'See how many people came to rescue you,' Renie whispered.

But Beth was staring at Chapman. 'He said he'd hurt me if you didn't give him money. I heard him. He's a bad man.'

'Don't come much worse than him,' Horry agreed.

The anger among the crowd was almost tangible, it was so strong. If the village constable hadn't turned up just then, more violence might have erupted against the three kidnappers.

A dozen people tried to explain to him at once what had happened.

'Let's get Beth home,' Gil said. 'Can you walk, darling?'

'Yes. But I want to hold your hand and Renie's. Oh, and there's Lizzie.'

They took the child away, leaving Horry and the villagers to make sure Chapman and his cronies were safely locked away.

Gil was limping badly now. Renie's wrists were throbbing and swollen, but both were smiling as they chatted to the child and tried to ease her fears.

'I knew you'd rescue me,' Beth said to her uncle.

'Did you?'

'Yes. Because I know how much you love me.' His voice was thick with tears. 'I do.'

'I love you as well,' Renie said.

Beth looked at her. 'You're nice. I like you being here.'

'And that man will be locked away so that he can never hurt you again.'

The little girl smiled tiredly. 'That's good. So when you marry my uncle, Miss Fuller, we can all live happily ever after, like in the story books. Can I be your bridesmaid?'

'Of course. With a pretty new frock.'

As they reached the house, Lizzie moved forward. 'It must have been very dirty in that hidey-hole. Your clothes are all tuzzled up. Every one of you needs a wash and change of clothes. I just hope we have enough hot water. Let me run and tell them in the kitchen, then I'll bathe this young lady for you.'

She was back within a couple of minutes. 'Come on, missie.' She held out her arms and Beth went running into them.

Gil stopped for a moment to watch Beth walk up the stairs with her nursemaid. 'I hope this doesn't give that child nightmares.'

'If it does, she'll have plenty of people to cuddle her and make her feel better. Let's go and have a wash.' Renie reached out to brush a cobweb off his jacket.

'Come and chat to me afterwards. You and I have some wedding arrangements to make.' He stepped closer and kissed her cheek, then turned towards his own bedroom.

Renie lingered to watch him go then went into her bedroom. Now all she had to worry about was Judson and where her sisters were.

Surely he wouldn't dare attack her again?

Surely she would find them again one day?

19

Mrs Tolson saw him coming from the landing window and went running to tell Dennis Carling. They stood by the window of his office, staring down at the street.

'It's him, isn't it? Judson,' she said anxiously. 'Where do you suppose he's been all this time?'

'Who knows? I'd hardly have recognised him, he's changed so much. He was always so well turned out.'

'He looks haggard and ill. Good heavens, he's coming across to the hotel!'

'I don't like the expression on his face. He looks absolutely furious. Better get some strong men. He's dangerous and violent.'

'Nonsense. He and I have always got on well. I'll speak to him, offer him some money if he needs help. He'll go quietly after that. You'll see.'

She watched Dennis go, fear clutching her heart. She didn't think Judson would listen to reason. In fact, she was so sure of it, she went running to the porters' office, taking care not to be seen from the foyer.

'Judson's come back,' she told the two men on duty, 'and I'm afraid he's going to attack Mr Carling. Do you think you could find something to do in the foyer and stay nearby?'

They looked at her in shock. 'Are you sure, Mrs T?'

'Very sure. Please. Go now.'

One of the porters took hold of a trolley and put a suitcase on it. The other one picked up a broom and began to sweep the floor near the door.

Other eyes were on Judson, but he'd spotted Eunice and was looking only at her. Oh, heavens! She'd let herself be visible through the open door of the porters' room.

He began striding across the foyer towards her, pushing people out of his way.

When Dennis Carlson approached him, Judson flat-handed him away violently, sending Dennis tumbling across the floor.

Eunice turned and ran, hearing the heavy footsteps thumping along behind her.

By that time customers were calling out and huddling together behind luggage or furniture. One woman began screaming but no one paid her any attention. The staff had all abandoned their duties and were also seeking shelter, except for the two porters and the commissionaire, but even they hesitated to approach such a wild-looking man.

Eunice fled up the stairs, but she wasn't young and nimble, and couldn't gain any advantage over him. He was behind her, cursing her, threatening her.

Just as she passed the lift, it stopped and the pageboy yanked her into it. He slammed the outer metal grill that served as a door to prevent customers walking into the lift well.

Closing the inner grill he locked it and set the lift in motion. It began to sink slowly down, then stopped part way.

Judson reached them, separated only by the metal grills. He reached out and shook the outer one, roaring curses and threats at her.

For a moment she thought he'd get to her, then slowly the lift began to move again. The last sight she had was of his legs and shoes.

'When we get to the ground floor, run for help,' the lad said.

But before they got there, they heard the screeching of metal above them.

'What's he doing?' the lad gasped.

'It sounds as if he's forced the outer grill open. Surely he can't do that?'

'I mustn't have shut it properly. But the lift ought not to have set off if both doors weren't closed. What's he doing up there?'

They could hear muffled shouting and roaring, but they couldn't see anything.

'I'm going right down to the basement, Mrs T. I know a room we can lock ourselves into, so even if he follows us down, he won't catch us. We can stay there till someone rescues us.'

They passed the foyer, watching people looking upwards, hearing people shouting, 'No!' or 'He can't!' or simply crying out in panic.

Two voices sounded louder than the rest, two men yelling at one another.

Then the sounds became muffled as the top of the lift passed the foyer and moved down again to the basement.

'It isn't far, Mrs T. Be ready to run.'

She nodded, but glanced up as someone began to yell again. It sounded like Judson.

Dennis Carling chased up the stairs behind Judson, too late to help Mrs Tolson, but not too late to see Judson heaving at the lift door, shaking the metal grill and shouting loudly.

The man must have run mad. He was trying to open the grill without a lift there. Well, it wouldn't work. There was a fail-safe to stop that.

Dennis came to a halt, not sure what to do next. To his horror, Judson did manage to haul the door part-way open. He stuck his head into the lift well, shouting down it, his voice booming and echoing, so that it was hard to make out what he was saying. It sounded like threats and curses.

The porters joined Dennis.

'He's mad as a hatter,' one of them said. 'Shall we catch him and lock him up? If you help us, sir, we should be strong enough.'

'We'll have to try, or he may attack the customers.'

The three of them crept towards Judson, but he must have heard them, because he swung round to face them.

'Stay back. I want to see where they go to. I'm going to strangle that bitch if she doesn't tell me where she's hiding Renie.'

As he turned to peer down the lift well again, the porters nodded to one another and all three men rushed towards him.

They grabbed him and tried to drag him back, but he fought them every inch of the way, landing a lucky blow on one porter's face that sent him spinning backwards.

'Come away, man!' Dennis panted, trying to keep hold of the heaving, bucking body. 'You'll fall.'

'If I fall, you'll go with me.' Judson clamped his hand on Dennis's jacket and tugged.

With a yell, Dennis let go of him and grabbed for the metal grill. The porter beside him stopped trying to tackle Judson at exactly the same moment.

The other porter had stood up by now and grabbed them both, hauling them backwards.

With a yell, Judson tried to regain his balance, reaching out to grab Dennis, but he missed. It seemed to happen very slowly. Arms flailing, he teetered on the edge of the lift well, then suddenly vanished from view.

There was a thump from down the lift well, then silence.

Dennis crawled to the gap and peeped cautiously down.

Judson was lying on top of the stationary lift cage on his back, eyes open, staring up in frozen surprise.

Dennis had seen that look before after a street accident. He edged back. 'He's dead.'

Silence, then, 'Let me help you to your feet, sir. Nasty shock, you've had.'

Dennis shuddered. 'If you hadn't been there to help, he'd have taken me with him.'

'I don't think he meant to kill himself,' the other porter said. 'Did you see the look of surprise as he fell. I'll not forget that as long as I live, not if I live to be a hundred, I won't.' He gulped and suddenly leant over a nearby ornamental plant and vomited.

'We need to call the police,' Dennis said, trying to pull himself together. If only he could stop shaking, he might manage to take charge again.

A man touched his shoulder, making him jump. 'Come and sit down. I'm a doctor. There's nothing you can do for that poor soul. Someone should call the police and fetch these men some hot, sweet tea.'

'What about Mrs Tolson and the pageboy?' one of the porters said suddenly. 'Do you think they're still in the lift?'

'I'll go down and check. They might not know they're safe.' His companion vanished through the emergency door.

Dennis gave up trying to take control. He had only enough energy to stagger along to his office and sink down in his chair, shuddering and struggling not to be sick.

★ ★ ★

A voice was calling, 'Mrs Tolson! Mrs Tolson, where are you? Are you all right?'

'That's Monsieur Leduc,' she said, pressing her ear to the door. 'I'm fine,' she called.

'You sure, Mrs T?'

'Yes, I'm sure. We're here,' she yelled back.

'Thank goodness. It's safe to come out now, madame.'

She unlocked the door and found the maître d'hôtel standing there, flanked by the commissionaire and Miss Pilkins.

'Have you got him safely locked up?' she asked, looking down the corridor behind them.

There was a moment's silence, then he spread his hands wide. 'I'm afraid he was killed, madame. He fell down the lift well.'

Eunice stared at him in silence, then closed her eyes in sheer relief. 'I can't be sorry.'

It wasn't until she was in bed, being fussed over by her senior staff, that she let herself think of Irene. She must set that tangle in order now that the girl was safe. No need to involve anyone else. It would only take a letter from her.

When Irene had escaped, Eunice had typed out a letter supposedly from the girl and sent it to the father's address, scrawling a signature at the bottom as near to Irene's as she could manage.

Now she had to write another letter and send that to clear up the deception. She was sorry to have come between the poor young woman and her family, but still felt it had been the safest thing to do.

As Judson's actions had proved. If he'd caught Irene, he'd surely have killed her.

He'd have killed Eunice, too. No, best not to think of that.

* * *

The following morning, Eunice went to find out Mr Rycroft's home address from the customer cards, then started to draft a letter.

It took her a long time to explain everything. Surely Irene would still be with Mr Rycroft? This time, Eunice wanted to contact Irene first and let the girl find her sisters for herself when the time was ripe.

343

She thought about it for a few days, then managed to put together a letter that more or less satisfied her. She hoped they'd forgive her for the deception.

When she posted it, she said a little prayer that it would find Irene and set things right for her.

★ ★ ★

Horry intercepted the postman and took the mail in to Gil, slipping a letter of his own into his pocket before he did so.

'Here you are. And there's a letter for Miss Fuller.'

'I'll give it to her.' Gil looked at the letter, saw the Rathleigh crest on the envelope and went straight up to the schoolroom. If this was bad news about Judson, better they find out about it straight away.

Renie was discussing Christmas and wedding preparations with Beth, her governess and Lizzie. Everyone in the house and village seemed to be getting together to make it a double celebration, and one to be remembered.

Chapman was safely locked away and a meek little woman who proved to be his wife had turned up to claim the tumbledown house for herself and his child.

To everyone's surprise, it was she who was distantly related to Miss Bennerden, but she denied any desire to lay claim to Oakdene. All she wanted was a home for herself and her child.

That left only Judson to worry about. Gil was considering hiring a private detective to find out what had happened to him.

He waited for a lull in the exciting discussion as to whether they should have the new square yoke collar to the bride's bodice, and how long her veil should be. 'There's a letter for you, Renie. I think you should open it straight away.'

She took one look at his serious face and got up, disentangling herself from Beth, who loved to cuddle up to people, as if that way she could make sure of keeping them nearby.

He handed the letter to her. 'Do you want to open it alone?'

She shivered. 'No. Let's go down to the sitting room.'

When she'd sat down next to him on the sofa, she stared at the envelope for so long without attempting to open it that he was hard put to keep quiet. But somehow he held back his questions and waited for her to slip her finger into the gap in the envelope and tear it open.

He watched her read it and then saw tears well in her eyes. She let the letter drop and turned to fling herself into his arms, sobbing uncontrollably.

Whatever it was that had upset her, he'd sort it out, he vowed as he cuddled her and hushed her.

Eventually she stopped sobbing and surprised him by giving him a beaming smile.

He looked at her in puzzlement.

'Sorry. I didn't even tell you . . . Oh, Gil, this is from Mrs Tolson. She knows where my sisters are.'

'I thought it must be about Judson.'

'No, he's dead. Is it wrong to be glad about that, do you think?'

'Not when it's a man so evil. Tell me about your sisters. That's much more important.'

'Read it for yourself.'

'Are you sure?'

Dear Renie,

I have to apologise to you for keeping some information from you, but I've been worried about your safety. Judson had vowed to me that he'd find you and take his revenge, and Mr Dennis Carling didn't believe how dangerous he was, so might have let some information about you slip.

So I told everyone you'd gone to Paris, including your sister Nell quite recently. I sent her a letter, typed, which I pretended was from you, in case Judson went hunting for you.

Now that he's dead, I can reveal everything and ask your forgiveness. I didn't even check that this was what you wanted, because I didn't know for certain where you were and wanted to be able to say that truthfully to anyone who asked, since I have difficulty lying.

Your sister Nell has found happiness with a man called Hugh Easton, who lives near Faringdon, which is near Swindon. And I gather she knows where your other sister is.

The letter I sent purporting to come from you was passed by the people in your old home to the Greenhills, then to your sister.

Oh, and I'm sorry to tell you your father is dead.

I've enclosed the address I have for Mr Easton, though you might also enquire at the publishing house where he works. He may have come back to live in London by now.

May I wish you all the best for the future, and if you need a job, you may always come back to the Rathleigh.

Eunice Tolson

'Good heavens!' He gave Renie a hug and wiped away a tear with his fingertip.

'Can we go to this Three Elms Farm today? I can't bear another minute to wait to see my sisters again.'

He checked the letter again. 'Why don't we telephone this publishing company and find out where Mr Easton is?'

'Yes, of course. Isn't the telephone a marvellous invention?' She tugged him to his feet. 'Do it now. Then phone your parents and tell them about us. Oh, and there's Walter and everyone else here. Not that it'll surprise them, but we want to make it official, don't we?'

Her expression as she looked at him was glowing with love and joy at the thought of being reunited with her sisters.

★   ★   ★

He had to wait till the operator connected him to London and then wait again to speak to someone at the publishing house. It took him a while to explain.

'Oh, you want to speak to Mr Easton, then,' the man said. 'I'll put you through to him.'

Another wait, then a voice said, 'Hugh Easton.'

347

'My name is Gilbert Rycroft, and I'm engaged to a Miss Renie Fuller. I believe you know where her sister Nell is.'

There was an exclamation, then Hugh said, 'Tell me where she is and we'll come to see you immediately. Nell has been so sad not to know where Renie was.'

'Why don't you bring Nell down to visit us?'

Hugh laughed. 'No, I have a far better idea.'

★ ★ ★

The following day Gil and Renie set off to find her sisters, with Horry driving them. Renie was so excited, her hat was awry and her hair kept tumbling down. When he looked, she was wearing two unmatching gloves. He didn't tell her.

She hardly said a word as they drove, but now and then he put his arm round her and gave her a hug, and she hugged him back fiercely, but without saying a word.

They passed through the small town of Wootton Bassett, where they asked directions, then drove on in the direction of Bath. When they turned off the main road, she roused herself enough to ask, 'Are you sure this is it?'

'Yes. Cherry Tree Lane.'

'And you're sure Mattie lives here?'

'Yes.' He didn't remind her that he'd told her that several times already.

When they got to the top of the slope and saw that the road ended at a large house, she looked round in puzzlement. 'We must have missed her house.'

'No. This is where she lives.'

Renie stared at the large house set in neat gardens. 'Here? Mattie?'

'Yes. We asked directions, remember, and the man was quite sure where Mattie Kemble and her husband Jacob lived.'

He'd expected Renie to jump out of the car as soon as it stopped, but instead she sat staring at the house.

'What if it's not our Mattie?'

'Of course it is. Mr Easton is married to your sister Nell, so you can trust what he told you.' He got out carefully and held out his hand to her. 'Come on.'

Her hand was trembling in his, but before they could take more than a few steps, the front door of the big house opened and two women rushed out, shrieking Renie's name.

She began to cry loudly as she rushed towards them, and her sisters were weeping as well.

Two men came to join Gil and introduce themselves, then one went to tell Horry where to take the car and find refreshments for himself.

One of the men limped slightly as he went across to the women. 'Come on now, my dears. Let's get you all inside. I don't know why you're weeping on such a happy occasion.'

One of the women gave him a quick hug, then went back to take Renie's hand. 'This is my youngest sister. Renie, this is my husband, Jacob, and this is Hugh, Nell's husband.'

'And this is my fiancé Gil, and you're all invited to our wedding at Christmas. I want two matrons of honour.' She plonked kisses on Nell and Mattie's cheeks. 'You both look so well. Oh, isn't it going to be blissful being able to see one another again!'

'Why don't I show you gentlemen round the gardens?' Jacob said quietly.

His wife overheard and gave him a smile and a nod.

Even before they'd left the room, the three sisters had their heads together and were busy catching up on all that had happened since the stormy day they'd run away three years ago.

Once they were outside, Hugh grinned. 'I have another surprise for them and I think I can hear it coming.'

A motor van came chugging up the hill, with the words 'Hal Keane, Photographer' written in large letters along the side.

'I thought they'd want a photograph or two to remember this day by. I'd better go and warn them.'

The three sisters shrieked again when he told them a photographer had come.

'We'll go up to my bedroom and tidy ourselves,' Mattie said, putting an arm round each of her sisters.

'I want a million photographs,' Renie said. 'This is the best day of my life.'

'Your wedding day will be even better,' Mattie said. 'We'll make sure of that.'

Renie hugged her, hugged Nell afterwards, then turned to the mirror. 'Come on. We want to look beautiful.'

And they did.

We do hope that you have enjoyed reading this large print book.

Did you know that all of our titles are available for purchase?

We publish a wide range of high quality large print books including:
Romances, Mysteries, Classics
General Fiction
Non Fiction and Westerns

Special interest titles available in large print are:
The Little Oxford Dictionary
Music Book
Song Book
Hymn Book
Service Book

Also available from us courtesy of Oxford University Press:
Young Readers' Dictionary
(large print edition)
Young Readers' Thesaurus
(large print edition)

For further information or a free brochure, please contact us at:
Ulverscroft Large Print Books Ltd.,
The Green, Bradgate Road, Anstey,
Leicester, LE7 7FU, England.
Tel: (00 44) **0116 236 4325**
Fax: (00 44) **0116 234 0205**

THE TRADER'S SISTER

Anna Jacobs

Ismay Deagan wants to leave Ireland and join her brother, Bram, in Australia. However, her father wants her to marry their vicious neighbour, the loathsome Rory Flynn. But after Rory brutally attacks her, Ismay realises she must escape. And, disguised as an impoverished young widow, she sets sail for Australia, hoping to be reunited with her brother. When she meets Adam Treagar on the ship, she believes her dreams of future happiness may come true. But before reaching their destination they are flung into adventures in Suez, Ceylon and Singapore ... Can Ismay tell Adam the truth about who she really is? What secrets does Adam hide? And will Ismay's past catch up with her and threaten her new life in Australia, before it's even begun?